W9-BNV-452

MEET MISS SEETON—

DARING, DARLING, UNDEFEATABLE, AND EVERYBODY'S FAVORITE AMATEUR DETECTIVE

Picture Miss Seeton
by Heron Carvic

POPULAR LIBRARY • NEW YORK

POPULAR LIBRARY EDITION
February, 1977

Copyright © 1968 by Heron Carvic

Library of Congress Catalog Card Number: 68-17039

Published by arrangement with Harper & Row, Publishers,
Incorporated

ISBN: 0-445-00442-8

A JOAN KAHN-HARPER NOVEL OF SUSPENSE

PRINTED IN THE UNITED STATES OF AMERICA

One

"L'*amour* est *tum* tum
De some*thing* . . ."

So colorful. Not romantic—no, one couldn't call it that; if anything perhaps a trifle sordid. Carmen herself, for instance, no better than she should be. In fact, if one were frank, worse. And the other girl, the young one; it was difficult to feel sorry for her. Her fiancé, quite obsessed with his mother —obviously weak and easily influenced—would have made a most unsatisfactory husband in any case. Still, for him to stab Carmen at the end like that—so unnecessary. Almost contrived. Though, of course, one must not forget that foreigners felt differently about these matters. One read that people abroad did frequently get emotional and kill each other. Probably the heat.

Miss Seeton stepped aside to avoid a pile of crates. She peered at them.

Seville oranges. How interesting. Spain. Such an odd coincidence. One might almost think that one was back in one's seat at the theatre, with the warm glow of the lights.

"Qui n'a jam*ais,* jamais
Tum *tum* some*thing.*"

Cracked, yes. Off-key, yes, but a warm glow had started up inside Miss Seeton. Her visit to the opera tonight was really in the nature of a celebration. Tomorrow morning she would set out on an adventure. No—no, that was putting it too strongly. Set out upon a new way of life—or at least the beginning of a new way. Which would be, of course, in its way, an adventure. For her.

Where was she now? If she turned right here—Gracious, how dark this alleyway looked. Should people park their cars all down one side? With their wheels on the pavement too?—it should take her toward Tottenham Court Road. Or she might even catch her bus in Charing Cross Road.

This walk had been a good idea. She felt quite a spring in her step. Was it her rubber soles? Or could it be—could it be just possibly that THEY were doing her good? Miss Seeton drew in her breath; braced herself. Of course it was ridiculous taking up exercises at her age—but that advertisement had looked so encouraging. Even when the book arrived and one realized the difficulties, it had still appeared to be worth trying. There was no question the tiresome stiffness in her knees did seem to be better. A lot of the positions were—well, embarrassing. Even to oneself. But, after all, if no one knew—and if it helped. Oh . . .

Miss Seeton prepared to hurry by a couple pressed into an adjacent doorway, when the girl spat:

"Merdes-toi putain. Saligaud! Scélérat, si tie m'muertes . . ." She ended on a gasp as the boy's arm hit her in her side.

Oh, no. Really. Miss Seeton stopped. Even supposing the girl had been rude—and it had certainly sounded so—that was no excuse. A gentleman did not hit . . . She prodded him in the back with her umbrella.

"Young man . . ."

He whirled and leaped. Deflected by the umbrella, he landed beside the prostrate Miss Seeton. Grabbing her by the coat, he jerked her toward him. A blaze of light froze him as the headlights of a car farther down the alley were switched on and an engine started. There was a scuffle of movement and, her coat released, Miss Seeton fell back on her elbows as the boy jumped to his feet and ran. With the help of her umbrella she pushed herself upright. Really! The foreign temperament—so impulsive.

A car door slammed. A man's voice called, "Stay where you are, Mabel." The thwack of running footsteps.

"Are you all right, madam? What happened?"

Miss Seeton looked around. A heavy middle-aged man appeared from behind the beam of light, hurried toward her and grasped her arm.

"That man who attacked you—did he hurt you?"

Miss Seeton, a little breathless, considered. "No—no, I don't think so. It was just the surprise."

"But you were on the ground," the man insisted. "He had hold of you."

"It was all so unexpected. I startled him, you see, and it made him jump. We both fell down. Then he pulled me. I think he was trying to help me up."

"Then why did he run?"

She appeared puzzled. "Well, there was the girl—such bad manners. But then, of course, he's not English."

"The girl? What girl?"

"They were in that doorway there. She cried out something that sounded rude and he hit her. I'm afraid I interfered. I do think, don't you," she continued earnestly, "that the young must learn to behave? Surely? Even abroad?"

The man glanced at the empty doorway, took a step and, leaning on the bonnet of one of the parked cars, saw the huddled body of a girl wedged between the wing of the car and the wall.

"Good God—you're right. He knocked her out. Just a minute, I'll prop her up against the door."

Miss Seeton moved to help. "Perhaps she's fainted, poor thing. Oh . . ." She gave a shocked cry. As the man shifted the body the girl's coat fell back and the glare of the headlamp shone on the handle of the knife in her side. "No, wait. Don't move her yet. We must get a doctor. She—look, she's been stabbed."

Stabbed. But of course. Stabbed. That was inevitable somehow. This dazzlement of light—spotlights. The slope of the alley steepened. To keep her balance Miss Seeton leaned against a car. Spotlights. Oranges. Seville. That was it. It had happened before. She'd seen it—watched it happen before.

Someone was speaking to her, urgently. "It's too late for a doctor. This girl is dead. We must get the police." The man gazed almost in awe at the little figure, hat askew, coat awry, gloved hands still clasping her umbrella. "You mean you actually saw this happen? What made him do it?"

Miss Seeton straightened. "He has to," she explained. "It's the last act." She shook her head. Suddenly she felt very tired. "But it's so silly really. And quite—it's quite unnecessary."

"Would you like another cup of tea, miss?" The constable at Bow Street Police Station made the suggestion as a conversational gambit to break an awkward silence.

Miss Seeton contemplated the emulsive remains of what appeared to be sweetened tar at the bottom of her cup. "How kind." Although the room was warm it was true, she still felt a little cold. "If I might have it very weak—nearly all water—and with no sugar, I should be most grateful."

"Sure you won't have something to eat while you're waiting?"

"No, really, I had a meal before the theatre. But—" she

hesitated, "I wonder if you'd be kind enough to ask about my handbag. I'm a little worried; you see, it's getting late and I have no money on me—also there's my latchkey."

The constable turned at the door. "Don't you worry about that, miss. We'll see you get home all right. And, as for your bag, the boys have got a description; if it's there they'll find it and let you know at once. Anyway, it won't be long now, the Yard should be here any minute. I'll go and rustle up your tea." He closed the door behind him with a sigh of relief. Funny little old trout. You'd think she'd be all of a twit, but she was as calm as you please. Probably came of teaching kids. Once you'd coped with kids these days you'd copped the lot.

Miss Seeton looked up as the door opened. A gray day on heathland came in briskly, followed by a footballer. No— really, this was too fanciful; she must be tired, next she would be seeing people as shapes with holes in them. A perfectly ordinary, tall, rugged, middle-aged man in tweeds, followed by a perfectly ordinary, though very large, scrubbed young man in a dark suit. It made no difference. She was still left with the impression of a gray sky and heather ruffled in the wind. And the young man's suit was entirely wasted. He might just as well have been wearing—in fact, more appropriately—several yards of striped wool muffler, shorts, and those stockings one associated with *Alice in Wonderland*; except, of course, the footballers' stockings were shorter and thicker.

The gray day—the older man smiled and spoke:

"Miss Seeton? No, please don't get up. I'm Superintendent Delphick of Scotland Yard and this is Detective Sergeant Ranger from the same locality." He moved to the chair behind the desk and sat down. The sergeant settled on an unobtrusive chair to one side. "Very good of you to agree to wait for us. Sorry if we've been rather long, but we both had to be dug out of our respective homes as we were not on duty."

"I'm so sorry." Miss Seeton looked distressed. "I'm afraid it was my fault. . . ."

The superintendent raised an eyebrow. "Hardly yours, Miss Seeton. Quite the reverse, in fact. They sent for us because there may be a tie-up with another case of mine, so it was thought better we should be in on it from the start. We knew the girl, you see."

"That poor girl who was killed."

"Not so poor as all that." His tone was dry. "She was a known prostitute."

"Oh, dear!" Miss Seeton exclaimed. "A very hard life; such late hours—and then, of course, the weather. And so unrewarding, one would imagine."

"Not necessarily. Like every other walk in life it depends on how far you rise in your profession."

Sergeant Ranger nearly dropped his pen. The Oracle was going it a bit, wasn't he? You didn't come straight out with words like "prostitute" and then a discussion on fees to somebody like this Miss Seeton. You wrapped it up. He tried wrapping it up. She was an—er—prostitute. The "er" didn't really make it any better and "um" actually made it worse. Perhaps the Oracle was right. Anyway the old girl hadn't turned a hair.

"I wouldn't waste too much sympathy on her," Superintendent Delphick continued. "She was a vicious little piece from all accounts. Yes?" in answer to a knock on the door.

The constable came in balancing a cup and saucer. "The lady's tea, sir." He put it on the desk beside her.

The sergeant was moved to protest. "Good Lord, what's that? Drain water?"

"Very weak, as requested. No sugar," he announced.

"Thank you," said Miss Seeton. "You see I don't really care for . . ."

"Burnt molasses any more than I do," agreed the superintendent. "You might bring me a cup of the same, if you can manage it, and some stewed treacle for the sergeant."

"Right away, sir." The constable left.

Miss Seeton sipped. Much better. Rather comforting.

"Now," he picked up a sheet of paper from the desk and scanned it as he spoke, "in your statement you say that your assailant was a foreigner. Is that right?" The sergeant looked up from his notes. Now they were getting some place. He underlined the symbol for foreigner. "You don't know his nationality, merely that he was definitely not English." Miss Seeton nodded. "Now, can you make any guess—from anything he said, for instance?"

"No. . . ." She thought. "No. You see, he never spoke." She ended on a note of faint surprise.

"But you still maintain he was not English. What makes you so certain of that? No, no," he added hastily, as he saw her troubled expression, "I'm not doubting your conclusions. What I want to get at are your reasons for drawing those conclusions. To put myself, as far as possible, in your place. To see and feel what you saw and felt at the time."

Miss Seeton's face cleared. "Well, it was really the girl, you see. She spoke to him—or rather snapped at him in what sounded like French, though I can't be sure. I didn't recognize the actual words but, of course, she was speaking quickly and my French isn't very good. And then he hit her—or that's what it looked like at the time. You see, if he'd been English, he wouldn't have understood her, would he?"

The sergeant studied his underlined "foreigner." He added a question mark. He added two more. They didn't express his feelings. He added three exclamation points and felt better.

"You're probably right," the superintendent agreed. "The girl, though she could speak English, was in fact French by birth. So if you heard her speaking in French, the likelihood is that any previous conversation was in the same language."

The sergeant surreptitiously crossed out all but the smallest of the queries after "foreigner."

"You also say," Superintendent Delphick went on, "that you can't give an exact description of the man, though you would recognize him again if you saw him. Is that correct?"

"Well, yes. It's difficult," Miss Seeton explained, "it was all so quick—and rather dark. And then, of course, I wasn't expecting . . . All I remember is long hair and his expression. An impression really."

Sergeant Ranger regarded his pothooks. That should help. An all-stations call for a long-haired expression should get them places. But fast.

"An impression—quite." The superintendent smiled. "Doubt anyone could do better in the circumstances. What I'm getting at is that that impression is photographed in your mind; and we've got to try and find some means of developing the photograph for our own use. I see from this," he tapped the paper, "that you teach drawing."

"But only at a very small school," she affirmed. "In Hampstead. And not on the regular staff, merely attached. I also teach at the Polytechnic—night classes, you know. And a few private pupils that I . . ." Her voice trailed off. "I'm so sorry. I'm wandering from the point."

"But you're not. That is the point. The point being that you are an artist. What I want you to do if you will," he leaned across the desk, "is to take this paper and pencil, sit quietly, concentrate on that impression in your mind, then see if you can get it down on paper. Don't worry if you can't. It's just a shot in the dark that might possibly come off. Take your time. It'll give me a chance to catch up on these statements. Come in," he called as he gathered up the papers and settled back in his chair.

The constable entered with a tray and placed two cups of tea on the desk. "One strong with, one weak without, sir." The superintendent nodded and the constable departed.

A shot in the dark. In the dark. Miss Seeton closed her eyes and concentrated. In the dark . . .

The superintendent skimmed through the longest of the statements. "Mrs. Mabel Dorothea Walters, 14 Lime Avenue East, Barnet, Herts. 'I have never been so shocked . . . di-da . . . My nerves . . . di-da . . . I was shattered . . . di-da . . . In all my life . . . di-di-da . . . I really feel I must . . . di-da-diddy.' " Useless, except to the woman's psychiatrist. He added a footnote: Stayed in car. Saw nothing. Suggest not called inquest. See coroner. He started on the next: "Edward Cyril Walters, 14 Lime, etc. . . . On leaving the Cambridge Theatre etc. . . . switched on lights and engine . . . figures on ground . . . he ran . . . I ran . . . I found . . . I tried . . . she said . . . I said . . . She said 'He had to do it.' And something about it being his last act 'but not necessary.' " He frowned and ringed the last two sentences. He made another note: Straightforward, factual, but saw nothing. Useless, except as confirmation of witness Seeton.

Sergeant Ranger drank his tea. H'm, not bad. At least it had some taste. Better than that hogwash the super went for. What did the Oracle think he was doing, sitting there browsing over all that bumph. At this rate they'd be at it all night and no forrader. He ought to be questioning the old girl; force a description out of her, not start art classes. Anyway, she'd gone to sleep. Tired, poor old thing, and no wonder. But it was no good them both sitting on their fannies while she had a kip. He got up and took his empty cup to a desk against the wall. Coming back, he stopped behind Miss Seeton and looked over her shoulder.

In the dark . . .

Be damned—she was having a go. No, she wasn't, she was doodling. Just some straight lines . . . and then a lot more lines scrubbed in, in a sort of mess. He looked up and caught the superintendent's eye fixed on him, daring him to move—almost to breathe.

In the dark . . .

Stripes . . . Hell, no, they weren't, they were bars. An eye . . . two eyes, staring among all those lines. No, he could see now: two eyes glaring in the dark. But why behind bars? What were those squiggles? . . . Hair—long hair . . . "Good God!" he exploded. "Caesar!"

Miss Seeton jumped. "Oh, no. More hair—and then, of course, no wreath."

The superintendent caught the drawing as it fell, glanced at it, pushed the telephone toward the sergeant: "Check that— we've got Lebel's photograph on file," turned back. "Nice work." He beamed at her. "I had a feeling you'd come up with it. Nice work, indeed. Saves a lot of fuss and fluster.

She looked pleased. "You do recognize him, then?"

"Yes, unquestionably César Lebel. Tell me"—he studied the drawing—"why the bars?"

"Oh, dear." She bit her lip. "I'm so sorry, that was quite unintentional. It is the sort of thing I'm always trying to stop. In my pupils, I mean—and, naturally, in myself. I do maintain one should draw only what is there; particularly when you're learning—and so it must apply to teaching too. Until you have learned. And then, of course, it doesn't matter, does it? I mean it's always permissible to break a rule, provided one understands what that rule is. But I do find it difficult at times to differentiate between what is really there and what one thinks one sees. Especially when working from memory. Somehow"—she hesitated—"I seem to remember that young man as a—a caged animal."

"You're dead on. Has been, and will be again. A violent tyke. English born, French parents. In trouble on and off since a kid."

"They've got mug shots, sir," the sergeant broke in. "Do you want to speak?"

"Yes." He took the phone. "Harry?" . . . "Good. Run some prints and to save me time get them to put out an allstations for him, would you?" . . . "No, not the 'Help with inquiries' lark. 'Wanted in connection with the murder of Mrs. Hickson; born Marie Prévost' and see the press get it." . . . "I know, but I want to give the impression the case is sewn up." . . . "No, no dabs, not a damn thing except one eyewitness ident." . . . "Exactly, that's the danger. I want Lebel and his lot to think there's more. That we've got him cold." . . . "Thanks. Be seeing you." He cradled the receiver and turned back. "Now, Miss Seeton, can you bear with us a little longer or would you rather we finished this in the morning?"

"I think now would be best. That is, if you don't mind and

if it won't keep you too late. You see," she apologized, "I have to set out early in the morning for the country. Also I don't think they've found my bag yet. They promised to let me know because without my latchkey I can't get in. My spare key is in my desk."

"Your handbag, yes." He regarded her seriously. "I wanted to talk to you about that. It's not at the scene of the crime and, I should say, almost certainly stolen."

"Stolen? But there was no one there. Only that nice Mr. Walters, so kind and helpful. He would never . . ."

"No, not Mr. Walters. Young César."

"But—but he hadn't time."

"Not when you were on the ground?"

Miss Seeton gave it thought. "Well—yes, I suppose it is just possible."

"Probable, I'm afraid. That is the main reason you were asked to stay on here. From your description of the contents," he referred to the papers, "some silver in purse, two pound notes . . ."

"Just for emergencies," she explained. "I don't keep more in my bag than I need because you never know, do you? And then, of course, at school—such a temptation. So unfair I always think."

"Very sensible," he agreed. "Now, let's see—handkerchief, comb, mirror, key to flat . . . ah, yes, here we are, diary containing name and address. The local police have been contacted and a watch is being kept on the house."

"A watch? But I don't understand."

"Don't you realize you could be in danger yourself? Lebel might very well make an attempt to kill you."

"Me?" Miss Seeton expostulated. "But that's ridiculous. I don't even know him."

"I doubt he's a stickler for the social conventions," the superintendent remarked. "If he thinks you're the only witness that can identify him, his best bet is to eliminate you. I'd like to suggest we arrange accommodation for you at a hotel for the night."

She became flustered. "I'm sorry, that would really be rather inconvenient. I—I've nothing with me. And then I still have some packing to do."

"Very well. In that case, with your permission, we'll have a policewoman spend the rest of the night with you. She can see you off in the morning. Meanwhile may we clear up one or two points in your statement? You say 'He had his back to me. Then he hit the girl. I spoke to him. Then he turned round and jumped and we both fell down.' I can't think why he jumped you—why didn't he just make a run for it? If he hadn't turned round you would never have seen his face at all."

"That was my fault, I'm afraid. I interrupted him and that rather took him aback, I think."

In defiance of control the superintendent's lip twitched. "I can see it would," he acknowledged.

"Actually—" Oh, dear, this was most embarrassing. It sounded so—so aggressive. But she must be exact. "Actually I was a little angry—at his rudeness, you know—so I poked him in the back with my umbrella. It was that that made him jump."

Holy cow! The sergeant's pen clattered on the floor. Only rigid training stopped him throwing his notebook after it. Go on, give her the George Medal and be done with it. Give her the bar as well. Give her the commissioner's job and get 'em all go home. Strong men thought twice about tackling young César in a temper. But not this little hen, oh, no. Stick him in the back with a brolly, right in the middle of a murder and tell him to stop it at once. A few more like her and crime would be all washed up and they could concentrate on traffic offenses like the public thought they did.

"When you're ready, sergeant."

The young man, red-faced under the stern gaze of his superior, retrieved his pen and straightened. "Yes, sir. Sorry, sir." How did the Oracle remain cool as a cold-blooded cucumber? Even a bit grim. Though, come to think of it, pinker than usual and sort of quivering at the edges.

"Thank you, Miss Seeton." The superintendent's voice was grave. "I have a very clear picture of events now." He had, too. Took him aback! He bet it had. Took him right back to his cradle, he shouldn't wonder. It was a delightful thought— but, no, not for now. For reflection later—preferably when he was alone. He set his jaw and conjured up serious thoughts. Car smashes. Murders—no, not murders—not just at the moment. Fire, famine, and flood. "There is one other thing," he continued, "it's in Mr. Walters' statement. With reference to Lebel, Mr. Walters quotes you as having said: 'He had to do it'—and something about it's being his last act, but not necessary. Can you remember what you meant by that?"

The sergeant shied. Oh, no, not again.

"But that was nothing to do with him," she pointed out, "that was the other one."

"Other one?" Delphick was sharp. Both detectives stiffened like pointers.

"Don José in the last act," she explained.

"Ah." The superintendent relaxed. He leafed through the papers. "The beginning of your statement reads: 'I was proceeding along Long Acre . . .' You had, in fact, come from Covent Garden. From *Carmen*?"

"Yes, of course."

"Of course," he agreed, "and I'm bound to admit I'm with you about his stabbing her—quite unnecessary. If he had to behave so stupidly in the first place, he'd have done far better at the end to mind his own business and stab himself. More sensible but less dramatic."

Sergeant Ranger reread his last notes. He had an uncomfortable feeling of weightlessness. Cloud-Cuckoo-Land? Or Outer Space.

The superintendent pulled forward a memo pad. "May I have your address in the country, in case I need to get in touch with you before the inquest?"

"The inquest?" For a moment she was at a loss. "I hadn't realized . . . I suppose I have to attend that."

"Unavoidable, I'm afraid. At least it should be short and straightforward. Did you intend to be away long?"

"About three weeks. I've got a little cottage in the country. The address is 'Sweetbriars, Plummergen, Kent.'"

"There was no note of this address in your handbag, by any chance, was there?" Delphick asked quickly.

"No, I hadn't put it in my diary yet. It would have been so final, somehow. You see, I hardly feel it belongs to me. Or rather it does, of course—but only just. My godmother, who was a cousin of my mother's, died recently and left it to me— she'd lived there most of her life. Also a little money, which makes it possible. I've been down once or twice to arrange things, but not to stay. I'd been thinking of retiring next year —though it's always so difficult to know what to do for the best and, then again, whether one can manage. It was like an answer, really. As my holidays started today, I thought I'd spend the time there, to see how I get on. With the idea of living there permanently, eventually. If it works, that is."

"Are you on the phone there?"

"Yes, Plummergen 35. Luckily my godmother had had it installed—though latterly she used it very little, I think. She was ninety-eight when she died and rather deaf."

He stood up. "Well, thank you, Miss Seeton. I mean that sincerely. You've given us more help than I could have believed possible. Certainly a great deal more than we had any right to expect." She rose and began to pull on her gloves. "I'll see that you're notified about the inquest and we shall meet there. I hope, for your sake, that we don't have to disturb you before. Though if we're lucky enough to lay our hands on Lebel, we might have to call on you for identification. It would depend what sort of story he cooked up. Meanwhile I hope you can put the whole unpleasant experience out of your mind and enjoy the Vale of Kent." He shook hands with her. "The sergeant will take you down and arrange for a policewoman to accompany you. The car's already waiting."

Miss Seeton moved hesitantly to the door; she appeared abstracted. Sergeant Ranger collected her umbrella, towered over her, and bowed. "Your small arms, ma'am."

She thanked him with a vague smile and looked past him to the superintendent. "You've been very kind. I'm sorry to seem insistent, but it's my key . . ."

"Not to worry." He grinned at her. "I think you'll find that, one way or another, the police will discover a means of opening your door. Though I'd feel happier if, before you leave in the morning, you'd arrange to have your lock changed."

He watched as the sergeant led her out and closed the door behind them. Comic little cuss. She'd be all right tonight with a policewoman there and the locals alerted, but he had a nasty feeling that when she'd stuck her brolly into César Lebel, she'd stuck it into a hornet's nest.

* INTERIM *

"Why?" . . . "No, not why you attacked her. Why you stole her handbag and went to her flat?" . . . "It was not. It was an unjustified and senseless risk which, I may point out, has put you further in jeopardy both with the police and with me. What could have passed almost unnoticed as a sordid killing of a prostitute is now, owing to your idiocy and this wretched woman, likely to become headline material with a blaze of publicity we can't afford." . . . "You will not. You will do nothing without instructions. You are paid to obey orders, not to think. If your salary depended on your mental processes

you would be permanently unemployed." . . . "That will be
for me to decide. You or this woman, whichever proves the
greater nuisance, may have to be removed. Meanwhile, get
under cover and stay there. You know where to go." . . .
"Your likes or dislikes are not in question. You will remain
there for as long as I deem necessary, and you will not set
foot outside without permission." . . . "Very well. If you prefer, I can make an arrangement by which you will be even
more 'boxed up'; but you will not feel it, nor will you be in a
position to make any complaint—at all." . . . "Good. You
will not attempt to get in touch with me again. I will make
contact when and if I have further use for you."

The telephone receiver was replaced.

Two

Miss Seeton waved; the platform at Charing Cross began to move past her; she settled back in her seat. What a charming girl; and the uniform, neat and becoming. How did she manage to look so fresh after sitting in a chair all night? What a tiring life it must be. She'd offered to let down the Put-U-Up, but no, the girl wouldn't have it; she preferred to sit and read. How clever the police were altogether; and what a lot they seemed to know. She'd been really worried about how to get into the flat, but one of them had just sort of fiddled with the lock and the door had opened straightaway. It would happen that that inquisitive Mrs. Perrsons from below—a most unsuitable dressing gown—should choose just that moment to come up and ask "Are you in trouble, dear?" How could she be in trouble when she was surrounded by police? Well, she hadn't been surrounded exactly; there were only two of them besides the girl; but it had seemed rather a crowd in a small flat; examining everything and asking her to see if anything was out of place. Thank goodness, nothing was. Except, perhaps, the kitchen window, which wasn't of course out of place, merely open. Surely she'd not forgotten to shut that? She couldn't remember forgetting it. Anyhow it had obviously interested them and they had insisted on dusting it for fingerprints, though you could hardly call it dusting when it meant blowing powder over everything and making rather a mess. One of them had even got out on the fire escape and powdered out there, too. However, apparently there weren't any fingerprints, not even her own; it was what they called "wiped clean" which sounded most satisfactory; she must have forgotten it after all.

This morning had been dreadful. The bell ringing the whole time, or else the telephone, or both together. So distracting when one was trying to remember if one had packed everything one needed. And that interfering Mrs. Perrsons coming up again, offering to help—when all was said, she hardly knew the woman—and asking endless silly questions. She wondered how she would have managed without that police girl, calm and efficient, arranging to have the lock changed, ordering a taxi and then getting them into it, with the help of the policeman outside, through that crowd on the pavement —newspaper reporters, apparently—you'd have thought they had more important things to do. Why should they want flashlights for taking photographs in daylight?

Nevertheless, they'd got away and here she was. She couldn't help feeling excited. It was exciting setting out for one's own place in the country. One's own. Well, she hoped it would become her own. Home. The country. Miss Seeton looked out the window at the endless vista of streets and buildings. Not quite yet of course. She picked up the *Times*. "Prime Minister Flies to New York." "The Moon Next Year?" "Road Deaths Up Again!" "Murder in Covent Garden." She opened the paper. Ah, now this was interesting. "How Does Your Garden Grow?" How indeed? That was what she must learn. "A simple, easy way . . . nitrogen . . . mulch . . . phosphates . . ." Oh dear, it sounded extremely complicated. Still, she had bought that book *GREENFINGER Points the Way* and she'd be able to look it all up in that when she arrived.

Tradition makes Brettenden the accepted station for Plummergen. It is also the main shopping center. Although a little farther than Rye, it is the inevitable choice since it satisfies that basic requirement of all English travelers that the end should resemble, as nearly as possible, the beginning of their journey. Brettenden is, in essence, an enlarged version of Plummergen.

The town of Brettenden consists virtually of one main artery, the High Street, a wide avenue, stretching over a mile from East Cross to West Cross, tree-lined for half its length and ranged with shops on either side. There are innumerable lanes and byways, but as these are, for the most part, shopless they are of little interest to visitors. At East Cross the High Street splits, the left fork becoming Virgin's Lane, which, after two slow curves, turns sharp left round a public house and sweeps up a long hill to the end of the town. Virgin's Lane, though a wide road and bounded by more shops than houses, is not regarded as part of Brettenden proper and the district is, in fact, subtitled Les Marys.

The right, and residential, fork at East Cross is labeled Plummergen Road—the Plummergen end is labeled Brettenden Road. This, though it leaves some doubt as to the road's official designation, leaves travelers from either direction in no doubt as to their destination. Despite the fact that it is necessary to visit the emporiums in Brettenden for many essentials, Plummergen itself is not ill-served in respect to shops.

The street, or, more properly, the Street—Plummergen has only the one and admits it—is straight, wide, and tree-lined, a quarter of a mile long, hedged on both sides by a medley of houses, cottages, and shops in a variety of styles ranging over some four hundred years, two public houses, one blacksmith, the police station, and a garage. It is not beautiful, but it has charm; it had also, on the last count, five hundred and one inhabitants.

Apart from the tiny, bow-fronted bakery—sweets, tobacco, cakes and bread, the latter no longer homemade since it has become no more than an outpost of Winesart's empire, which supplies most of Kent and Sussex—and the old building which houses the admirable butcher—meat, eggs, and white turkeys any time of year on a few days' notice—whose hideous clapboard shop front has been giving it an oddly temporary effect for at least two hundred years, there are three shops: the grocer, the draper, and the post office. All three sell groceries, green and otherwise, sweets, tobacco, wines and spirits, and all have well-stocked deep-freeze compartments. The draper also sells china souvenirs, picture postcards, clothes, cotton materials, and wool. The post office, the largest of them, deals in ironmongery, china, glassware, cosmetics, rubber boots, books, and has even, in a rather dim corner at the back behind the bacon, cheese, and butter, a small counter with a grid devoted to postal perquisites.

Miss Seeton's cottage, set back from the road and with a small front garden, stands at one end of the village facing down the Street. The name on the gate, Sweetbriars, serves as a postal address for foreigners. People from abroad, anywhere outside a thirty-mile radius, cannot understand that brevity is the essence of good writing. Attacked by verbal voidance they are not content with "Plummergen, Kent" but give the locals such gratuitous information as that they are "near Brettenden" (6 miles north) or "near Rye" (5½ miles south) which can delay correspondence up to three days while a blue pencil is found, the "nearness" removed, and the letter readdressed "Ashford" (15 miles east), which is "nearest" from the postal point of view. The cottage's local name at the present time is "Old Mrs. Bannet's." Most of the houses and cottages around are known by the names of previous owners; not because of any parochial prejudice against change, but due to practical considerations. Houses are continually bought and sold, occasionally by newcomers to the parish, but more often by the parishioners themselves. As families increase they move into larger accommodations: when the children grow up and the family is scattered, the process is reversed; thus it is not unusual to finish where you started, ending your days in the house where you were born. In Mrs. Bannet's case, that latterly her name should have won house recognition during her lifetime was something of an accolade. It had been deemed presumably that the old lady, when rising eighty and having lived in the same house for some fifty years, was unlikely to shift again until her final move across the road to the cemetery.

The church—part of the existing fabric was built before the Norman Conquest—stands modestly from sight at the southern end of the Street, on the opposite side of the road to Old Mrs. Bannet's. Next to it is the vicarage with a garden that adjoins the cemetery. It is a Victorian building of which the unpleasing façade is screened from view by evergreens. Its size, designed for a Victorian family and their retinue, has proved excessive in modern times, and it has been divided into two homes with separate entrances. Even so the remaining half is overlarge for the present incumbent, the Rev. Arthur Treeves, a bachelor whose maiden sister runs the house for him; she does more, she runs him, all church matters, and is in fact the power behind the vestment. In speech she is as direct and practical as her brother is wind-tossed and unworldly.

Somewhere along the line Arthur Treeves had lost his faith; not lost in the sense of mislaid, but an erosion, a slow whittling away, a dwindling over the years. He was acutely conscious that he lacked the moral courage to leave the church and take up other work; but it is not easy, late in life and with no independent means, to change your vocation simply because that calling no longer appeals. He was conscientious and active in the discharge of his duties, but had to steel himself to make his visiting rounds, always in dread that some among his parishioners, thinking to please him, might wish to discuss theology; a greensward that had turned to a bog beneath his feet, wherein, one day, he feared to be engulfed. The tenets and rules that at twenty had looked such positive solutions to all problems had by now become problems in themselves. He could see·so many sides to every question in human behavior and sympathize with all of them that the question itself had no answer: every question but one: deliberate unkindness.

"Your coffee, Arthur." Miss Treeves put down the paper and handed him his cup. It was not their own morning paper; there had been such an eager exchange of newspapers throughout the village—"Schoolmistress Scares Stabber" swopped for "Covent Garden Murder Heroine," "Battling Brolly" for "Art Teacher Routs Gang"—that no one was now sure whose paper they held. "Don't you think it might be kind to call on this Miss Seeton before tea?"

The Rev. Arthur started, spilling coffee into his saucer. "So soon? Surely not." He sought an excuse for delay; found it. "Next week, perhaps, when she's had time to settle in."

"She's only here for a few weeks, I believe," his sister pointed out. "After all, Mrs. Bannet was an old friend and this is her goddaughter."

"Ah, yes. Yes, of course." He got up, went to the window, looked out: the grass needed cutting. "I must express my sympathy." He returned to the table, stirred his coffee. "When's she coming?"

"She's arrived already. The Bloomers told me she'd be here for lunch."

"For lunch? Here?" He dropped his coffee spoon and looked apprehensively round the room."Good gracious! I'd no idea . . ." He made for the door. "I must . . ."

"Sit down, Arthur, drink your coffee and don't get in such a tiz; we've just finished lunch. Not here for lunch—there for lunch; in her own house," she explained patiently. "Mrs. Bloomer was very kindly going to stay on and have it ready for her. The train was on time; I saw the car arrive."

"She's got a car?" The vicar's mind jumped ahead: the Old People's Party—she could give lifts; the Seaside Outing; endless possibilities. "Can she drive?" he inquired anxiously.

Miss Treeves sighed. "I've no idea. I shouldn't think so. Why don't you listen? Crabbe's car from the garage met her at the station, drove her to the cottage, and Bloomer helped her with the luggage."

"Bloomer?" He was cheered; one of his flock in the right place at the right time, doing the right thing. "That's fine. An excellent man with hens. I'll drop by this afternoon and say how sorry we are."

"No, Arthur, no." She spaced her words as though to a child. "Glad. How glad we are to welcome her."

"Yes, that, of course." He finished his coffee and jumped up. "Naturally. Surely you can trust me to say the right thing. But a word about her bereavement is only fitting. After all, we knew her mother well. I buried her."

"Oh, do pay attention, just for once. Her godmother, Arthur. How many more times?"

"Yes, yes, that's what I said," her brother answered testily. "Don't muddle me, Molly." He looked out the window again: the lawn really did need cutting.

"And try to find out exactly what happened last night."

"Last night?" He turned, surprised. "But she wasn't here, I understood . . ."

"Oh, Arthur, it's the talk of the village. It's in all the papers. There was a murder last night in London and Miss Seeton was mixed up in it. The accounts vary, but apparently she hit the man."

For a moment she had his full attention; the vicar was shocked. "It hardly seems a suitable topic," he reproved her.

Molly Treeves was exasperated. "Nonsense. It must have been a most dreadful experience. It would be a kindness to encourage her to talk about it and get it off her mind. If I hadn't got a committee, I'd go myself."

"H'm, yes, I see." He ruminated. "If you put it that way . . . Naturally, anything I can do—any way I can help . . . I really think you can leave it to me to know what to say." He opened the French windows. "I think some air—I'll get on with mowing the lawn." He escaped. Poor Molly, so well-meaning, but didn't always quite realize . . . Someone in trouble; there he flattered himself he could be of use. It all sounded most unfortunate. A brawl in London—dubious company—and ending in death, too. Very distressing. Yes, he really did feel he might be of service. To talk it over rationally with someone like himself would give her a different perspective. He trotted off to collect the mowing machine.

His sister watched him with a smile. Poor Arthur, the mere idea of meeting new people did upset him so. Note: She must remember Milk of Magnesia tonight. It was just as well he always took his agitations out on the garden. It kept the place tidy and the exercise was good for him.

"More coffee, anyone?"

"Thank you, m'dear." Without lifting his eyes from the

sporting page, Sir George pushed his cup toward Nigel who handed it to his mother. She filled it and gave it back; he gently lifted the bottom of his father's paper and pushed it underneath. Sir George grunted.

Lady Colveden opened wide innocent eyes. "Busy this afternoon?"

Her son's equally wide eyes narrowed. "Why?"

"Just a little errand I thought you might do for me in the village. I meant to go myself only I can't get away, my committee isn't over till five."

"Come off it, mother darling. When you go all innocent, you're finagling. What are you up to?"

"I'm not up to anything. It's simply that I thought it would be a kindness, that's all. Considering the aunt was our oldest inhabitant and with the niece coming here today, I thought the least we could do was try to make her welcome, take an interest, you know."

The newspaper moved a fraction: Nigel caught his father's eye; it winked. He grinned. "Yes, we know." He finished his coffee, got up and started to stack the luncheon plates. "Do you think I'd be good at welcoming heroines? Anyway, what d'you want me to do? Present her with a gold-plated umbrella, or a press-cutting book on a salver?"

Lady Colveden considered. "Well, I thought some eggs."

"But she's got hens of her own—at least, she and the Bloomers between them."

"I know, but I can't think of anything else. I ought really to have baked a cake, I suppose, but you know what happens when I do."

There was a strangled noise from behind the newspaper.

"We do," her son agreed.

"Well, there you are then." She collected Nigel's cup, took the coffee tray over and pushed it through the kitchen hatch. "I'd have got Mrs. Bloomer to do it, only she changed her day this morning so as to see Miss Seeton in. And you can't go armed with cabbages or cauliflowers, it look so silly, so what else is there except eggs?"

"A nice bottle of homemade wine?" Nigel joined her at the hatch with the dishes and the plates.

"Don't be revolting."

"Right, eggs it is. What do I do?" he asked. "Cross-question her, or get a signed statement?"

"Your trouble is you're vulgar." She returned to the table,

picked up the cruet and the butter dish and put them on the bread board. "It's only natural to sympathize over that dreadful affair last night. How would you feel if you were an elderly spinster, coming to a new place where you knew nobody, after a terrible adventure and you're all alone and nobody calls, nobody cares—I think it's very sad." Sadness was tilting the bread board; things started to slide.

Nigel reached for it. "Better let me have that before it's overcome."

His mother brightened. "I'll collect the glasses. Of course," she added, "if you manage to find out a little more of what really happened, surely there can't be any harm in that?" Sir George folded his paper and put it down. "Oh, George, you're back with us. How nice. Nigel has just decided to call at Old Mrs. Bannet's this afternoon with some eggs."

"Why?" Sir George took his coffee cup and went into the kitchen.

His wife carried the glasses to the hatch and poked her head through. "Why? As a gesture of sympathy and welcome, of course." She closed the hatch, retrieved the newspaper and followed the men into the kitchen. She opened the dishwasher. "Will you do the pans in the sink, Nigel, and, George, you hand me the rest of the things; I'll stack."

Her husband passed her a pile of plates. "Why eggs?"

"Don't be tiresome, George. Because there isn't anything else, that's why. There was a murder last night." She took the newspaper and started to hunt through it. "You wouldn't know anything about it, you never read the interesting bits, but it's here somewhere; she was in a running fight with the police all round Covent Garden, or something, Old Mrs. Bannet's niece, I mean."

He gave her the vegetable dishes. "Second cousin."

"Who's a second cousin, what are you talking about, George?" she accused. "I don't believe you've heard a word I said." She ruffled the paper. "Why do things always disappear when you look for them?"

He put the trays on a shelf. "Page one, headline column four."

She made a face at him. "Pig. You'd read it all the time."

"Old Ma B cousin of mother. Makes Seeton second cousin. Also the old girl's goddaughter."

"Don't be ridiculous, George, how could you possibly know?"

"Asked her."

Nigel hung up the last saucepan. "Father, you've been holding out on us. When did you meet up with the battling brolly?"

"Met her twice. Once visiting Ma B for the day. Once clearing up after the old girl's death."

"And you've been keeping it from us all the time." She slammed the dishwasher shut. "George, I could kill you."

"Stupid." Sir George bent down, picked up the dispread newspaper, smoothed it, folded it neatly, and laid it on the table. "Wife always first suspect. Hire someone. Don't let 'em overcharge."

"No, but honestly, George, knowing her all the time and not a word. What's she like anyway and why didn't you tell us?"

"No murder then."

Nigel snapped his fingers. "I've got it. You know her, you take the eggs."

His father's plump figure headed for the door. "Can't. Going to bed."

"To bed?" Lady Colveden echoed. "What on earth for?"

"Sleep."

"But you can't sleep in the afternoon." All at once she was concerned. "George, you're not ill, are you? No, please tell me what's wrong?"

"Rabbits," he told her and shut the door.

"Another cup of tea, Eric?"

"What?" Erica Nuttel looked up from the newspaper. "Yes, thirsty. Dunno why. 'Less there was too much salt in that mock beef. Thought it tasted salty meself." She passed her cup. Mrs. Blaine poured lime tea and handed it back.

Miss Nuttel and Norah Blaine had shared a house for eleven years in the center of the village opposite the garage; thus ideally situated to watch all the local comings and goings, on foot or otherwise. There was little they didn't know, much they speculated on, and a deal they invented about everybody's business. People complained that they spread malicious and unfounded rumors; unfounded was true, but malicious was unfair and for the spreading the people themselves were equally to blame. Faced with any untoward event which had no immediate explanation, an interpretation would present itself which, improved on and garnished in discussion between the two ladies, emerged finally as positive fact. That these in-triguing myths lingered long after plain truth had been estab-lished was as much the fault of the disciples as it was an error in the preachers of the gospel.

They were dedicated vegetarians, known collectively as the Nuts. Miss Nuttell, tall, angular, with the face of a dark horse, was generally referred to as Nutcrackers. Mrs. Blaine, whose dumpy geniality was belied by the little black-currant eyes, was called by everyone Hot Cross Bun; this derived largely from Miss Nutel's pet name for her of Bunny, but it may have been also a tacit acceptance of the shrewish temper which flared through the placid surface when she was thwarted. Their house, Lilikot, a modern innovation with large plate-glass windows screened by nylon net, was inevita-bly the Nut House.

"Salty?" Mrs. Blaine did not like criticism. "I can't think why you should say that. You've always liked the mock beef before. It was precisely the same as usual. I followed the rec-ipe exactly. More likely to have been your parsnips, I should say; I thought you were a bit free-handed there. You should know by now parsnips won't stand too much salt, it spoils the sweetness."

"Could be, could be—no need to get into a flap, Bunny. This Seeton woman—" Erica Nuttel jabbed a blunt forefinger at the paper—"think we should call?"

Bunny responded at once. "Oh, yes, do let's, we must find out what really happened. What excuse can we make? I know, we can take her some dandelion wine. We've got plenty and it's full of vitamins."

"Good idea. Stimulating—good as whiskey any day. Better make it last year's—a bad year. Don't suppose she'll know the difference."

"All right, we'll get it out as soon as we've cleared away lunch. When shall we go along to old Mrs. B's? At teatime? I think this Miss Seeton sounds terribly brave, don't you?"

"Sounds more of a damn fool to me. Not teatime—too ob-vious. Wouldn't look well. Better make it three, sharpish."

"Mummy—" Angela raced into the house and flung open the door of the sitting room. "Mummy, she's here—that woman who's in all the papers this morning."

Mrs. Venning stopped typing. "Have you had anything to eat?"

"No." Angela chucked her coat onto a chair, danced over to the writing desk, kissed her mother, and looked at the pile of paper beside the typewriter. "How's the new book going? Sorry I missed lunch."

"Have you been over at the Barn again?"

"At the—the Barn? Oh, don't be daff, mummy, what on earth should I go there for? I told you the boys there are bores—just fuds. No, I—I got talking in Brettenden, and one thing and another—oh, you know how it is."

"Nigel Colveden rang you up."

"Nigel? What did he want?"

"He didn't say."

"Oh, well—" She perched on the arm of the sofa, taking cigarettes and matches from her bag. "I'll give him a ring sometime. On the way back I took the car into the village to get her filled and heard all about it from Jack Crabbe, he had to pick her up from the station."

"Hadn't you better get something to eat?"

"Oh, puff food," she threw the match in the fireplace. "I'll get it in a minute." She came back to the desk. "But, mummy, isn't it ultra about this woman?"

"What woman?"

"Oh, darling," she hugged her mother, "don't be such a fud. I told you—the one who's in the papers, who was mixed up in a murder last night in London, she's here in the village, she arrived just before lunch. I can't wait to meet her, she must know masses of spicy people."

"Who are you talking about?"

"Oh, I don't remember her name, Miss Something-or-other."

Angela collected her coat and tossed it over her shoulder. "But she's taken Old Mother Bannet's cottage or rather I think it's hers now, or something like that, old Ma B was a relation of some kind. Let's go and look her up, shall we?"

"Certainly not. We don't know her and from what you say I should prefer not to. Go and ask Mrs. Fratters to give you some food."

"Oh, all right, but I think you're drab, you never want to do anything spicy." The door banged.

Sonia Venning sighed. She remained still, gazing out the window. The roof of Meadows' Barn showed through the trees beyond the hedge that divided her garden from the field. Her mouth tightened; then, with a shake of her head, she referred to her notes and continued typing.

Jack the Rabbit jumped nimbly over the stile. He swept off his cap with its tall red feather. He made a courtly bow and held out his paw to little Lucy.

"Well, you're looking better, Miss Angie, I must say." Mrs. Fratters dried her hands on the roller towel and bustled over to switch on the electric kettle. "Thought you were coming down with a cold this morning from the look of you. What d'you want to go and miss your lunch for? Upset your ma, and not the first time. What's got into you these days? You should have more consideration."

"Oh, don't harp so, Frat." She dropped her coat on the kitchen table, moved over and started to hunt through the store cupboard. "I felt all hung this morning, now I'm fine."

"What you looking for?"

"Some of your apricot jam."

"You don't want jam now, it's not enough." Mrs. Fratters bent down and pulled open the hot-drawer at the bottom of the cooker. "I've been keeping some of the steak 'n' kidney warm for you just in case. There you are now." She dumped the plate on the table and took a knife and fork from the drawer. "You just sit down there and get on with it."

"Yes, yes, in a minute." Angela took a pot of jam from the cupboard, tore a sheet off a memo pad, and sat down at the table. She rummaged in her handbag for a pen and an elastic band. She wrote: "Greetings from Mrs. and Miss Venning, The Meadows, Plummergen." She put the paper round the jampot and slipped the band over it. "There, that's prime."

"Well, I'm off now, dear, so I'll say ta-ta." Mrs. Bloomer came into the living room, shrugging on her coat. Miss Seeton turned from the French windows which opened on to the lawn. She smiled. "I've washed up and put everything away and laid the tea ready, the cold meat's in the fridge, the rest of the apple pie's on the table with a cover over it, there's plenty of vege, so you're all right for your supper, unless you fancy something else, if so there's tins—or eggs of course, you can say what you like but it makes a difference when you lay your own, stands to reason, when you buy them there's fresh and fresh, but when you lay your own you know where you are, I've left you six, but if you wanted more for your breakfast, Stan'll be collecting after tea when he waters the hens."

London-born and married to a local farmhand ten years previously, Martha Bloomer had come to clean house twice a

week for Mrs. Bannet. Since she lived close by, this was to
lead to an arrangement advantageous to them both. As with
most houses in the village, the main garden of Mrs. Bannet's
cottage lay at the back. The Bloomers lived in one of a row
of small dwellings divided from this garden by a narrow lane,
a continuation of the Street, which ran down the side of Mrs.
Bannet's, over the canal, and eventually connected with the
main coastal road. The Bloomers had no garden, except for a
small front patch. Mrs. Bloomer suggested that Mrs. Bannet
should buy some chickens and provide their feed. Stan
Bloomer repaired the disused chicken house, looked after the
birds, kept Mrs. Bannet and his own family supplied with eggs
and poultry, and sold any surplus for his own profit in place
of wages. The agreement had proved so satisfactory to both
parties that it had spread to flowers, fruit, and vegetables.

"Now," Martha concluded, "is there anything else you
want, dear, before I go?"

"No, nothing, Martha, thank you. You've done everything
possible and I'm more than grateful."

"Right, then off you go to bed, I've put a hot-water bottle
in."

"But I can't go to bed in the middle of the day," Miss Seeton protested. "I must unpack and . . . and . . ." How curious, now she came to think of it there was nothing really urgent, nothing that couldn't wait.

"And what, dear?" demanded Martha. "You've got out all
the things you need for the moment. You get to bed, it's the
right place for you, you're looking tired and no wonder."

Miss Seeton was not used to being organized; she found it
comforting. "I must confess I am a little tired. I was rather
late last night and I'm not used to such a large lunch, deli-
cious as it was." She moved to the door.

Martha followed her into the passage and reached past her
to shut the heavy oak door to the cupboard under the stairs.
She shot the bolt. "You want to watch it, dear, you nearly
walked right into it. The latch doesn't hold right and it
swings. You keep it bolted or you'll be getting a nasty knock
one of these days. Need to keep your strength up with all
your gallivanting about and then the journey on top, so up
you go and have a nice lie-down, there'll be nobody coming
so you won't be disturbed and if they did you wouldn't hear
them with your bedroom at the back. Then you can have a
nice quiet evening settling in and you'll feel fit as a flea in the
morning."

"I think perhaps you're right." Miss Seeton started up the little twisted stairs. "I will lie down, after all. And, Martha—" She stopped and looked down.

"What, dear?"

She still hesitated. "I—I don't know how to thank you. I feel—you and Stan have made me feel—as if I'd come home."

Martha chuckled. "So I should think, what have you done if you haven't? I'll slip out the kitchen way, I need a lettuce for Stan's tea so I'll pull a couple on the way down and pop out by the back gate, it's quicker. Ta-ta, dear, see you Friday if not before."

How lucky she was. Dear Martha, she talked as much as ever: Cousin Flora had maintained that Martha must have been born in the middle of a conversation. In the bedroom Miss Seeton placed her hat and bag on the dressing table and stood for a moment, discovering the garden. One's own garden. So different from London, not being overlooked. She pulled the curtains to keep the light from her eyes when she lay down, put her coat and skirt on a chair and got into bed. Warm. Comfortable. And so quiet. Nobody to disturb one. So silly to feel guilty, resting in the afternoon. Martha was quite right. It was just what she needed. Sleep.

Three

"Well, I must say, Eric, I think it's too peculiar."

"A bit odd, yes."

"It's more than odd, it's peculiar. You don't go to sleep as soon as you've arrived in a place, and in the afternoon, too, unless of course there's a reason. Well, would you?"

"Not myself, no. Not without a reason."

"Do you think she drinks, or something, and is sleeping it off?"

"Could be."

"Oh, Eric, how terrible. We should never have left that dandelion wine, it will only make her worse."

"Might not be. Might be something else. Could be she's ill."

"She can't be too ill, or she'd never have made the journey from London. Though I did just happen to notice the bedroom curtains were drawn, because I slipped down the lane to see. I mean you don't pull your bedroom curtains in the afternoon unless there's some terribly good reason, do you?"

"Not 'less you've something to hide."

"To hide? Yes, that would explain it. But what could she . . . Oh, Eric, it's too terrible to think of, it couldn't be it's—not possible—drugs, do you think? Could it be that, do you think?"

"Possible, of course. Could be. Could very well be."

The two ladies entered the post office and took their places at the grocery counter.

"It's dreadful to think of, really——" Mrs. Blaine dropped her voice; persons more than six feet away had to strain to hear—"when you remember Mrs. Bannet and imagine how she'd have felt if she'd known."

"Don't forget, Bunny; can't be sure," Miss Nuttel encouraged her.

"Of course not." Her turn to be served had come; she smiled at the assistant. "Two boxes of dates, a packet of digestive biscuits, oh, yes, and a large packet of prunes, please." The shop assistant turned to the shelves; Mrs. Blaine returned to her theme. "But what other explanation is there? I mean, there has to be a reason, Eric, even for the oddest behavior, doesn't there?"

"Woman's something to hide, certainly," her friend agreed.

"Obviously, and I'm afraid it is the only answer. Of course it would never do to say so. Thank you." She helped the shopgirl to stow her order into her carrier and took out her purse. "There, eight and eightpence halfpenny. Too lucky, I have the exact change. I don't even like thinking about it." She moved away.

Several customers, seed borne on the breath of scandal, had drifted between them and the door. "Oh, good afternoon, Mrs. Goffer, how's your dear little girl, Effie? Not been up to mischief again, I hope. Excuse me—Why, it's Mrs. Spice. Looks like keeping fine, doesn't it? But it's too true, I'm afraid," she went on as they threaded their way, "that you're always reading in the papers how the drug habit is increasing everywhere, aren't you, especially in London." The ladies left the shop.

"Wanted more of that puce wool, didn't you?"

"Of course, too silly of me, I nearly forgot." They started across the road. "And anyway it's not puce, it's magenta. I only meant to use it as a border, originally, but I think the all-over pattern is much better, don't you?"

"Don't think it a bit strong against that mustard?"

"Oh, no, Eric, mustard's all the thing at the moment, but it needs a strong contrast to go with it. I can't think what Mrs. Venning was doing sending a pot of jam."

"Jam?"

"Yes, you remember those pots of jam, they were all from people in the village and I just happened to notice the card on the apricot one said: 'Greetings from Mrs. and Miss Venning.'"

"A bit odd for the Venning."

"It's too peculiar. After all, Mrs. Venning never goes anywhere these days, you practically never see her. I wish we could find out why. I mean it's too funny when you think she used to be quite gay and go out a lot and then she suddenly stopped."

"Since she had that barn rebuilt."

"Exactly. I can't think why the council allowed it. And then letting it to some boys' club or something. The whole thing's too odd."

"Don't see much of them."

"Well, that's what I mean. If you don't know what people are doing it can't be right."

"She'd've done better to let it to sheep, like anyone else."

"I feel sorry for poor little Angela."

"Not so little as all that. Seventeen or eighteen, must be."

"Yes, I suppose she must be about that by now. She's so gay always."

"Too gay, I'd say. Or too moody. Too much up and down altogether. Hysterical type, if you ask me."

"Oh, nonsense, Eric, she's just young and high-spirited and that always leads to moments of depression. I was just like her as a girl. You wouldn't understand because you've always been the blunt, forthright type. I used to think she and Nigel Colveden would eventually make a match."

"Doubt it. She's always gadding about in that little car. Drives too fast. And that club outside Brettenden she's always at, that's too fast, too."

"Well, it must be terribly dull for her now that they never invite people to the house any more. That's what makes it so funny that Mrs. Venning should send greetings to a new-comer." They stopped to look in the draper's window. "Do you see, they've got that mango chutney we've always had to get in Brettenden. Do you think perhaps they've met in London?"

"Could be. The Venning used to go to London a lot. To see her publishers, or so she said." A bell pinged as she pushed the door.

"Those silly children's books of hers—" Norah Blaine followed Miss Nuttel into the shop. "Good afternoon, Mrs. Welsted," she greeted the proprietress.

"Good afternoon, Mrs. Blaine."

"—yes, that would explain it, if they knew each other in London." She reached the counter. "I need some more of that magenta wool."

"Yes, Mrs. Blaine, how much?"

"Of course, with what we now know about Miss S, it's too obvious in that dreadful affair last night, there must have been more in it than meets the eye. How much?" she echoed. "Well, you see, I've decided to do the patterned, instead of the plain with the border. I mean, Eric, you don't get mixed up in murders and things without good reason, do you?"

Mrs. Welsted called her daughter. "Margery, how many

ounces of magenta will Mrs. Blaine need if she's doing the patterned twin set?"

"Matter of fact, Bunny, I don't get mixed up with murders at all myself." Miss Nuttel held out a pair of stout gardening gloves. "How much?"

"Ten and six," said Mrs. Welsted, "and very good value."

"I'll take 'em."

Margery Welsted finished her calculations. "Mrs. Blaine will need sixteen ounces."

"Well, there you are, Eric," Mrs. Blaine exclaimed, "it must have been some of those terrible people she'd be bound to know, to do with—you know what—and that sort of thing always leads to trouble."

"There's the wool and gloves." Mrs. Welsted handed her the parcel. "I'll credit any of the mustard wool that's over to your account. Is there anything else you want, Mrs. Blaine?"

"No, nothing else, thank you, Mrs. Welsted." She accepted the parcel and turned to go. "In my opinion that would explain about Mrs. V, I mean why she suddenly took to staying at home and seeing no one. If you want to know what I think," she held the door open, "I think Mrs. V's frightened."

Miss Seeton put on her hat. Yes, that coxcomb effect in stiff ribbon gave it character, she considered. Half past three; goodness, she'd slept over an hour and a half. How right Martha had been; she felt much less tired now. Some air, yes, that's what she needed and with the sun shining it was an ideal moment: she must go round the garden. She went down the stairs.

She'd always liked the cottage; but it was curious how much more personal—no, to be honest—how much more lovable a place became when it belonged to you, when you got that first little awareness that, perhaps, you belonged to it. Good gracious, what were all those? She turned from the kitchen door and moved down the passage. Beside the telephone, on the narrow table just inside the front door, were several parcels with notes stuck into the wrapping. These weren't here before. Who in the world . . . had people been calling while she was asleep? Oh dear, she hoped they hadn't thought her rude not to have answered the door. She began to read the labels. But she didn't know any of these people. It was plain, and naturally one understood, it was for Cousin Flora's sake; she must have been much loved in the village. But, for all that, to make her, a stranger, welcome like this was so kind—so kind . . . There was a knock at the door. She opened it.

"Miss—er—Seeton, is it?"

"Yes?"

"I'm—er—Treeves, your—the vicar."

"How do you do, but how nice of you to call." She stood back. "Won't you come in?"

"Oh—er—I—" Arthur Treeves hesitated, then took the plunge. "How very good of you. I—er, that is, it's so nice to meet you."

Miss Seeton closed the door and started for the kitchen. "Can I offer you some tea?"

"Tea? Oh, no, I wouldn't dream of putting you to the trouble."

"But it's no trouble."

"Oh, well, in that case—but, no, my sister wouldn't approve."

"Your sister?" She stopped in surprise. "Doesn't approve of tea?"

"Oh, no, good heavens, no. No, she drinks a lot, she lives with me. She wouldn't approve of my imposing on you."

"But it's not an imposition, I promise you. It's all laid ready. I'll just put the kettle on, if you'd like to go into the sitting room."

She repaired to the kitchen, switched on the electric kettle, and came back to find the vicar still hovering in the sitting-room doorway. He stood aside, bumping into the hall table.

"Ah, been shopping, I see," he remarked as he followed her in. "What do you think of our local stores?"

"No, I haven't been out. I've only just seen those parcels and I'm rather overcome; they're presents, I think, a form of greeting from some of the people in the village, I imagine. I was about to read the cards when you called." She sat in an armchair near the fireplace. "Won't you sit down?"

"Ah," he brightened as he perched on the edge of the chair opposite her, "that shows generosity of spirit, that pleases me very much. That's how I see people, you know—like to see them, that is—warmhearted, well-intentioned friends. Friends," he assured her, "that's what people should be. And to see a true example of it here makes me very happy indeed." The brightness clouded. "But, dear me, I'm forgetting one of the chief reasons for my call. To offer our condolences, my sister's and mine, and our sympathy in your loss. Your grandmother was an old and valued friend."

Miss Seeton smiled. "Not grand-, Mr. Treeves, but god-."

Not grand, but God? The vicar flinched. A deist possibly? And fanatical at that. "Quite, quite." He jumped to his feet. "We all have our own views, beliefs, faith—call it what you will. Live and let live is my creed. Dogma and doctrine may differ, but at bottom—or perhaps I should say heart—I like to feel we're all the same. And now I really must go, I mustn't keep you."

"But, vicar, your tea? The kettle must be on the boil." She rose.

"Tea? Oh, no, certainly not. Wouldn't dream of giving you the trouble." He hurried from the room. "I'm late already, I must fly. Good-by, Miss—er—" he grabbed the latch—"so nice to have met." He threw open the door. "Oh . . ." Confronted by a policeman in uniform, he stepped back hastily, knocking against the table; the parcels teetered, Miss Seeton was in time to save them. "I'm so sorry, clumsy of me."

"It's all right, there's no damage done. Excuse me for one minute, I must switch off the kettle." She hastened to the kitchen.

"Ah, Potter," the vicar was geniality itself—law and order had come to his rescue, "you were looking for me?"

"No, sir."

"No?" Pure chance then—providence was abetting his flight. "In that case I must be off. Nothing I can do, eh? I quite thought for a moment you were coming here."

"I was, sir. A Miss Seeton is here, I understand."

"Seeton?" The Rev. Arthur hesitated—and was lost. "Yes, that's right. But you don't want her, my boy, there's nothing she can do for you, she's only just arrived." But a small doubt was burgeoning in his mind. Something Molly had said. Something he should have said. Something—what was it—London? Trouble of some sort. Something distressing. And one of his people. He must stay. He might be needed; perhaps be able to help.

Miss Seeton came back. "I'm so sorry to have kept you waiting, I had to open the kitchen door to clear the steam."

"Miss Seeton?" P. C. Potter inquired.

"Yes?"

"I've been instructed to give you notice of the date of the proceedings that you are required to attend."

"Proceedings, Potter?" The vicar took up mental cudgels and waved them. "I can't have this . . ."

"It's all right, Mr. Treeves," Miss Seeton reassured him, "I think I understand."

"But I don't." He was stern. "Attend what? Explain yourself, Potter."

"The inquest, sir. Miss Seeton is required as witness."

Arthur Treeves was shaken. "Inquest? Good heavens, but nobody's died." But somebody had. Wasn't that what Molly had said? Somebody dead in a brawl in London. And this Miss Seeton—oh dear, oh dear. Doubtless not wholly to blame. Extenuating circumstances, if only one understood. His duty was plain. He must go with her; lend support. "When and where is this inquest, Potter?"

"The day after tomorrow, sir, at eleven-thirty. I took down the details for you here." He handed a paper to Miss Seeton.

"Eleven-thirty, good heavens, that means an early train. Leave it to me, Potter, we shall be there."

"No, not you, Mr. Treeves," Miss Seeton protested, "I wouldn't hear of it. They told me it would be quite short. It's all most unfortunate."

"The more reason for me to be there."

"No, really, it's very kind of you, but . . ."

"Not another word; I go with you. I'll let you know tomorrow the time of the train and I'll order a car from Crabbe's. Well, I must go on my way. In the meantime, don't let yourself dwell on this unhappy affair. We must face things as they come." He went on his way and P. C. Potter went with him. "All most unfortunate," murmured the vicar, "but I feel it is my duty to be there."

"I'm sure she'll be glad of your company, sir. Between you and me, the London chaps, the Yard in fact, have instructed me to keep an eye on her." The pride of direct contact with the head of all headquarters shone in every button.

"Have they?" His unhappiest surmises appeared established facts. He shook his head gloomily. "Have they indeed?" The vicar walked home deep in thought.

"Miss Seeton?"

Nigel, having failed to get any response to his knock, came round the side of the cottage and into the main garden. Like so many of the afternoon's callers, he could have left his parents' offering with a note, but he had his own reason for wanting to see Miss Seeton personally and his mother's commission had given him the excuse he needed. At first he had thought the garden to be empty and that both Miss Seeton and his luck were out, but noticing a movement behind the shrubs which backed the herbaceous border at the end of the lawn and screened the hen houses and vegetable garden from view, he crossed the grass to investigate. He found that it was Miss Seeton's hat and not the wing of a bird as he had at first thought.

"My name's Colveden," he continued as she turned to face him. "I hope you don't mind me butting in. There was no answer at the door, so I wandered round the side and saw you were down here. You know my father, I believe."

"Yes, indeed, I met Sir George twice, I think. How do you do, Mr. Colveden."

"Nigel. Actually I'm my mother's stand-in at the moment. She would have floated in herself, to see you touch down, but she was committed this afternoon and as Father's up to his pillow in rabbits there's only me, I'm afraid—with a dozen eggs."

"Oh, no, Mr. Colveden, it's very kind and please thank Lady Colveden most sincerely, but I can't accept any more, it's so embarrassing and especially eggs, you see—" she indicated the hen house—"we lay our own."

For one split but glorious second Nigel was vouchsafed a vision: Miss Seeton, in that hat, enthroned on an outsized nesting box, led her hens in a countdown—three . . . two . . . one . . . The vision faded. Nigel guffawed. "Sorry." He gulped. "A passing thought. But, apropos the hens, that wall at the back of the hen house should be at least three feet higher, you know."

Miss Seeton studied it. Now one came to examine it, that back wall was quite a bit lower than the side wall down the lane. Of course, with that tree in the corner one didn't really notice it at first; in fact she doubted if she ever would have noticed it if it hadn't been pointed out. It was only just higher than the roofs of the hen houses themselves and not as high as those wire cages in front of them. She looked back at the house: ah, yes, that would be the reason; so as not to break the view sloping down to the trees bordering the canal and over the fields beyond. Then, surely, it was better left as it was. Why make it higher? "Why?" she asked.

Nigel laughed. "Some of the local talent hop over egg hunting. Crazes up the hens; you'd think it was foxes at least and makes Stan Bloomer madder than a hornet."

"Oh, I see. That's why Martha keeps the second key to that side door and insists we keep it locked."

"I say . . ." He stopped. It was ridiculous. She was so completely different from anything he'd expected. From what he'd read in the papers he'd imagined . . . now he came to think of it he didn't really know what he had imagined. Probably some rather overbearing, militant female; positive, an organizer, a boss type, in fact. Certainly nothing like this little old innocent. And he'd been so sure somehow. The Miss Seeton of his imagination had looked like a possible answer to his problem at last. But this Miss Seeton wouldn't even understand the problem or, if she did, would be likely to have a fit. To his embarrassment he realized she was looking at him expectantly, waiting for him to go on. He was pained and surprised, while still trying to think of some social pleasantry to cover the awkward pause, when he heard his own voice asking, "Do you mind if I ask you something?"

"I shouldn't think so, Mr. Colveden."

"These detectives—you know, the Yard men you met in London . . ."

"I beg your pardon?" She was startled.

"Well—" Nigel was a little jolted. "Well, I mean, you did, didn't you?"

She gazed at him in astonishment. "But I don't see . . . how could you possibly know about that?"

"Everybody knows about it, it's in all the papers." The penny dropped. "Good Lord, didn't you know?"

"Certainly not. No, I . . . oh dear, how dreadful—the newspapers." For the first time she saw last night's events objectively in relation to herself. "How vulgar. Then that's why, this morning . . . how stupid of me not to realize. I never thought"—her repugnance grew—"those photographers, too—how very shocking." For her the worst had happened. "It's so vulgar," she repeated helplessly.

"I say, I'm awfully sorry to've upset you. I'd no idea you didn't realize . . ."

"It's all right, Mr. Colveden. It's my own stupidity, I'm afraid. You see I'm not used to that sort of thing. It never occurred to me . . . oh dear."

Nigel almost laughed. It was incredible. She hadn't even realized her own predicament. And he'd been thinking of asking her help in his. But there was a chance he might be able to achieve his object without involving her at all. "They'll be coming down here to see you?" he asked casually. "The detectives, I mean."

"Good gracious, no. Why on earth should they?"

"No, of course not. I'd just imagined there'd be interviews, statements, and all that sort of thing. But naturally you'd have done all that already. Silly of me."

He tossed the subject lightly away. It landed on Miss Seeton's ear with the sad thud of despair. She studied his profile. "What's the matter, Mr. Colveden? And why did you wish to meet these detectives?"

"I?" said Nigel innocently. "Oh, no reason. I was vaguely interested, that's all. I don't particularly want to meet them." She continued to watch him. "No, naturally not."

That did it. The same words—the same tone of voice. He was back in the headmistress's study at his kindergarten accused of catapulting ink pellets round the classroom. His denials had been met by her slightly bored "No, naturally not." The contemptuous indifference of the adult agreeing with a tiresome child. Now, as then, he promptly blurted out the truth.

"I'm in a mess," he stated. "Or rather I'm not, but a friend of mine is. Or soon will be. And I'm a bit boxed in down here, there's no one I can ask advice from, no one I can even discuss it with."

"But surely, Sir George . . ."

"Lord, no, my father's the last person, as you'll see in a minute."

Miss Seeton collected herself and made for the cottage. "Have you had tea, Mr. Colveden?"

"Tea?" Nigel stood bewildered, then hopped after her. "Tea? No, why?"

"Because," she said practically, "I haven't, and I don't know about you, but I could do with it. We can go and make tea, then we can take it outside and sit in the sun and you can tell me anything you want to in comfort."

She entered the kitchen, and switched on the kettle which, after its recent and abortive boiling, began encouraging noises almost at once. "I'm afraid, from what you say, I can't imagine I shall be of any use." She selected the larger of the two gift cakes and began to unwrap it. "I don't think I know anything about messes, as you call them, or what to do when you're in them." She put the cake on a plate, added it to the tea tray and surveyed the result: bread and butter, biscuits, jam, sandwiches, small cakes, large cake—that should be ample. Martha's idea of tea for one was her idea of supper for two. But the young needed a lot of food. "It does help sometimes to talk over one's troubles. It's saying them aloud that helps, I think. And sometimes they shrink. But then, of course, sometimes they don't," she added with honesty. "As for anything to do with the police," she continued, "I'd be no use at all. I've never had anything to do with them." Looking up she saw Nigel's left eyebrow rise as he hovered in the doorway; she turned slightly pink and laughed. "Well, hardly ever." The kettle was boiling, she picked up the teapot. "You take those folding chairs and table out while I make the tea."

Sitting in the sun, with the food spread before him and told to help himself, Nigel found he was hungry. Miss Seeton put down her cup and refilled it.

"Now, Mr. Colveden . . ."

"Nigel, please."

"Very well, Nigel, what is this trouble or mess and why can't you discuss it with your father or anyone you know?"

"I suppose," he answered slowly, "I suppose it's just because I do know them. The whole thing's so local—that's the trouble. Father would be the ideal person to talk to, of course, but I can't as things stand because he's a J.P. and I'd be putting him in an impossible position later as a magistrate if I told him all I know now. I mean, if I do manage to keep this friend of mine out of it when it busts wide open, as it's bound to, Father can't very well sit in judgment on a case knowing that someone else should have been involved and that I'm covering up for them."

Miss Seeton nodded. "I see. This friend of yours has done something actually against the law?"

"And how," Nigel agreed. He took up the cake knife and toyed with it brooding on the result of his one attempt to lecture Sonia Venning on the duties of motherhood and the upbringing of daughters. Talk about a packet of deep-frozen raspberries. "To mind his own business"—nicely chilled; "Since when did he presume"—served on ice; "Did he really imagine"—in fact frost on everything. Miss Seeton, wise in her experience with children, said nothing further. She waited. Nigel, in face of her cool gaze—no judgment there, merely detached sympathy and interest—fell. "It's a girl I know," he stated abruptly. "She's very young, only seventeen and irresponsible." He grinned at her, stuck the knife into the cake and cut it. "All right, I know; so I'm only a year older, but I'm not irresponsible. I've known her for years; she was only six when she and her mother came here to live, so we've sort of grown up together and I can't let her go on as she is without doing something about it. Anyway, it's all her mother's fault. Mrs. Venning . . ."

"Venning?" Miss Seeton sat up. "Wait, I'm almost sure— yes, a Mrs. and Miss Venning left a pot of jam this afternoon."

"You mean—" Nigel put down his cake and gazed at her. "You mean you know them then?"

"No, indeed, but several people left things and I'm afraid I missed them because I was asleep. But there were messages and one of them was from a Mrs. and Miss Venning."

"From Mrs. Venning?" He frowned. "That's strange, she never goes out these days, never sees people, or anything, if she can help it. That's the whole cause of the trouble; that's why Angie's gone wild. To sort of compensate, I suppose."

"But, surely, Nigel, there can't be many opportunities for wildness in a small village."

"Little you know." He laughed shortly. "It was all right until about a year ago. No—come to think of it—as far as Angie's concerned, the barn business must have been the beginning and that's nearer two years."

"The barn?"

"Yes. Angie's mother converted the old barn in their field —they never used it—and let it to a chap called Noyes. He runs it as a sort of holiday place for young men—some club or something, I don't know—anyway there's usually two or three of them there. From the little I've seen of them it looks more like a delinquents' home."

Miss Seeton nodded. "I see. And it's these young men who are a little wild?"

"What?" Nigel was surprised. "Oh, Lord, no. They're harmless enough, I suppose, they just look awful, though you hardly ever see them about. The point is, Angie started mixing with them and some of them took her to the S.S. Actually I don't think they go there much themselves, but she does— now. And that's what's got her mixed up with what's going on and—"

"Nigel." Her voice pulled him up. "What exactly is an S.S.? And what has got Miss Venning mixed up in what? And what is going on?"

Nigel smiled apology. "Sorry. Well, you wouldn't know about our local troubles, but there's been a lot of vandalism lately round the Brettenden district. And it's getting serious. There've been two robberies I know of and in the second, last week, a man and his wife were badly beaten up."

"But this is quite, quite dreadful." She was scandalized; and in the country too—it made it even worse. "But surely if you say you know—I mean the police . . ."

"I know, all right, but I doubt I could prove it. And even if I could, I'm hamstrung. You see Angie was with them in the car both times."

"But you must go to the police," she insisted, "surely you see that. I mean it's quite dreadful, robbery and violence. You say this man and his wife were hurt. You can't leave it like that. Even without proof you must tell them what you know. Quite apart from the danger to other people, it makes you partly responsible for anything else that may happen."

He stared down toward the canal, unseeing. "Think I don't know that? But would you go to the police if your sister was involved—that's pretty well what Angie is to me—without making one final effort to get her out of it before the balloon goes up?"

"A final effort?" She seized on this. "You've done something already? You've tried speaking to her, reasoning with her?"

He smiled ruefully. "Yes, I've tried both those. I've also tried shouting and yelling at her. I think I've tried everything but a whip where Angie is concerned. We quarrel every time we meet and now she avoids me like the plague. A few months ago the police raided the 'Singing Swan'—that's the club where they all meet: hot music and supposedly soft drinks—the other side of Brettenden, beyond Les Marys—but they got nowhere, the police, I mean. They raided again last week—the night before the robbery with the beating up, a night when Angie wasn't there—because they'd had an anonymous tip-off. But no dice—everything as innocent as all pie." He shrugged. "Maybe the club got an anonymous tip-off too; I wouldn't know."

"But how did you find out about the information the police had, did one of them tell you? I would have imagined they would have kept very quiet about that sort of thing."

"I would have hoped so, too." There was a wry twist to his mouth. "I found out about it quite easily by phoning the tip myself, did a break-and-enter at the Vennings' garage, put the car out of action, and then managed to hijack Angie by offering her a lift to the Singing Swan and driving flat out for

Brighton." He gave a reminiscent chuckle. "We had an unholy row." He stood up, restless, stuffed his hands in his pockets, and began to pace. "I'd known there was something on for that night from a slip she'd tried to cover up and from the way she was behaving, all glitter-eyed and galvanized."

"Oh dear," she watched him, helpless, "I don't know what to say. You seem to have done everything possible and more. I don't see what else you can do—on your own, that is."

"Nor do I. It's no good trying to do anything more locally, as they appear to get wind of it somehow. And I guess my next move's likely to end in me being beaten up by Angie's little playmates. I thought," he turned to her, "if it was possible to interest Scotland Yard in any way and set up something from a distance, it might work. But if there's no chance of their coming down here," he sat down, leaning forward, eager, "I suppose you couldn't have a word with the fellow in charge of your case, could you?—say you'd seen someone like this Lebel type round the S.S."

"Oh, no," she exclaimed in dismay, "I couldn't possibly do that, it wouldn't be true."

"It could be," he argued, "or near enough. From the description I read this morning he sounds very much in their line at the S.S. I borrow Mother's car and hang around there quite a lot, trying to keep an eye on things. You could come with me one night and from a distance you could mistake any of the boys for this Lebel."

Miss Seeton shook her head and got up. "No, Nigel, I'm sorry, I'm afraid it's impossible. It would be untrue and misleading the police. I think it would be very wrong. Also I don't know about these things, but can Scotland Yard interfere without being asked to?" She saw his defeated expression. It seemed such a shame, so unfair that he should get involved in something like this. She did wish Sir George . . . But, no. She agreed with Nigel, that was quite impossible. As a magistrate he could never countenance any suppression of charges against Miss Venning if, as Nigel seemed to fear, such charges could legally be made. But to appeal to her, of all people . . . What could she do? She hated the idea of being so useless. It was ridiculous, of course, but she felt as if she'd betrayed a trust. "The only thing I can think of," she began tentatively, "and what I will do if you like—if you think it might help at all—is to tell Superintendent Delphick what you've told me without, of course, mentioning your name or Miss Venning in any way, and explain the difficulties

as far as I can and ask his advice. He told me he would be at
the inquest, so I shall see him then. He's such a nice man, so
understanding, that I'm sure if he can make a suggestion, or if
there is any way in which he can help, I'm quite certain that
he will."

Four

There was little conversation on the return journey after the inquest. The morning event, though short as Superintendent Delphick had foreseen and the verdict of murder against César Lebel a foregone conclusion, had given both Miss Seeton and the vicar food for thought.

Miss Seeton had been grateful to Nigel Colveden for making clear to her the notoriety she had brought upon herself. She had wisely decided to endure what she could not avoid and to ignore it so far as was possible. She had resolved to be careful and to do nothing which could give rise to further comment, happily unaware that her own nature was bound to betray her. Little as she realized it, Miss Seeton was situation-prone. She was conventional to the core, but natural and logical behavior in unconventional situations can appear the height of eccentricity to onlookers.

When the coroner had praised her bravery and gallantry, she had winced at the mention of her name in public but otherwise had shut her ears to what he said. After the verdi[ct] the superintendent had asked her to lunch. Finding her a[c]companied by the vicar, he had included him in the invitati[on]. The vicar, however, excused himself, saying that he woul[d] meet her at the station in time for the train.

It had been a delightful lunch with a charming companion who, with a mixture of tact and frankness, had largely succeeded in reconciling her to the part she had played. He did make her see that publicity is a penalty you sometimes have to pay for doing what you believe to be right, but he failed to make her realize that she herself might still be in danger and that, in spite of the coroner's verdict, the case against Lebel was liable to collapse if she was no longer available as a witness. The vicar's absence had made it easy for her to broach the subject of the Singing Swan. The superintendent had surprised her by his interest. Instead of polite and rather offhand attention, which was what she had expected, he had cross-questioned her closely, embarrassingly closely, and she had been hard put to it to give the facts as Nigel had told them

47

without mentioning names or Angela Venning's connection with the club. However, she felt she had accomplished this and had been much gratified by his promise that he would quietly look into the matter and see that something was done.

Superintendent Delphick, too, was pleased. He found Miss Seeton's company refreshing and had managed to keep her away from the press. Obviously there would be talk in her own village, but it didn't seem likely that such talk would reach London.

There was, indeed, talk in her own village. The superintendent was not to know that the talkers were rapidly splitting into two main parties: those who favored Miss Seeton as the agent of a London dope ring come down to have it out— though what "it" was, was so far unspecified—with Mrs. Venning; and those that looked upon her as a victim of the drug habit who, having failed in her battle for further supplies in London, had arrived to see the chief supplier, Sonia Venning, in person and insist upon her rights.

Delphick had detailed a man to travel down on the same train as Miss Seeton and to keep a sharp lookout for any sign that she was being followed, so he felt that he had done all that was humanly possible to ensure that her address was not known to any interested party. He had reckoned without the vicar.

For Arthur Treeves the inquest had been a humiliating revelation. He had come to stand by one of his parishioners in trouble who, probably through thoughtlessness or lack of experience, had got into bad company and might need a guiding hand, would need moral support, only to find that he was escorting the heroine of the hour. He felt deeply distressed at the thought of his previous unworthy misgivings and could not but feel that his sister was partly to blame for misleading him. Between embarrassment and humility he was quite unable to face the lunch that the superintendent had proposed; he needed time to sort out his thoughts and formulate a fitting apology to her for his baseless suspicions. Consequently, when the newspapermen, who had noticed him sitting with Miss Seeton in the court, being balked of their quarry by the superintendent, had descended on him in a flock like pigeons on a crumb, he had been only too glad to seize on this opportunity for atonement and say how proud they were in Plummergen of Miss Seeton's arrival in their midst; that her example was an inspiration to them all, shining even more brightly than that of her grandmother who had lived among them so long and whose cottage she now inhabited. Thereby at one stroke undoing all the superintendent's planning of the past few days.

They were nearing Brettenden before Arthur Treeves finally resolved his problem and had the exact formula of his apology worded in his mind. He cleared his throat.

"I—er—h'rm," said the vicar. Miss Seeton looked inquiry. "I—er—feel . . . that is to say, I must own—or rather it is my duty to tell you that it's all most unfortunate," he explained.

"Oh, I do so agree," she replied, "most unfortunate, but I do feel myself to blame. I see now that if one interferes in people's affairs one must be prepared to take the consequences. It's horrid of course but it's over. I don't want to talk about it any more. I've quite made up my mind. I simply shan't read the newspapers for the next few days and then everyone will have forgotten about it and I shall be able to, too."

She found Nigel at the cottage when she got back. For a moment her heart sank. She was tired and would have liked to be alone. But after her first qualms she found his gay takeover comforting. He had the kettle on the boil and refused to let her talk until he had taken her hat and coat, ensconced her in an armchair, made and brought in the tea which was laid ready in the sitting room, poured it, and seen her drink her first cup. He had even brought some plain chocolate biscuits, by chance a favorite of hers, as his own contribution. She leaned back in her chair and smiled at him: he was so very eager, but thoughtful too. It wasn't fair to keep him in suspense. She must collect her thoughts and try to remember everything Superintendent Delphick had said; even though, when you summed it up, it didn't really amount to a great deal.

Nigel forestalled her. "Hope you don't mind me pinching tea off you two days running and making myself at home, but I thought you might be tired when you got back so I went down to see Martha and persuaded her to let me in and get things ready."

"I'm most grateful," murmured Miss Seeton.

He chortled. "You should be. Martha had made up her mind to be here herself when you got back, but she'd been in one of her Grand Slams and the whole thing was so noisy that I'm afraid I told her you were expecting me and got her to go away."

"Oh dear." She sighed. "What's the matter with Martha? And what is a Grand Slam?"

"Haven't you met her in one of her Slams?" She shook her head. "Good Lord, you haven't lived. 'If people tittle-tattle about people, what people need—' that would be the people of the first part," he explained—" 'and what people are likely to get is a piece of somebody's mind.' The somebody of the third part being Martha, of course. All to the accompaniment of a lot of slamming doors, pans, brushes, anything to hand. If only she'd go and slam the people she's got it in for instead of everything within hearing, it would be a lot quieter and much less wearing. It might even do some good."

She laughed. "It's silly of me, but I hadn't realized you knew Martha so well."

"Oh, help, yes. Martha's been doing for us at the Hall for years. I've known her since I was knee-high to nothing."

"What is it that's so upset Martha?"

"Gossip," said Nigel darkly, and then looked sheepish. "About you, I'm afraid. Based on some splendid misreading of the newspapers. I know," he hurried on, seeing her expression, "don't let it get you down, it'll blow over. Meanwhile the village gossips are having themselves a fancy-dress ball with orders and, as far as I can make out from Martha, have linked you with Mrs. Venning in sundry dark deeds in the woodshed."

"But I haven't even met Mrs. Venning," she insisted.

"Trifles like that don't make any difference. At a guess," he continued, "that would be the Nuts—Miss Nuttel and Mrs. Blaine to you. They're the parish substitute for a Hollywood scandal sheet. There's nothing unpleasant they can't brew up at the Nut House—and throw in a few adders' tongues for good measure. They must have 'just happened to notice' the pot of jam here that afternoon when they left their own tiny token, and 'just happened to peek' at the message with it. I wouldn't be surprised if they didn't 'just happen' to taste the jam as well."

Miss Seeton sat forward, put down her cup, and pushed the tea trolley to one side. "Well, it can't be helped. What you want to hear is what the superintendent said."

Nigel grinned. "Yes, I do a bit," he admitted, "but I was trying not to rush you."

They discussed exhaustively all that Miss Seeton had said to Superintendent Delphick, all that he had said to her, and all the possible meanings, double meanings, and innuendoes that could have lain behind or between everything that either of them had said. Something had been done: a move made; a little nebulous, perhaps, but at least something, and Nigel felt cheered. He pushed the trolley through to the kitchen, his offer to help wash up was firmly refused, so he took himself off, assuring her that if his mother's M.G. sports was available, he would continue his watch on the club in the hope of being able to gather more information.

After clearing up Miss Seeton decided that she would have a light supper and go to bed early because she was tired. But first she must do her routine. She repaired to her bedroom. She put a folded traveling rug in a corner against the wall, removed her shoes and her dress, got out her book, and sat down. Opening the volume of *Yoga and Younger Every Day* she was faced with a photograph of a gentleman doing a solo imitation of the statue of the Trojan priest Laocoön and his children fighting with the serpents. "The Star Posture—advanced Yoga." A little too advanced perhaps. In any case, even if she could ever achieve it, she saw no advantage in being able to put one leg behind the back of her head, with the foot on the opposite shoulder. Such a strain. She turned the pages back. Ah, yes, here she was—"The Headstand." "Put a clock in a place where you can see it. Close your eyes and breathe slowly." Really, what were they thinking of? What place did they imagine you could see a clock when you were upside down with your eyes closed? Miss Seeton set her egg timer to ring in three minutes. She knelt down, clasped her hands, placed her head against them on the floor, arched her body, walked her feet forward, then launched herself at the wall.

Superintendent Delphick pushed the overflowing out-tray to one side and regarded the empty in-tray with satisfaction. There was a knock on the door. In answer to "Yes," a constable entered carrying a batch of papers; he dumped these into the in-tray, collected those in the out-tray, saluted, and left the office. Heroically Delphick refrained from comment.

"Bob."

Sergeant Ranger put down the file he was studying. "Sir?"

"Get me Ashford on the line, will you? A personal call to Chief Inspector Brinton. If he's not in, scrub it."

He glanced quickly through the new lot of papers, decided

there was nothing that couldn't wait, took a notebook from the drawer of his desk, and began to write. After a few moments the sergeant interrupted him.

"Chief Inspector Brinton on the line, sir."

Delphick picked up his receiver. "Chris?" . . . "Yes, too long, that's your fault. Either things are too quiet your end or you're too efficient." . . . "Don't say you've grown modest since I last saw you." . . . "Tell me, Chris, strictly between ourselves, have you any gen on the Singing Swan down your way?" . . . "Come, come, you forget, my spies are everywhere." . . . For some time the superintendent listened in silence, taking occasional notes. "I see," he said at last, "interesting. But you've no idea where the leak was—supposing there was one?" . . . "No, no, not yet, but I have a feeling it may. Anyway, if it does, I'll let you know, and thanks a lot." . . . "See you." He hung up and looked across at the sergeant. "Bob, you don't by any chance know anybody living at Brettenden, I suppose—or even better, at Les Marys?"

"I've never heard of either of 'em, sir."

"Pity. A spot of leave, to visit friends or an aging relative would have done you good. But I've an idea that gap in your geographical knowledge may be filled shortly."

"Where are they, sir?"

"In Kent, Bob, in Kent. The one adjoins the other and both are near to Plummergen."

"Plummergen? But that's where Miss Seeton . . . Don't tell me she's biffed anybody else, sir."

"Don't be common, Bob. The Miss Seetons of this world don't biff people; they indicate displeasure with the ferrule of an umbrella." He paused and added thoughtfully, "But when they lie, that interests me."

"I can imagine Miss Seeton doing almost anything, sir, but not lying."

"You're quite right, it would be against her principles. Prevaricate is the proper world. We lunched together after the inquest and she told me a lot of flapdoodle, serious, but flapdoodle all the same, about a club called the Singing Swan near Brettenden. She knows nothing about it—only what she's been told. But for some reason she's not telling me all she's been told. But the reason why she was told—and then told me—and the reason why she's not telling me all she was told are what interest me if you follow me."

"No, sir."

"She's covering up for someone who's covering up for

someone. And that, in case you didn't know it, is intelligent deduction."

Bob Ranger considered the Oracle and Miss Seeton having lunch together. His imagination boggled. If the Oracle was going to get matey with Miss Seeton, he wondered if he himself should apply for a transfer.

"You look worried, Bob," his superior commented.

"Well sir, you can be bad enough on your own—you say things. But she not only says 'em, she does 'em."

"You sorrow me, Bob. You should cultivate Miss Seeton."

"God forbid, sir."

"I mean it. It's another gap in your education. Until you can learn to understand her you'll get nowhere as a detective. She's everybody's conscience, Bob—the universal maiden aunt, cousin, or sister. Humanity's backbone. Throughout history she's gone to the stake for you again and again; not with any sense of heroism, but as a matter of principle and because it would never occur to her to do anything else. She scrubs for you, sews for you, cooks for you, nurses you, and is your unfailing support in times of trouble."

The sergeant pictured himself supported by Miss Seeton in times of trouble: a transfer wasn't enough—emigration—Canada, perhaps. The Mounties. After all, they always got their man. It said nothing about women.

Delphick threw down his pen and sat back. "The whole damn case is so nebulous. I know those two girls' killings are connected—same method; both prostitutes, both drug addicts, both pushers. We've Lebel pinned for the second, if only we could find him, but nothing to connect him or Prévost with the first girl. And now Ashford think they've got drugs down their way. They say that club I asked about smells wrong and there've been reports of trouble but nothing they can pin down. A couple of raids got them nowhere. They've a feeling that drugs are in the background, but they haven't found anything. So they can join us in the dinghy. What's the good of feelings if you can't find sufficient evidence to support them? Just have to wait for the next move," he finished in exasperation.

A telephone rang.

"Chief Superintendent Gosslin, sir."

Delphick reached for the telephone. "Delphick here, sir." . . . "The evening papers? No, not yet, sir." . . . He listened with a gathering frown as the instrument quacked. Finally: "No, nothing. Just one of those things." . . . "Thanks a lot, sir." He put the receiver back. "Blast!"

"What's happened, sir?"

"Nothing yet," Delphick said savagely. "But all my puerile precautions to keep Miss Seeton's whereabouts under wraps have been blown sky high by that doddering half-wit, the vicar of Plummergen. He came up with Miss Seeton as escort, refused to join us afterwards, and then, it appears, improved his shining lunch hour by giving an interview to the press. I gather he gave her family's life history, her address, and what time she would be at home to visiting assassins—in fact, everything except details of the parking facilities. The chief's just seen the late editions and it's all in the reports on the inquest. So the next move may come any time. In Kent, I guess."

* INTERIM *

"There was no bargain as to the extent of your commitment. Your practice as a solicitor is your own affair. Your extracurricular activities are mine and I am the judge of their compass." . . . "I'm glad you do. It would have been more convenient to wait until interest in her had abated, but her appearance down in your district puts pressure on me." . . . "No. With the press as well as the police watching her, they're liable to start prying round Plummergen." . . . "Precisely. You will deal with her at once." . . . "Then you won't be acting for her much longer; except for winding up her affairs. However, since you know her cottage and its layout, you will put Noyes in the picture and save the boys a reconnaissance." . . . "No. It will be done locally. There isn't time to brief anyone and send them down; in a village as small as that local knowledge is essential." . . . "Quite unnecessary. Tell Noyes he will use that tall, dark boy, with the ginger-haired one as driver. They're new down there and won't be known by sight. They will attend your club during the evening as visiting strangers, go over and do the job, then drive north before circling back to Meadows' Barn by the Common road. That will divert police inquiries to London." . . . "Naturally. Noyes will finish processing the present lot and get it off at once. Hold any further consignment until this business is finished and forgotten." . . . "Nothing should go wrong. If there is a hitch, you will lay on something else at once. This infuriating woman has a positive genius for interference. Next, she'll go calling on Mrs. Venning or poking her umbrella into the Barn."

The telephone receiver was thrust back.

Five

Nigel lurked. He was chilly and uncomfortable and he felt like a badly cast minor conspirator in an indifferent melodrama, but he continued to lurk, grateful that he had had the forethought to bring a couple of garden cushions. For such information as he could gather he had been wont to rely on occasional visits to the club, the overhearing of unconsidered scraps of conversation, and above all on his translation of Angela Venning's moods and ill-considered chatter. Now he was aware that his appearance at the club was viewed with suspicion by those few whom he, in turn, suspected; a suspicion which might turn ugly at any time. Since the Brighton episode Angela had avoided him. Lurking was the only solution.

There were five boys and two girls whom he had pinpointed as the main troublemakers. Two of the boys owned or had the use of cars. During the past week he had contented himself with parking some way off and then following at a distance one of these or Angela's, whichever seemed the most promising. He had decided that if another break-in was tried, either he would light up the scene with his own headlights in the hope of frightening them off, attempt to join in himself, or go for the police, according to what seemed best at the time. What he would do if Angela was again directly involved he had never quite faced. This watching and waiting had produced nothing except the conviction that the monotonous and tiring role of a private investigator was not for him. Individuals had been dropped at their homes, good nights screamed, and the cars parked for the night. The group appeared to be resting on its laurels.

That drugs in some sort were in question he knew; but whether it was merely a matter of pep pills or whether it embraced anything more serious he had been unable to discover. In particular how far this had been carried in Angela's case was his chief worry. Some months earlier she had persuaded him to try a couple of what she called her boosters. He had taken the pills and had awaited the effect with interest, thinking the experience might make him understand her better and so be more effective in dealing with her. It had not helped. Either the dose was too strong or he was allergic. He had just begun to feel slightly dizzy and relaxed when he realized that the relaxation was of a different order and he was sick.

The car park at the club was fenced by wooden palings. Behind the fence Nigel squatted under close-growing shrubs. The leaves were damp with dew; the ground likewise; he had the definite impression that creatures from above, spiders, earwigs and their ilk, were on their way down via his collar, while creepers from below, ants, centipedes and their kind, were on their way up by way of his trouser legs, for a social convention around his midriff. He was, as stated, chilly; he was also wet and he tickled.

Disappointed after Miss Seeton's report that armies of policemen were not already on the march, a little reflection had shown him that the fact that the Yard had questioned her closely and had assured her that something would be done was a big step forward. This encouragement had determined him to keep vigil as long as he could or as long as his mother's complacency about lending him her M.G. lasted. Her only comment that afternoon had been that with a husband who slept by day and shot rabbits by night and a son who fly-by-nighted in her car she was not only grass widow and grass mother but was left stranded on the grass as well.

Over the fence Angela's car was parked next to one of the suspects' with the other not far away, so he felt he was in a good position to hear anything of interest. The club was emptying, it was getting late. The door was thrown open and in the shaft of light a shrill group of youngsters clattered down the steps. The door closed and the dark figures, growing clearer as moonlight took over from electricity, headed volubly toward Nigel's hiding place.

"Who you think you kidd'n, chick?" The accent was outer Odeon. "Heroines for gossakes, down here? You kidd'n?"

The voice of one he didn't know. Nigel peered through his leafy screen. Yes, there were two he hadn't seen before: one rather tall. What he'd told Miss Seeton had been quite right. Any of these seven youths could be mistaken for Lebel, judging from his picture in the papers, even at fairly close range.

"But it's true, I tell you." Angela's voice, light and clear and feverish.

"No more'n six mile away," one of the other girls chimed in. "C'mon."

"A real live heroine—now I guess that's the kinda broad I'd like t'see. What say we go call on her—look her up like?"

"That's a spicy idea, I've wanted to meet her," cried Angela above the squeals of delight from the other two girls.

Four of the boys swelled the chorus, but one held back. "Don't be so daft. It's late enough," he pointed out, "she'll be sleeping."

"Well, for gossakes we c'n wake her up. She's not deaf or sump'n?"

There were shouts of approval. "Yes, why not?" agreed Angela. "Let's get going."

"Tell you you're daft," the other boy countered. "Her place's right on the Street. We'll have the whole village out on us."

This started an argument that the newcomer quelled. "I guess I'd still like to see where a slap-up heroine lives," he persisted. "If they go t'bed so goddamn early can't we jest drive by? We c'n always dip our lights in salute or sump'n."

"Come on then," called Angela. "I'll lead. We'll go round the marsh and come up from the back. That'll leave you heading your right way and you can carry on." She ran for her car, jumped in, and started the engine. The others bundled noisily into the remaining vehicles except for the newcomer who, accompanied by his tall, silent companion, headed for a car parked near the entrance.

Nigel held his breath as Angela's car shot out into the roadway swinging right with protesting tires, followed by the two locals, the strangers' car bringing up the rear. He scrambled from his hiding place, made a quick survey—no one in sight —threw the cushions over the fence, vaulted it, scooped them up and ran for the M.G. Should he phone the police? Once that gang worked themselves up there was no knowing what they might do or where they'd stop. On the other hand, they didn't seem too bad tonight and the one he knew as Art had been putting a brake on the proceedings—at least he didn't want the whole village roused. It should be all right, he decided, and, as they were going the long way round, if he got weaving he ought to be there nearly as soon as they. If everything was quiet he could carry on home without stopping. Yes. He'd risk it. He reached the car, flung the cushions in the back, and leaped into the driving seat.

Good gracious, what was that?

Miss Seeton, suddenly awake, found it difficult to orient

herself. Of course. It was the hens. What a noise! Oh dear.
Really. She got quickly out of bed, into her slippers, pulled
her dressing gown round her, and hurried down the stairs.
Without stopping to put on a light she instinctively snatched
her umbrella from the drip tray in the passage as she passed,
unlocked the kitchen door, and sped down the garden. No,
really. It was too tiresome of them. Of course Nigel had
warned her. Upsetting the hens like this. Well, she'd soon put
a stop to it. Thank heaven, there was enough moonlight to see
one's way. Poor Stan; he'd be so cross.

The squawking from the hen houses continued unabated.
Miss Seeton arrived at the runs. She beat on the wire door
with her umbrella.

"Stop that," she called. "Stop that at once, do you hear
me?"

"Sure, lady. I hear you."

She gasped. A shadow moved forward, reached through
the wire and unhooked the door. With the moon behind him
Miss Seeton could see little but a dark shape muffled in a
coat, a hat pulled low. But the moon shone on the barrel of
the pistol he held.

"Now, just take it nice and easy, lady. Back to the house
and no noise, see."

"Don't be so childish," she snapped. "And put that toy
away at once or I shall send for the police." She brought her
umbrella down smartly on his wrist.

There was a flash. A sharp blast. There was a howl of min-
gled rage and pain. The gun fell.

"Oh dear," cried Miss Seeton in startled dismay. "I'm so
sorry, I'd no idea . . . I hope you didn't hurt yourself." She
was talking to the air. The figure, dancing in wild abandon on
one foot while clutching the other, had hurled itself at the hen
house, heaved itself onto the roof, and vanished over the wall.

There was a thud, a yelp, a curse. There were stumbling
footsteps, running footsteps. Windows thrown up, doors
thrown open. The hens redoubled their efforts in the face of
competition.

People calling: "What is it?" "Murder." "Shots." A man's
voice: "Quick, for gossakes, quick." Two loud reports, yells of
pain. Doors slamming, engine revving. And trumpet-tongued
above the tumult Sir George's triumphant bellow:

"Got him, by God—a barrel a buttock."

Two speeding cars, one close behind the other, headlights

at full coming round the second curve of the S bend ahead. This would be the Brettenden contingent, Nigel decided. That was a relief. Nothing could have happened. To have got this far in the time meant that the cars hadn't even stopped. Angie must have turned off already down the lane to the Meadows and the other car would be on its way back to wherever it had come from.

He slowed down and took a powerful torch and dark glasses from the dashboard. He had been prepared for their ditching game for some time, but this was likely to be his first chance to test his countermeasures. As the cars came into the straight he put on the glasses and dipped his lights. They didn't. He smiled: so they were going to try their usual trick. He'd seen them at it often enough, but he'd generally been behind them.

The leading car, headlights blinding, drove straight at him. At the last moment when he knew they'd veer, Nigel eased his off-wheels from the narrow road onto the grass shoulder, flipped up his headlights, and shone his torch full on his opponent's windshield. There was a yell of dismay and curses, followed by the heartening sound of tearing branches and rending metal. One in the ditch and one to play.

Nigel, his lights and torch still on, drove straight by the second car, which had slowed to give its mate room to maneuver, resisted the temptation to take a swipe at the head sticking out of the driver's window and screeching abuse, flung his glasses and torch on the seat beside him, switched off his lights and drove for the bend, thanking the moon above for enough light to steer his course.

Once round the first curve he flicked his lights on again and exulted. Hoist with their own petard. For once some devils had been given a slice of their due. They'd no chance to read his number plate nor was there room to turn and follow. In any event, they'd be too busy getting their fellow travelers out of the ditch.

A few moments later he drove happily into Plummergen. All quiet at Miss Seeton's; no lights—good. He was turning right at the end of the Street into Marsh Road, heading for home when the hen house war broke out behind him. He slammed on his brakes, reversed into a gateway, and raced back.

Windows were lighting in many houses. He cut his engine in front of Miss Seeton's and leaped out. What a racket! The hens—of course, it must be down there. He ran forward. As he reached it, the entrance to the lane beside Miss Seeton's flooded with light. A car rocketed out and down the Street. The stranger's car. He rushed back to his own, jumped in, slewed the M.G. round to follow, jammed on his brakes again to avoid by inches the stocky figure of his father as Sir George ran from the lane, double-barreled shotgun at the ready. Nigel threw open the passenger door, catching a glimpse of the vicar cantering out into the road, arms and nightshirt flapping, a ghost from the graveyard, shouting: "Stop, thieves, stop!"

Sir George stepped into the car without breaking stride and slammed the door. Nigel raced through his gear changes. Light poured from open doorways, torches flashed, people in strange array ran out, ran back, waved hands, waved pokers, brooms, and sticks, all shouted and the mechanized cavalry swept into action as the M.G. roared down the center of the Street in pursuit of its quarry, with Sir George, gun still at the ready above the windshield, standing braced for battle.

Six

The men at Rytham Hall slept late next morning.

"Anybody up yet?"

"Up, but not down, m'lady."

"Boiled eggs," said Lady Colveden.

She closed the front door. Thank heavens, it was one of Martha's days; someone to help with the lunch. She took her shopping through to the kitchen and began to lay a tray. Ten past ten. One egg and two pieces of toast each; that was quite enough as late as this. She heard the vacuum start. Right, if Martha was doing the dining room, they could have it in the morning room. For the hundredth time she wished they could eat in the kitchen, but with all the plumbing arranged under the only window it wasn't feasible. To alter it apparently meant a major operation.

They both looked a bit sheepish, she decided, as they finished their eggs and toast—like schoolboys caught out in a peccadillo. So they should from the stories going round the village—and the state of her M.G. beyond the over-casual good mornings, followed by eye avoidance, nothing so far had been said. She handed them tea.

"Did you have a good night?" she asked brightly.

Sir George spluttered. Nigel choked. Both hurriedly put down their cups. They looked at each other, then at her. Sir George gave a strangled hiccup, Nigel whooped, and they collapsed in helpless merriment.

It was most unfair. For a few seconds Lady Colveden managed to maintain her air of innocent inquiry, but an irrepressible giggle tricked her and she joined the happy throng. There was a knock and Martha put her head round the door.

"The police've come for you," she announced.

That finished them. Superintendent Delphick followed by his sergeant had a fleeting impression that they should have been carrying pails of fish to throw to the sea lions.

Order partially restored, introductions made, Martha

61

Bloomer dispatched for coffee and biscuits and the detectives seated, apologies were offered.

"No, please," disclaimed Delphick, "the police so seldom get an uproarious reception; it's a refreshing change. It was primarily Miss Seeton we came to see," he added.

"Wrong house," croaked Sir George.

"No," murmured his wife weakly, "right house, wrong time. She'll be back for lunch." She collected herself. "Please, superintendent, you must forgive us. I know it's very serious, but I think we're all a little overwrought this morning. My husband and son have only just come down to breakfast, so we've had no chance yet to catch up on each other's activities. I've heard various versions of theirs in the village—all colorful and dramatic and all, I'm sure, inaccurate—but they don't even know that Miss Seeton came back here for the rest of the night."

"You fetched her, m'dear?"

"Yes, George, in that monstrous estate wagon of yours, as my own car was out on another mission at the time."

"I'm sorry about the M.G., mother, I'm afraid we . . ."

"It's all right," she assured her son with a smile. "I quite understand. At least . . ." the edge to her smile was a little keener, "I'm sure I shall—sometime. I went into Crabbe's garage this morning, when I saw the car wasn't back, to ask if they knew anything about it. They'd found it outside when they opened up, with your note under the wiper, and got busy on it straightaway. They'd already beaten the dents out of the fender, mended the lights, and were putting the bumper back on. Crabbe told me there's nothing serious and he hopes to bring it back before lunch."

"Yes," commented Delphick, "we heard something of that particular episode from the Ashford police. I'll go into that later if I may. The only firm fact I've gathered so far is that there was a disturbance last night and as this disturbance would appear to have centered round Miss Seeton—" Bob Ranger let out an audible sigh—"we were called in since there was the obvious possibility that there might be a connection with the case in which she is already involved as a witness. The Ashford police told us that it was very late when they brought Sir George and Mr. Colveden back here, so we didn't like to bother you too early. We called at Miss Seeton's but she was out, so we had a look round her place to get the lie of the land. Then we were informed by a Miss Treeves—

that would be the vicar's sister, I take it—that Miss Seeton was staying here. Miss Treeves, an eyewitness, I understand, very kindly gave us her account of last night's affair. And the vicar, another eyewitness, very kindly gave us his. Several people came forward, all eyewitnesses, and they very kindly gave us theirs. The accounts differ: ranging from the stealing of eggs, through Miss Seeton threatening to shoot up the village, to a full-scale invasion by troops. So we came here, I'm afraid a little earlier than we had intended, to try and get some facts to fit these fancies. If you'll bear with me, we would be very grateful for a full statement from each of you in turn which should put us in the picture. I think it would probably be simplest, if that's all right with you, Lady Colveden, if we hear your side of it first as you seem to have been more on the fringe of the affair."

Fringe? That irked her. "Well, I didn't really do anything, superintendent," she replied airily. "I just went over there and disarmed her and brought her home with me."

Sergeant Ranger was startled into speech. "Disarmed her? You mean you took her umbrella away?"

"Certainly not," Lady Colveden answered, "she had that in her other hand. I took her pistol away."

"Good God!" said Sir George.

Having made her point, Lady Colveden gave them a straightforward account of the little she knew at first hand of the night's events.

Rytham Hall, up a winding drive off Marsh Road, was about five hundred yards from Miss Seeton's cottage. Lady Colveden had been reading in bed. Soon after midnight she remembered being vaguely conscious of fowls making a noise somewhere and then a crack that might have been a shot. She had gone to the window and leaned out. She had heard distant cries and then two more reports, followed by screams and somebody shouting. It had sounded, but she couldn't be sure, like her husband's voice. She had dressed quickly and, seeing that the M.G. was not yet back, had taken Sir George's car. Arriving at the Street, she had found several people converging on Miss Seeton's cottage, some with torches although there was enough moonlight to see by. The vicar had rushed up, trying to persuade her to give him a lift in pursuit of the thieves who had driven off only a few moments before. She had seen no point in careering round the countryside with the Rev. Arthur in his nightshirt and no slippers—she did hope

Molly Treeves had made him take a hot bath when he got back—after an unknown car traveling in an equally unknown direction.

Miss Seeton's hens were still vociferously indicating the center of the disturbance, so she had gone round the cottage and down the garden to find Mr. and Mrs. Bloomer, Martha armed with a broom and Stan with a billhook in one hand and a torch in the other, standing as bodyguards to Miss Seeton who, in her dressing gown and leaning on her umbrella, was holding a pistol aimed at a cluster of bewildered villagers gathered by the side door in the wall, with the beam of Stan's torch illuminating them as if for target practice. She had broken up this tableau, told everybody to go home, taken Miss Seeton's pistol away from her, and persuaded her to return to the cottage, pack a few things for the night, and come back with her to the Hall. She had made up the spare bed and put in two hot-water bottles, Miss Seeton and she both had Veganin and hot milk and both had gone to bed and to sleep.

"Not, I'm afraid," Lady Colveden concluded with a look at her husband and her son, "in the tradition of high heroism and romantic endeavor, but I like to think it was practical."

"Practical and very wise," agreed Delphick. Lady Colveden glowed. So much for that "fringe." "There is just one point which is not quite clear," he continued. "What did you do with the pistol?"

"The pistol?" She was disconcerted. "I—er . . . George," she rounded on her husband, "if you laugh I swear I'll leave you. And, Nigel, if you snigger, I'll make you pay for the M.G.'s repairs." She gazed back at the superintendent, wide-eyed. "How awful. I'm not quite sure," she confessed.

"Well, don't worry about it," Delphick reassured her. "There was no reason for it to seem important to you—at the time. But I think we ought to find it. It can't be far away. Let's see. You didn't put it down to help Miss Seeton pack?"

Lady Colveden reflected. "No, I don't think so. At least I don't remember doing so."

"No? Then you certainly wouldn't want it when you were driving. You might have put it in the back of the car."

"Superintendent, you're brilliant!" she exclaimed. "I remember now: that's exactly what I did do. I put Miss Seeton's case in the back and threw the pistol in after it."

Sir George went hot; Nigel cold. Delphick gave an inward shudder. It had, presumably, been fired. Therefore on the same presumption the safety catch was off. What with Miss

Seeton waving it at the villagers and Lady Colveden tossing it lightly among the luggage, it was a miracle that no one had been killed.

"Is the garage locked?" he asked. She shook her head. "Sergeant." Bob Ranger left the room.

"Well, if no one wants me any more I'll go and help Martha prepare lunch," suggested Lady Colveden.

"No, nothing further at the moment, Lady Colveden, except to thank you for a very clear statement and also to thank you for your prompt action in removing Miss Seeton from the danger zone last night. I'd be grateful if you'd tell her that we'll call and see her after lunch, if we may."

"Certainly, superintendent. And see if you can't persuade her to stop here. She's talking about going back to her cottage this afternoon. Apropos, Nigel, if she does insist on going back—and always presuming that my car has been returned by then—will it be all right for me to use it? Or had you any further maneuvers in mind?"

"It's all right, m'dear. The boy can drive. Decided it's time he had a car of his own."

"What a good idea, George. I do so agree. I would suggest an armored car, or perhaps a tank." Her exit was spoiled by her bumping into the sergeant as he entered with the coffee tray. "Oh, good," she remarked, seeing the automatic pistol lying on a clean handkerchief beside a plate of biscuits. "You've found Miss Seeton's gun all right. Thank goodness for that. I suppose," she added wistfully, "it would be against the regulations for you to slip me a copy of your notes later on. It appears to be my only chance of ever finding out what everybody got up to last night."

The door closed. The sergeant put his burden on the table, picked up the handkerchief and took the pistol to his superior.

"I've put the safety on, sir. There won't be any fingerprints, of course, or if there are they'll be everybody else's but."

Sir George sat up. "Safety catch?"

The cups of coffee Nigel was bringing them wobbled in their saucers. "Do you mean they've been running round with that thing and chucking it about cocked?"

"I'm afraid so, Mr. Colveden, but as fortunately nothing's happened, it might be better not to mention it. No point in spreading unnecessary alarm and despondency. Now, Sir George. Where were you exactly when the shooting started?"

"Down by the canal."

"With a gun?"

"Rabbitin'."

"Ah, yes, that would be just beyond Miss Seeton's boundary. Do you get many rabbits down there, sir?" Sir George reddened. Delphick smiled. "Would I be right in assuming that you have been patrolling—I beg your pardon—rabbiting just these last nights since Miss Seeton's arrival?"

Nigel leaned forward. "Good Lord, father, why didn't you tell me? We could have shared watches."

Sir George avoided his son's eye. "Thought you had other things to do." Nigel subsided.

The superintendent watched them with interest. How alike they were in some ways. But if they must form themselves into a kind of private Home Guard, why not have a discussion and plan their campaign together? Sir George evidently knew what his son had been doing; whatever that might be. No, wait. Did he know? Perhaps suspected was a better word. Nothing had been said openly. Yes. That must be the clue. Nothing said. But why? Major General Sir George Colveden, Bart., K.C.B., D.S.O., J.P. Yes, J.P., that could be it. Sir George was a local magistrate. In which case, though he might be able to ignore suspicion, he could not overlook actual knowledge. Which meant . . . All that rigmarole of Miss Seeton's about the club. Yes, Nigel was probably her informant. And all that idiotic covering up must mean that some friend of his was involved and his father mustn't know. How complicated. Also stupid and tiresome. But it did shed an obscure light on certain aspects and meant, if he was to get anything out of the boy, he'd have to question him on his own. He repressed a sigh. Well, back to his muttons. He addressed Sir George.

"We had, of course, asked the local police to keep an eye open."

" 'Course. Good lad, Potter. But only one of him. Can't be everywhere."

"Precisely. Which is why I should like to express my most sincere thanks for your sudden interest in rabbits. You said you were down by the canal."

"Four cars came over the bridge. Went up the lane. Last one stopped. Damn chickens started quacking. Moved in closer. Heard a pistol shot. 'Fore I could get there, chap fell over the wall. Began to run, had a limp."

"A limp? H'm, he could have twisted his ankle jumping down. Can you describe him?"

"Never saw him. Back view, overcoat and hat. Let him have both barrels. Peppered his bottom—tell from the way he jumped. Youngish from his movements. Reached the car and was off before I could reload. Chased up the lane after him. People comin' out everywhere, they'd see to Miss Seeton. Thought it important to catch the car, shoot its tires off. Found my son there: entrained and got crackin' after 'em."

After them? Which way now? Maidstone Road through Brettenden or the Ashford by Ham Street. Hoped the boy knew. Apparently did. Without hesitating, Nigel took the right-hand fork for Ashford. Sir George narrowed his eyes to slits against the rush of air. Wished he'd got goggles. Huh? Oh, good boy. He took the pair of dark glasses Nigel handed to him and put them on. No use sitting down, if they got a view he'd never have time to scramble up again. Silly little car this of Meg's; stand up or lie down, no proper sitting. He braced himself against the back of the seat and hoped they'd hit no bumps.

This couldn't go on. Have to put a stop to it. So far as Nigel was concerned anyway. All very well for Meg to say not to interfere, let the boy try his own methods; as it was her car he was using she ought to have most say. He smiled briefly, remembering his wife's logic. But it wouldn't do—too serious. Let Angie go to hell her own way. That had been her car, the first of those four tonight. Knew the sound of it. Admit it hadn't stopped, but she'd been there all right, he'd bet on that. Silly little chit, needed discipline. Why the devil didn't Sonia . . . ? Something very wrong there, nice woman once. Angie, too, nice little girl. But lately . . . These youngsters, doing everything for kicks. But not a damn about the people they kicked.

"Car ahead," shouted Nigel.

Sir George peered forward. Yes, headlights. Traveling fast. He bent down. "Know the number?" he yelled.

"No. I think I'd know the car."

Think. Not good enough. Silly ass. Couldn't go shooting up cars on speck.

"Try to overtake. Get level. Force 'em into the side and stop 'em. Can't keep apologizin' for shootin' up wrong cars."

He straightened. Light coming from the side at the crossroads ahead. Damn these hedges. Growing brighter. Instinctively his son eased his foot.

"Keep goin'," howled Sir George. "Ours major road;

they've got Halt sign, have to stop. Keep goin'. You—" he bawled into the night, "you, you goddamned . . ." A car shot from the side road, turning on two wheels into the straight in front of them. "Halt. Halt, you fools. Our road. Major roa—"

His voice was drowned by the wail of a siren and the skidding scream of the M.G.'s tires as Nigel, between braking and changing down, fought for control. Sir George dropped his gun which exploded forlornly into the hedge, and clung to seat and windshield as with a twanging crunch they slithered inexorably into the illuminated sign at the back of the other car. There was a tinkle of glass and POLICE vanished as the light went out. There was a reek of petrol.

Both drivers sprang into the road. Recriminations were stayed by the sound of an engine. A lonely figure on a Velocette puttered into view. Waved on by the police driver, P. C. Potter, the only mobile pursuer left, helmet straight and wireless antenna riding high, passed with a salute and phut-phutted on his way.

"A first-class man, Potter," commented the superintendent. "He was taking particulars of an accident about a mile from the village, on what I believe is the Brettenden Road, when he heard distant shots. Having been warned to expect trouble he radioed a report, alerting patrol cars north and south of Plummergen. On the outskirts of the village he was told that two cars had been seen streaking north. As they hadn't passed him, it had to be the Ashford Road, so he followed up as best he could."

"No luck?" asked Sir George.

"I'm afraid not. The car you hit sent messages and road blocks were tried, but there was never much hope. There were too many possible routes and too little description available. Incidentally, Sir George, the driver of the car you unfortunately immobilized admits that he was late in sounding his siren, forgetting that the hedgerow would have hidden the flashing of his rooflight. He gives your son full marks for avoiding a serious accident."

"Generous," said Sir George.

Delphick smiled. "Give credit where it's due. The car wasn't too badly damaged, I take it?"

"No," agreed Nigel. "It looked a bit sorry for itself. I'm afraid the police car came off worst with a bashed petrol tank. We told them everything we could and then they radioed for a tow for us, because a fender was binding and one headlight was a goner. We dropped the car off outside Crabbe's garage in the village and the tow brought us on home before going back for the police car."

Delphick got up. "Well, thank you, Sir George. I think that's all quite clear and I needn't keep you any longer. We only need Mr. Colveden's statement, then that's all till we can get in touch with Miss Seeton. Just one thing," he added as Sir George opened the door, "grateful as we are for your help, I'm bound in duty to remind you that the license for your shotgun is for sporting purposes and not, in this country, for big game however pepperworthy. Whatever one's personal opinion on the types we are hunting, the law insists they are treated as being on the police reserve and not as vermin." He grinned. "However, I feel there is little likelihood of a complaint being lodged in this case."

Sir George gave a short bark of laughter and left the room.

The superintendent did not return to his chair. He moved to the window and stayed there for a time admiring the garden.

Beautifully planned and, considering the difficulties these days, amazingly well kept. Whoever had planted the trees bordering that long vista must have done so with loving care and forethought. Brown, copper, scarlet oak, the crimson and purple of maples, dark gold and primrose yellow hazing to the blues of cedar and eucalyptus, interspersed with every shade of green. And below, the present owners had extended and sharpened this massed coloring in the flower beds, shrubs, and borders that framed the sweep of lawn.

Bob Ranger watched him warily. Not a good sign with the Oracle, this long pause.

Delphick swung back to the room. "Now, Mr. Colveden," —yes, he was right, the sergeant concluded, he knew that tone; the storm signals were out—"your name I know, your address is here, your occupation is what?"

Nigel stared. "Occupation?" This curt tone was a surprise after the superintendent's urbane and friendly manner of a few moments ago. "Occupation?" he repeated. "I'm still training."

"For what?"

"Agriculture. I go back in a fortnight. Father's done wonders with putting the farm on its feet, but it doesn't make money and it could be made to. Pay its way properly, I mean. And that's what I intend to do."

"Hard work."

"So's anything else, but this happens to be work I like."

"You're the only child, then?"

"No, I have an older sister. She's married and lives in London."

"During this training period, then, you're not at home a great deal. Is that right?"

"Not this last year, no. Only for holidays."

"Your arrival on the scene last night was timely."

"I—I suppose it was."

"It was. Why?"

"Why? I was on my way home."

"From where?"

"Brettenden."

"Where in Brettenden?"

"I'd been out."

"Obviously. Where?"

"At a place outside Les Marys."

"Its name?"

"Does that matter?" Nigel was becoming resentful under the terse questioning.

"If it didn't I shouldn't ask. You were, I should imagine, in a club called the Singing Swan."

"I wasn't in it."

"Don't let's indulge in sophistry," rapped Delphick. "Where exactly were you?"

"Under some bushes behind the car park."

"Alone?"

"Of course I was alone. What do you suppose?"

"I suppose nothing, Mr. Colveden. I'm trying to get facts. You were alone under some bushes behind a car park. Why? Or is it part of your agricultural training?"

"I was trying to keep a watch, if you must know."

"On whom?"

"I don't know all their names," he snapped in exasperation. "They're a group that use the club a lot. One of them's called Art and another Micky or Nicky, I'm not sure which. And one of the girls is called Sue."

"Allow me to help you." Delphick went to the table where his sergeant was sitting and picked up a piece of paper. "Susan Frith, Diana Dean, Arthur Grant, Michael Hughes, Percy Davis, James Trugg, John Hart. Were they all there?"

Nigel gaped. "If those are their names, yes. They all came out together."

"Anybody else?"

"No," he answered quickly, thinking of Angela—then: "that is, yes, there were two other fellows whom I didn't know. They were talking to them, but they weren't with them. I mean they had a car of their own. I got the idea they didn't belong down here."

"What gave you this idea?"

"Only that one of them spoke in a terrible sort of Cockney version of American. Also I think something was said about their car—that it would be heading back in the right direction —which gave me the impression they came from a distance."

"Can you describe them?"

"Not really, no. The moon wasn't all that bright and I didn't notice. One of the girls was wearing a dress, but otherwise they all looked much the same. Tight trousers, loose jackets, and mops of hair."

"Was either of the two you didn't know wearing a hat and overcoat?"

"No . . . Oh, wait, one of them, the tall one, I think, was carrying a coat."

"Did you hear much of what was said?"

"Yes, they were quite near me, I could hear all right. There was some talk about Miss Seeton. It sounded as if they'd been reading about it in the papers and the Cockney American said he'd like to meet a heroine. But the one called Art said they couldn't, it was too late. So in the end they decided to drive round the other side of the marsh and come back up the lane past Miss Seeton's cottage. Oh, yes, that's when somebody said that they'd be on their right road."

"Who said that?"

Nigel frowned as if trying to remember. This needed care. "I don't know. That is, I'm not sure. One of the girls, I think."

"What happened then?"

"They drove off."

"All four cars?"

"Yes . . . no," he floundered, then recovered, "three cars. The Brettenden lot have only got two cars. The other fellows had a car over near the entrance. I didn't see it clearly. It was a dark saloon, that's all I know."

"Oh, no, Mr. Colveden, not all you know," said Delphick enigmatically. "Aware, then, that these slightly—irresponsible shall we say?—friends of yours," he glanced at the list of names he was still holding . . .

"They're not friends of mine," retorted Nigel.

". . . these slightly irresponsible acquaintances were converging on the cottage of an elderly woman living alone, it didn't occur to you to give her a friendly warning; nor, even more to the point, get in touch with the police. You just," he dropped the list back on the table, "went home."

"No . . ." Nigel began to protest.

Delphick overrode him. "No. You took time off, on the way home, to play dangerous road games with these acquaintances of yours and put one of their cars in a ditch."

For a moment Nigel was too startled to speak. How could he know about that? How could he have found it out so quickly anyway? He thought back over what had been said. There was nothing . . . one minute—an accident on the Brettenden Road with Potter taking particulars. That must be it. They'd guessed it was his car. But they couldn't know for certain. "You couldn't possibly prove that," he stated.

"If it interested me at all or was of the slightest consequence, I should imagine it could be proved a dozen ways. The prints of your tires on the shoulder should be enough."

"All right, then," Nigel answered savagely, "I did ditch them. I only wish I'd been able to ditch the other car as well. And it's not a game, as you seem to think. They tried to put me off the road, but they didn't expect me to be ready for them. I've watched them do it to other people before."

"I see. So you not only lie about under hedges listening to other people's conversations, you watch them too—you follow them about."

He didn't think he liked this, decided Bob Ranger. Not a bit. What was the Oracle getting at? After all, this youngster had tried. Done pretty well, too, he would have thought. They were always asking the public to have a go. Well, he'd had one. And look where it was getting him. The Oracle was forgetting that the boy was only a boy. Reaching back to that callow horizon of eighteen from the staid maturity of twenty-eight, Bob readily admitted that if he'd copped the Oracle in this mood at that age he'd have rolled himself up the carpet by now and had himself carried away.

"Perhaps you'd like to explain why you've been watching and following these people."

It was pathetic, Nigel thought, that he'd actually wanted meet these Scotland Yard detectives. Wanted to see them. Wanted to talk to them. Wanted to ask their help. Wanted . . . With regard to this particular specimen at all events must have been out of his miniature mind. He'd even be eager to give them information. After a session with this type, he wouldn't give them the time of day.

"Well, Mr. Colveden?"

Why had he been following them? No harm in telling them that, he supposed. "Because they're—well, I can't prove it, therefore it's not a fact, so I don't see how it can help you. But I know—sorry, wrong again, it's just another of my ideas —that they've started raiding people's houses. Stealing."

"Sarcasm and rudeness aren't exactly helpful."

"I quite agree," retorted Nigel, "but I don't see why it should be one-way traffic."

"Whatever you may suspect these people of doing, from the little you've told me so far you appear to have no grounds for these suspicions."

"No grounds?" he exclaimed. "Well, if you don't want to believe anything else, what about last night?"

"Last night, you yourself, Mr. Colveden, helped to give them an unshakable alibi. Both cars were a mile away on the Brettenden Road, one of them in a ditch. The occupants of those cars were making statements to a police constable at the time when the shooting took place. They could not possibly be concerned. It sounds to me far more likely that you're trying to get your own back on these youngsters for some imagined slight or injury; including, unless I'm mistaken, trying to involve the police in your private vendetta by anonymous telephone warnings of events that never took place."

"Never took place?" Nigel's fury was beginning to loosen his tongue. "What about that poor wretched man and his wife who were robbed and beaten up the next night? I suppose that was fancy too."

"A specific accusation." Delphick returned to his chair, sat down, stretched his legs out, and stuffed his hands in his pock- . "At last. Now, perhaps, we shall get somewhere. How do know these same people were involved? Were you re?"

No, I wasn't." He was sullen. "I'd kept too far behind and them. I didn't get there until just as they were driving from the house. Didn't even know what had happened ext day."

Delphick frowned. "I saw the file on that case this morning. mention of your evidence. If you knew so much, why n't you go openly to the police?"

A fat lot of good that would have done."

"Yes, it would. The only reasonable conclusion, if you're not involved yourself, is that you're trying to protect someone who is."

"I . . ."

"Don't bother to protest. I've neither the time nor the inclination to play ring-around-a-rosy with you. If I'm right, you won't admit it and in any case I shall very soon find out. One thing I wish to make quite clear: I do not like," deliberately he spaced out the four words: "vicious, shallow little hooligans who endanger other people's lives and property simply for their own entertainment. They mostly take drugs to foster their excitement and become as filthy in their persons as they are in their habits. I know it's correct these days to look upon them as sick and in need of help and treatment, but if you'd seen as much of them as I have and of the effects of their mischief, you'd realize that with the number of worthwhile people in the world, it's a waste of time and money to try and save the scum. Better and simpler to flush it down the drain where it belongs."

Nigel sprang up stammering with rage. "How d-dare you speak like that? You kn-know nothing about it. Just b-because you're older you think you can s-solve all the world's problems, know the answer to everybody's t-troubles. What about the p-parents? Have a look at them for a change. You—you couldn't even imagine what it's like to be young, with no brother or father or sister, with nobody except a mother who writes stupid books all day long and never goes out—or allows anyone in either—you'd damned soon try to find friends of your own age to go about with, t-try to find some amusement and you'd end by getting mixed up with the wrong sort and into a mess just like Angie has."

Seven

"There. That's the last signature. The last. I think we may say that concludes everything. Yes, that finishes it. For the moment at all events." Hubert Trefold Morton, solicitor, alderman, and mayor-expectant of Brettenden, sat back and beamed. "Probate shouldn't be long delayed. Not long. A perfectly straightforward estate. No bequests, other than the small one to Mr. and Mrs. Bloomer. Shall we say three months at the most? Your cousin was a wonderful woman. Wonderful. She did me the honor to leave her affairs entirely in my hands and I flatter myself I didn't do too badly by her. Not too badly at all. Of course, placed as I am with my knowledge of local affairs, I have my finger on the pulse so to speak and when there's just that extra little bit of capital lying around I'm in a position to know when is a mortgage not a mortgage, as one might say." He laughed lustily. "Property. That's the thing. When you own land you own it, I maintain. And while we're on the subject of property, Sweetbriars itself is a very nice little place. Very nice indeed. I don't know whether you intend to live there or are considering selling."

"I've not made up my mind," murmured Miss Seeton.

"No, no, quite. Early days yet. Early days. If you should consider it, remember we could probably do a very satisfactory deal there. Very satisfactory in fact." He beamed again. "Now, is there anything you wanted to know? Any little point on which I can be of assistance?"

Miss Seeton pressed her fingertips to her forehead. "No, nothing that I can think of, thank you." Really, this Mr. Morton, so overpowering, though she was sure he meant to be very helpful and kind, did boom at one so. She didn't know how Cousin Flora . . . But then, of course, and certainly latterly, most business would have been transacted by correspondence and at least letters didn't make a noise. She sighed and stood up.

Mr. Trefold Morton came ponderously to his feet and leaned on the desk. "I hope you don't mind my saying so, Miss Seeton, and with no wish to be ungallant, you seem a little tired. Not quite the thing, you know. Not the thing at all. Of course it's not to be wondered at, from what one reads in the papers you've been having a most distressing time. Very distressing. And there's a rumor—only just a rumor, but you know how these things get about in small communities and, after all, Plummergen's not so far away, not far—there was another distressing incident last night. Of course I don't believe half I hear. Very little of what I hear, in fact. But they say there were shots . . ." He paused expectantly.

Miss Seeton collected her things. She couldn't—no, she really couldn't—go into all that.

Mr. Trefold Morton passed off his disappointment. "All wildly exaggerated, I've no doubt. No doubt at all. But nonetheless tiring. You must take more care of yourself. After a certain age we all have to take that little extra care. Would you like me to call the garage and order a car to take you home?"

"No, please. It's quite unnecessary." Miss Seeton was firm. The thought of having to wait for a car while this Mr. Morton continued to boom at her was unendurable. Also he seemed to say most things at least twice, as if one was slow of understanding. But then he was on the council and she believed he did quite a lot of public speaking; that probably accounted for it. "I'm perfectly all right," she assured him, "it's only that I have a rather bad headache. But I'm sure that a little fresh air will soon put it right."

"A headache?" Mr. Trefold Morton looked at her sharply. "Come, we can't have that. Oh, no. We certainly can't have that. Wait here a moment. I think I have just the thing for you. Unless I gave them away, that is. But I don't think—no, I'm sure I didn't. They'd be just the very thing." He opened a door behind him and hurried out.

The office contracted into a grateful silence; the furniture shrank to normal proportions; the air and Miss Seeton's head ceased to vibrate. Not for long. Ebullience returned with Mr. Trefold Morton holding up in triumph a small phial of pills.

"Eureka, dear lady, here we are. When you get home, lie down and take one of these. Miraculous you'll find them. Miraculous."

"It's very kind of you, Mr. Morton . . ."

He winced. "Trefold Morton. We use the full name."

". . . Mr. Trefold Morton, but I seldom take drugs."

"Drugs?" He swelled. "Good heavens, no. Nothing of the kind I assure you. Homeopathic, I believe. They were given me by a friend. A dear friend. Some time ago, when things were—er—a little difficult. They did wonders for me. Wonders. Now, not another word." He pressed the phial into her hand. "Don't forget. Take one as soon as you get home. And take one again whenever you find the strain too much, with this trying time you're having. Tremendously relaxing you'll find them. Tremendously."

Disgraceful. Truly scandalous—those two women in front. And at the top of their voices, too. Should she interfere? wondered Miss Seeton. Tell them there wasn't a word of truth in what they were saying. But it would be so embarrassing to make a scene. And in a bus, too. Somehow that made it worse. Anywhere else you could say what you thought and walk away. But you couldn't walk away in a bus, at least not far. Unless you stopped it and got off. Then, of course, you would have to walk—rather too far. Or wait two hours for the next one. Oh dear, she wished she had agreed to Mr. Trefold Morton's suggestion of a car to take her home. Miss Seeton sat and seethed. The woman on the other side from them had called the fat one Mrs. Blaine. So the thin one must be Miss Nuttel. Nigel had been quite right about them. Dreadful women. To dare to say that Miss Venning had attacked her last night. And that she, of all people, had tried to shoot the girl. How on earth did they dream up such fantastic ideas? Just because some silly boy tried to steal some eggs. To drag Miss Venning's name into it was monstrous.

The bus slowed and stopped to pick up a plump, fresh-faced little woman, standing at the side of the road at an opening where a lane wandered quietly between hedgerows. The white-painted sign pointing down the lane was lettered in black "The Meadows."

Miss Seeton rose and hurried down the aisle. She'd remembered: this must be where the Vennings lived. They weren't far from Plummergen now, only about a mile. She could perfectly well walk back from here. How very fortunate that she'd noticed. She'd go at once and explain. Apologize. She'd scotch this mischievous rumor before it had time to do any damage. She swept past Miss Nuttel and Mrs. Blaine without a glance and the plump little woman stepped aside to make room as she descended.

Mrs. Fratters looked back in surprise as she climbed aboard the bus. Someone calling on madam. That wouldn't go down well. But it couldn't be helped. She hadn't time now to go traipsing after her and find out what she wanted. She'd never get back in time for lunch with the Kenya Continental. And if madam had to go without her coffee, that wouldn't go down well either. They'd had quite enough to-dos for one morning, with Miss Angie in the state she was in.

The Nuts watched Miss Seeton's hurrying figure and exchanged pregnant glances. The bus started; drew away. Through the open window floated a brighter titter and the words: "What did I tell you? If ever proof was needed . . ."

Miss Seeton's wave of indignation carried her crest-high until she was halfway down the lane, then treacherously receded, leaving her to flounder in crosscurrents of doubt.

She'd had no idea that Mrs. Venning lived so far out. So— so solitary. It was quite possible, in fact, now she thought of it, even probable that Mrs. Venning might not have heard of this dreadful rumor. Or at all events not yet. It was one thing to deplore malicious scandal and reassure an innocent victim, but it was quite another thing if the victim didn't know she was a victim—and one had to explain what it was one was deploring before one could deplore it. To reassure someone who didn't know that they needed reassurance would mean that one would have to make it clear oneself what the reason for reassurance was and why the need to . . . oh dear, how complicated. And, of course, embarrassing. On the other hand, if Mrs. Venning and her daughter knew nothing as yet of what was being said, surely it would be better—kinder, for they were bound to learn of it in time—to forewarn them. To, so to speak, remove the poison from the sting before it stung. In which case it was one's clear duty. But then, again, bearers of bad tidings. There were too many ways of looking at it.

Looking at it from every conceivable angle, Miss Seeton went forward on doubtful feet. Facing her was a high brick wall, partially covered with evergreen honeysuckle and variegated ivies. The lane turned sharp right.

Miss Seeton was about to follow suit when she delayed on hearing a protest of raised voices round the corner.

". . . can't git a bit o' long-eye fer cryssake."

"Noysey said fer t'stay in. If yer needs a stash-in, do t'Venning poult."

How very awkward. One didn't want to eavesdrop—even if one didn't understand. But then, equally, one didn't want to interrupt an argument. So dreadfully embarrassing. For both sides.

The first voice rose to a wail. "That ole scrubber, fer crys-sake, s'bin scrubbed so often t'bristles're worn."

Miss Seeton relaxed. Only a domestic difference. She went forward.

On her left the wall ended in a pair of huge wooden doors, closed and reminiscent of the entrance to a barracks. In front of her the lane continued through an ordinary barred gate to run along the side of a field. In this open gateway was a car. Beside it, standing in the lane with their backs to her, were three young men.

These must surely be some of the boys Nigel had spoken of, who lived—no, holidayed—at the Barn. People were fre-quently unfair to the young, dismissing them as pleasure-seeking and feckless, whereas here were three lads having a heated discussion on house cleaning.

Miss Seeton approached them with confidence.

"Go on. Git goin' back. Y'know what Noysey said. Fer t'stay outta sight till Ginger's finished it arter Lofty's ballin' it. Till t'ole trot wi' t'mush's bin done."

The old trot hung the handle of her mush over her left wrist, stretched out her right hand, plucked a sleeve. The sleeve jerked away. Three blank faces confronted her.

Her confidence waned. Really, until one turned the corner of the lane and was out of sight of the road one didn't realize how isolated it was here. How very isolated. No—this was ri-diculous. They were only boys. Miss Seeton smiled.

"Excuse me, is this where Mrs. Venning lives?"

Six blank eyes. Silence.

"Mrs. Venning?" articulated Miss Seeton. No doubt they found her speech as difficult to understand as she did theirs.

A dark boy, the tallest of them, jerked a thumb. Miss See-ton followed the indication: a small wooden door to one side of the two big ones; no bell, no knocker, no letter box even. Just a plain wooden door with a ring-handled latch. She smiled again in thanks, opened the door, and went through. The effect was strange. She hadn't realized there was quite a wind today, until it was cut off as she closed the door behind her. Such peace. No, peace wasn't the right word. Stillness. If one were fanciful one might almost say a brooding stillness.

On her right was a courtyard and a garage. On her left an attractively blended shrub border. In front of her a concrete path ran to the back of a small outhouse of some kind. To its right a glasshouse; to its left the path curved out of sight be-hind a high clipped hedge.

No one about. No sound. Rounding the curve she was faced with—yes, it must be—the back of the house. The steep tiled roof sloped down to a low oak door. A miniature ship's bell hung near the door which, like the windows on either side, was closed. But a latch window farther on was ajar; the nearest to a sign of life she'd seen. Did one ring the bell? Should one go round to the front? It was so difficult to know what was right. Many people in these old houses used the back door all the time. Perhaps it would be more correct to go round.

The front door was of plain oak with a heavy wooden drawlatch. No bell. No knocker. No letter box. What did the postman do? she wondered. She tapped on the door with the handle of her umbrella. There was a period of silence, broken abruptly by the rattle of the bolts being drawn. The latch lifted and the door swung outward, forcing Miss Seeton to step back. A tall woman with a handsome haunted face looked at her in silent inquiry. Unnerved, Miss Seeton flustered.

"Oh dear. Have I come to the wrong door?"

"Yes."

Miss Seeton fled. The bolts clanged back into their sockets. Mrs. Venning walked through the house, Miss Seeton hurried round it, to arrive breathless at the back door as it opened and she faced the same situation, the same woman, the same look, the same silence.

It was ridiculous to let oneself be agitated by a little thing like going to the wrong door. After all, it was a very natural mistake and obviously Mrs. Venning thought so too, or she wouldn't have come straight to this one and opened it ready, as she had. But, somehow, it did make it even more difficult to explain why she'd called. How to put it? Really, the best thing would be to state the facts quite simply. Let them speak for themselves.

"I really came to apologize," she began. "Well, not to apologize exactly—at least not in that sense—for, of course, it was nothing that I'd done, myself. Only I was so very, very shocked to hear it. And, as I of all people knew there wasn't a word of truth in it and as I happened to be passing by your lane, I thought it only right to make that quite clear straightaway."

Sonia Venning regarded her visitor. Finally: "I haven't the remotest idea what you're talking about."

Miss Seeton looked worried. "You are Mrs. Venning?"

"I am."

Miss Seeton smiled with relief. "That's all right, then. It was foolish of me, I should have asked that in the first place. I quite understand your not understanding what I'm talking about. I did realize that was very possible, but on thinking it over I felt it was essential that you should be put in possession of the facts, so that you could ignore it or refute it when you did hear, as you'd be bound to eventually."

"What are you talking about?"

"Eggs," Miss Seeton told her earnestly. "They said that your daughter had stolen my eggs. It's outrageous."

Mrs. Venning was calm, her voice acid. "Who said this?"

"A Mrs. Blaine, I think their names are, and a Miss Nuttel."

"Then I don't think we need let it disturb either of us. They'd say anything."

"But it was on a bus, in public."

"Angela is supposed to have stolen your eggs on a bus? It's too puerile to bother with."

"No. You don't understand. It was said on a bus. Everybody could hear. I thought of protesting, but I'm afraid I couldn't bring myself to make a public scene. And then I saw your signboard, so I got off and came straight here. What actually happened last night was just childish and silly. But with the shooting, and then the police becoming involved, the whole thing could easily become a scandal. And to bring your daughter's name into it, wantonly like that, is unforgivable."

Mrs. Venning's face was an expressionless mask. She moved aside. "I think you'd better come in and clarify this absurdity."

Sonia Venning considered her visitor; considered her story. Certainly it wasn't true. What was less certain was how much truth the story contained. No village boy would have gone searching for eggs after midnight. Conceivable, but unlikely, that he might have been after the birds themselves. Inconceivable that he should have been armed. The various members of the Colveden family appeared so promptly on their cues that one was tempted to suspect that the cues were prearranged. All this must be connected with the police action last night of which she'd heard from Mrs. Fratters, who, in turn, had got her information from the milkman. Not just the local bobby at that, but mobile police in cars. More than one car. Was there a trap here? Or was this woman telling the truth so far as she knew it? Angela had arrived home soon after midnight. And alone. But it was easy to see how the village would link her with the affair. And, in point of fact, they were probably right. The essence being, how far was Angela involved this time? And could it be proved? On the whole, she decided, Miss Seeton was genuine, with this story of some pot of jam that they were supposed to have left on her. Well, maybe Angela had. This female was presumably giving the facts as she knew them and activated solely by a desire to help. She rose.

"You've been more than kind in coming here and I'm extremely grateful. I know how inaccurate and malicious village gossip can be. Or any gossip, for that matter. But it's always better to be forewarned. I'm sorry if I seemed a little abrupt when you first arrived, but my housekeeper is out shopping and I was working," she gestured toward the typewriter and the litter of papers on the desk, "and one gets immersed. It's so difficult to switch one's concentration. Particularly," she smiled apologetically, and put her hand to her head, "when one has an extremely bad headache."

"I'm so sorry. How dreadful for you," sympathized Miss Seeton. "Shouldn't you lie down? But what a curious coincidence." She opened her bag and began to hunt in it. "I was given something for a headache only this morning. It's in here somewhere. I'm most unlikely to use them as I don't care for taking drugs myself."

"Why not? Who's not caring about taking drugs?"

Both women turned at the interruption. Mrs. Venning went quickly to the door.

"Angela, what are you doing down here? Go back to your room."

"Oh, don't be so fud. What gives? What's that old . . . ?"

"Don't argue with me. Go back to your room at once. You aren't well. You weren't well last night, if you remember. Go back to bed and stay there as I told you or I shall have you seriously ill. It could easily be serious, do you understand? Now, will you do as I say?" Reluctantly her daughter retreated up the stairs. A door slammed. Mrs. Venning forced a smile. "I'm so sorry . . ."

"Please." Miss Seeton was distressed. "It is I who am sorry. Such a worry for you. And the young—so impatient. Always sure that they know best. Now what was I . . . ? Oh, yes, of course. I don't know if they'll be any good to you, but I'm told they're excellent." From her handbag she brought the phial of pills. "These, for your headache. Do try them if you think they'll be any help."

The smile froze on Sonia Venning's face. She gave a high-pitched, ugly laugh. Miss Seeton recoiled. Mrs. Venning stepped forward and slapped the phial out of her hand.

"Get out," she flung at her visitor. "Get out, you lying filthy little spy. Go on, get out. If you want money, try some other game. You've made a bad mistake this time. Go on. Go on, get out."

Lunch at Rytham Hall, for which Miss Seeton, having misjudged either the distance or her walking speed, was late, was not a success. With a guest who appeared abstracted, a son who was sullen and preoccupied, and a husband who was never a brilliant conversationalist, Lady Colveden's efforts to enliven the proceedings gradually petered out and they finished the meal in silence.

After lunch Miss Seeton announced her intention of going back to her cottage. The superintendent, arriving with his sergeant to interview her, joined his arguments to the protests of the Colveden family in an attempt to dissuade her, but she stuck to her decision. Grateful as she was for shelter the previous night, she could see no reason to remain. Simply, she had fallen in love with her cottage and wanted to return. So Delphick and Bob Ranger drove her back, to conduct the interview in her own home.

Miss Seeton and the superintendent were at their ease on either side of the fireplace, while the sergeant, with his inevitable notebook, sat at a table near the front window looking onto the Street.

"So we must accept that this time the sound was working, but the vision was switched off. Or rather the lighting was faulty."

Miss Seeton smiled. "I'm afraid so, superintendent. But I think that you could be wrong in imagining it was the same boy as in London. This one was completely English and looked very tall, though that may have been the light."

"Lebel's parents may have been French, but he was born and bred in London, he's got no foreign accent. What was this man's voice like?"

She thought. "No. I can't help you, I'm afraid. It was just a voice. Very ordinary. Not well educated. I remember he called me 'lady.' He said 'Go back to the house, lady'—or something like that."

"Did you see him walk at all?"

"Yes, he came forward when I first got there—to the hen house, that is."

"Then can you remember if he limped at all? Sir George thought he did. I wondered if he genuinely has a limp, or whether he might have risked his ankle getting away."

"Oh." There was a pause. A flush stained Miss Seeton's cheeks.

"You don't remember?" he prompted.

"Well—yes. I'm afraid I do. I feel very guilty about it. You see I was worried on account of the hens, knowing that Stan would be upset. I felt responsible. So I told him to stop—stop upsetting the hens, I mean. When he defied me and told me to go back to the house and pointed that gun thing at me, I'm afraid I lost all patience and smacked his wrist. And the thing exploded. I think it must have damaged his foot. I did ask him if he was hurt, but he didn't say. He only cried out and hopped about, holding his foot, before he scrambled up on to the hen house roof and disappeared."

This was beyond. This was way, way over the odds. The sergeant was impelled to speak. He addressed his superior: "She—hee-hee!" he tittered. Shocked at the sound and wilting under the Oracle's quelling eye, he clenched his teeth. Through tight and trembling lips he said: "I'm sorry, ma'am. For the record, was it your umbrella you smacked him with?"

"Why, yes," agreed Miss Seeton. "How did you know?"

"B-because it had to b-be. Only you—hoo-hoo . . ." Heroically he silenced himself by biting his tongue—hard.

"If you've quite recovered, sergeant?"

Bob's glowing face gazed at the Oracle in mute appeal. Between pain and suppression, water welled in his eyes. Two large tears ran down his cheeks. Hastily Delphick looked away. One tear splashed on the notebook, made a blot, to remain in testimony to the emotion of the interview.

"Well . . . yes." Delphick had the rare experience of finding himself at a loss. He reversed his gambit and tried again. "Yes . . . well, that disposes of his limp. And very nice marksmanship too, if I may say so." He drew a deep breath. "Now, two other matters." He smiled. "Poor Miss Seeton, it must seem to you like one unending catechism. But I'm afraid police work consists of information. Volumes of information. All of which has to be filed, tabulated, correlated, and what-have-you. And from this process, if we're lucky, emerge facts. Information is occasionally given to us, but mostly we go out and dig for it—with endless questions."

"But of course, superintendent. I'm only too willing to help, if I can. I don't see how you can do your work if people don't tell you things."

"Right. Now, there's an authoress, living locally, who writes what some people refer to as 'stupid' books."

"You mean Mrs. Venning? I don't know about stupid. I believe her books are very successful. I've never read any myself. They're books for small children."

"And she has a daughter called Angie."

"Angela, yes."

"Have you met them?"

"Yes."

Give him credit, thought the sergeant. Hadn't been able to find out the name of young Colveden's "stupid authoress" at lunch time because the local P.C. was out on his beat, he'd now winkled the information out of Miss Seeton without her even knowing she'd given it. He'd be asking for a description next.

"What are they like?" asked Delphick.

"I'm sorry—I can't say. I've only spoken to Mrs. Venning once. And I haven't met her daughter, only saw her. She wasn't at all well."

"But you must have formed some impression—of the mother, at least. What kind of woman is she?"

She balked. "I—I don't know, superintendent, I can't tell you."

"Then tell me, how did you happen to meet her? I understood she was something of a recluse."

"I called on her."

"Recently?"

"Yes. This morning, on my way back. Just before lunch. I'd overheard something spiteful and, knowing it was quite untrue, I thought she should be warned. So I called on her and . . ."

"And?"

"And . . ." She faltered again. Her hands moved restlessly. "And that's all."

"I'm sorry to badger you, but it is important for me to learn more of the Vennings. If you remember, you agreed we couldn't do our work if people didn't tell us things."

"It isn't that I won't—it's that I can't. Oh, I could tell you that she was a little strange in her behavior. And that she was very rude to me. But it would be wrong, don't you see? It wouldn't be the truth." Again the uncharacteristic restlessness of the hands. "Not the real truth."

Delphick had been watching her intently. He jumped to his feet. "Got it. Off you go. Find yourself paper, your drawing block, pencils, paints, whatever it is you need. The sergeant and I will take a turn round the garden if we may. We'll examine the chicken houses, the wall, the ground beyond it. We'll crawl about on our hands and knees and spoil our trousers. We'll observe blades of grass through magnifying glasses. Have you got your magnifying glass, sergeant?"

"No, sir."

"Good. Then we'll use the eyes our National Health has given us and see sweet nothing at all. But at least we shall look like sleuths. While you stay here and do some proper work." He swung round on her with a broad smile. "I'm right, aren't I? That's how you resolve your problems, find out about people, get at the truth—your fingers tell you, don't they? You put it down on paper and then you can see it—then you know? Am I right?"

Miss Seeton was acutely embarrassed. "I don't think . . . well, perhaps. Yes—in a way, I mean—it's true I do draw things. And people. I always feel one shouldn't. But I can't help myself, somehow. It's—it's compulsive really. But it does help—help me, that is—to see things more clearly. But, of course, they're quite private. Rather, in a way I suppose, like a very private diary. I never let anyone else see them."

"Except us. We're the confessional, remember. We're doctors, priests; we're that anomalous anodyne for society's ills, detectives. To think that I nearly didn't recognize a drug-taker's craving because it happened to be paper and pencil, not pills. I ought to be put out to grass." He grinned at her. "We'll leave you to it. Come along, sergeant, grass it shall be."

Miss Seeton watched them go through the French windows and down the garden. What an understanding man the superintendent was, very comforting somehow. And that enormous young man with the notebook, who so rarely spoke. They were both—dependable, that was it. She sat at the writing desk near the window, pulled open one of the long drawers, and took some cartridge paper from her portfolio, collected pencils, charcoal and erasers, shut the drawer, pulled down the flap, and spread out her things. For a few moments she enjoyed the air from the open window, the view of the garden and the quiet. How pleasant it was. How lucky she'd been.

She turned back to the writing desk, to find that her hand, of its own volition, had taken up a piece of charcoal and had started blocking in. Mindlessly at first, then with increasing concentration, Miss Seeton began to give vent to her feelings.

The hens, who had shown a slight interest on the detectives' arrival, now, since no food had been forthcoming, ignored them. Bob clambered back and sat astride the wall.

"Were you expecting to find anything down here, sir?"

"Such as a few packets of heroin wot slipped out of 'is 'and while 'e was scarperin'?" The Oracle grinned amiably. "No, Bob. And if he dropped a few in on the chickens, I'm all for letting sleeping birds lie. Who am I to interfere with their simple pleasures. And I don't think we can have you searching the hen houses, for even if we could get you inside, if you let your breath out, or had another fit of hysterics, you'd blow the whole structure down."

Bob was abashed. "I'm awfully sorry about that, sir— laughing. I just couldn't help myself."

"Forget it. But another time, if you must cry, have the decency not to look at me during the performance. That was almost my undoing."

"You. You never batted an eyelid, sir."

"I'm delighted to hear it, but I should hate to guarantee that I haven't ruptured something rather serious inside. All we're doing down here at the moment is filling in time and going through the motions, in case there's anything to see. It's a pity that back wall's so low," he reflected, "it probably improves the view from the house, but at that height it's a positive invitation to the dance."

"Do you think Lebel's got contacts down here, sir?"

"Not accomplices in the sense you mean it, no. But people he could contact, yes. You must remember, Bob, that drugs mean big money and big money means big organization. I should imagine that Lebel's no more than a small-time runner and hatchet man for them, but an organization, if it wants to run smoothly, must protect its own people, or eliminate them. At the moment Miss Seeton is inconvenient to them because she can put the finger on someone who is evidently useful to them, but if we can catch up with him, or make things sufficiently hot that he becomes an inconvenience, with any luck they'll kill him and leave her alone which, though it may not please the Narcotic Squad, will save us a lot of leg work."

"And you think Mrs. Venning is mixed up in it, sir?"

"Entangled in the fringe, I should guess."

"It seems odd for someone like her. She's quite well known."

"Don't tell me you're a fan?"

"My sister's kids—they love her books. They're all about a character called Jack the Rabbit."

"Such erudition," said Delphick admiringly. "Well, it's possible that the mother's only covering up for the daughter, who sounds like a mainliner to me."

"You think the girl is hooked, then?"

"Merely speculating. But young Colveden has evidently been worried about her for some time. From what he didn't say, she was obviously in on the party with those young punks last night. And according to Miss Seeton, she's ill this morning. It sounds a drearily familiar pattern."

"Pity," commented Bob.

"Oh, yes," agreed Delphick. "And 't will be pittier still if 'tis true. However, cheer up, it may not be like that at all. It's . . . I don't like amateurs without the weight mixing it with the professionals. It's dangerous. That's why I slapped the Colveden boy down. Making him lose his temper was the only way to get him to talk. But all his running around playing peekaboo and I spy, while trying to cover up for the Venning girl, could easily have landed him in hospital, or worse. And a lot she seems to care. He did a good job putting those other young disasters in the ditch, it gave us all their names and addresses on a plate, so the Narcotics boys can now concentrate on them, instead of just vaguely on the club. They don't matter in themselves, it's who starts them off in the first place and who supplies them in the second. But the Vennings, I feel . . ." He shrugged. "I don't know; I'm not happy about it. Come on. Perhaps Miss Seeton can give us a clue. She's had time to fill Burlington House by now."

"I don't see what you expect to get, sir, by her trying to draw Mrs. Venning. After all she's not likely to stick her behind bars, like she did Lebel."

"It would be highly informative if she did. I'm not sure what I expect, but I've a shrewd suspicion that woman's psychic, without knowing it. But whether, by drawing the subject, it will clarify her mind and she'll be able to tell us what she thinks or whether there'll be something helpful in the drawing itself I can't even guess. Come on, let's go and find out."

As they approached the French windows they could see

Miss Seeton was absorbed. She was working with charcoal, smudging and shading with thumb, fingers, and bits of cotton wool. They stood to one side and watched. After a few moments she sat back and studied what she'd been doing, then took a piece of charcoal and scrubbed it across the top of the paper, working it in with the heel of her hand. She pushed away her chair, got up, and surveyed the result. Delphick moved forward.

"May we come in?"

She turned, startled, looked at them blankly, then, coming back to earth: "Oh, superintendent. Yes, of course, come in. I was just going to clean myself up. Charcoal's such a messy medium." She held out two grimy hands; she had managed to get smears on her face as well. "I won't be a moment."

They stood contemplating the littered desk. On top was the charcoal drawing on which they had seen her at work. Well, you couldn't win every time, reflected the sergeant. The Oracle had fallen down on this one. Or rather Miss Seeton had. They'd been trotting round the garden while she was supposed to be running off a few front and side views of the Venning family. Only she'd forgotten all about it and settled down to a bit of landscaping. Pretty gloomy at that. Clever enough, he supposed, but he wouldn't want to live with it. All those mountains at the back, with that dark sky on top. It was— brooding. Yes, that was the word, brooding. And that cliff on the left—no, not a cliff exactly—a rock. Just that one ray of light catching the stream as it trickled down—there were two streams actually, but one disappeared over the other side— lighting up the pool at the bottom where—good Lord—some girl had come a purler and dropped a bottle or something that had smashed. He wouldn't give much for the girl's chances. She looked as if she was lying half in the water. Bit ominous, the whole thing. Not his cup of tea at all. Delphick pulled a sheet of paper from underneath the drawing. Bob chuckled. This was more like it. This was something you could understand. It was a quick pen sketch, done in a few lines. On a rostrum, behind a table above which was festooned a mayoral chain in place of bunting, a portly, pompous figure was delivering a speech while holding up a phial in his right hand: a wicked likeness to Mr. Trefold Morton in the role of a huckster selling quack medicines.

"Who," laughed Delphick as Miss Seeton returned, "is the gentleman you don't like?"

"Oh," exclaimed Miss Seeton. "You weren't supposed to see that." She looked at him reprovingly. "It was underneath."

"I know," agreed Delphick, "but the corner was sticking out and I couldn't resist it. It's very funny."

"It was naughty of me, I admit. But he did boom so. It's my cousin's solicitor. I had to see him this morning about probate and he would insist on giving me pills for a headache. I didn't want them, but it was easier to take them than argue."

The superintendent considered: it certainly was funny. And yet . . . A con man if ever he'd seen one. What a cartoonist the woman would have made. And the odd coincidence of a bottle or phial in both drawings. Coincidence? A little probing there might pay off. A few inquiries into this man's financial standing and that of his clients . . . But with a solicitor any such investigation would need to be discreet.

He put the sketch down and regarded the charcoal drawing. Miss Seeton watched him anxiously. "I don't know that it's very clear. Does it help at all?"

"Oh, yes. I think so." The sergeant glanced at him in surprise. "I'm not too happy about it—or the implications. But, oh, yes, I think it helps. 'Like Niobe all tears.' "

She glowed with pleasure. "Then you do understand how I felt."

"You say she was rude to you?"

"Well, yes—in a way. But I'm sure it was a misunderstanding. She had a headache and I offered her Mr. Trefold Morton's pills. She knocked them out of my hand and said something about spying and told me to get out. But I'm sure she didn't mean it. It's just that I think she's very unhappy and on edge."

Delphick pointed to the picture. "Hence the broken bottle down here?"

She nodded. "You see, I'd interrupted Mrs. Venning in the middle of working and creative people don't like that. It's very understandable."

"What's worrying you, sergeant?"

Bob was looking perplexed. "It's that I don't get this Niobe business, sir. I know the statue and I thought she was a Greek lady who couldn't stop crying because all her children were dead."

"A Greek myth," corrected the Oracle. "Artemis and her brother killed all Niobe's children except one daughter and turned Niobe herself into a rock and her tears became twin

streams that ran from it. The rock, sergeant. Can't you see
the woman's face in it?"

Suddenly Bob could. Those shadows and vegetation were
the eyes, the nose, the mouth. Like a tragic mask. Couldn't
think why he hadn't seen it before. Couldn't see it any other
way now. All the children except one daughter. He looked at
the bottom of the drawing again. The girl lying crumpled half
in the water. He didn't like the implication either.

Eight

Really, it was very muddling. "Tread the earth well down when planting so that no air-pockets are left round the roots." That seemed clear and sensible enough. Then, a few pages later, under "Care and Attention," it said: "Fork well round the roots to let in air." Surely it seemed a pity not to have left the air there in the first place. And now it said on page 53: "Never fork roses as, being surface rooters, you may damage the roots." Miss Seeton closed the book and put it on the grass beside her. *GREENFINGER Points the Way.* Yes, but which way? It pointed in so many directions. Was gardening, perhaps, like some of the other professions? she wondered. One knew that, in many cases, unsuccessful singers taught singing, unsuccessful authors taught writing, and, as one knew oneself only too well, unsuccessful artists taught drawing. In fact one liked to console oneself that such persons made the best teachers. And there was no question that, if one was successful, one would hardly have the time to teach. So could it be, she mused, that unsuccessful gardeners wrote gardening books? Or was that heresy? Certainly one got the impression that if one did half the things that appeared to be vital if any plant was to survive, one would have no time at all, even for meals. It really was very muddling indeed. She must ask Stan. She heard a tapping. Probably someone who had tried the front door and failed to get an answer. She got up, crossed the lawn, took the key off its nail and opened the side door in the wall.

"C'n I int'rest you in sump'n, miss?" Bright eyes gleamed under a tangle of ginger. The sinuous, eager movements of youth—appealing; the clear complexion fading, the puppy fat receding; guileless cherub yielding to disingenuous ferret.

Miss Seeton was puzzled. "Interest me? In what?"

"Anything, miss, for gossakes. Fresh vege, bottles of pop, eggs, cheese, canned stuff. No kidd'n—you name it, we got it."

"Really, I don't think there's anything I need just at the moment, thank you."

"Aw, c'mon! Cheaper y'see, cuts out the middleman. We bring it right to your door f'you to choose. C'mon, take a look-see," he wheedled, "can't hurt you none to take a look."

Miss Seeton moved forward as he stepped to one side. Backed at right angles across the lane, the back doors open and touching the wall on either side of her, was an elderly car, the rear half converted to a van. On the floor inside were two or three cabbages in sere and yellow leaf, some bottles of ginger beer, and a cardboard box out of which were sticking tins of soup and packets of detergent.

Miss Seeton regarded the disheartening array. "I'm afraid I really don't think that . . ."

Her sentence finished in a muffled squawk as a sack descended over her head, her ankles were seized, and she was pitched among the merchandise. The doors were slammed, a jolt as the driver jumped into his seat, a jar as he banged his door, the engine roared and Miss Seeton, accompanied by bottles, was rolled from one side to the other as the van lurched forward, backed, then sped up the lane.

Miss Seeton squirmed and writhed to free her arms; to free herself from the stifling mustiness of sacking which enveloped her. But the sway of the car made coordinated movements difficult. Objects with sharp or blunt edges would move in to unexpected attack. If she found something on which to gain purchase for her feet, she no sooner braced herself than that something melted to nothing and she was once more rolling helplessly at large; rolling on, rolling off, endless bottles—surely there hadn't been so many. On one of these excursions something jabbed her painfully in the neck, catching the sack, holding it. She wriggled downward, freed her elbows. Now it was simple. She pushed the sack over her head and sat up in the dark to take stock of her position, drawing grateful breaths of stale cabbage and petrol; ozone after her enmuzzlement. Miss Seeton, rarely angry on her own behalf, was cross.

This was beyond a joke. It was outrageous. Perhaps that redheaded boy was the one who'd been after the eggs and this was his idea of revenge. He probably thought it was a lark. But it wasn't funny. Not in the least. A perfectly good hat, and almost new—it must be ruined. Leaning back against the side of the van she put up tentative hands. Yes, she'd thought so—squashed. Her indignation rose. It was no good knocking, calling him to stop. If he'd intended to stop he'd never have started. Where were they going? And what did he imagine he could do when they got there? Really, the young—so thought-less. Never considering the consequences. No, she must shift for herself. But how? How did you stop a car when you were shut up in the back of it?

Patting and feeling, she began to crawl about the floor. At one side something jutted up with what felt like a large rubber cap. She clung to it for support as the car heeled round a corner. The cap came away in her hand and she fell back-wards. The reek of the petrol grew overpowering. Miss See-ton crept back to its source.

Yes, there was a slopping sound down there. If only one could see. It was so difficult trying to guess in the dark. Really, the smell was quite awful. But how odd. Of course she knew nothing about cars, but surely the petrol was usually on the outside. Perhaps vans were different. She put out her hand to replace the cap. Now—wait. Something . . . Now what was it? Yes. Water in the petrol. She'd heard people complain of that. "It wouldn't go because water had got into the pet-rol." Water. Well, she hadn't any. But—remembering—would ginger beer do? She began to search. The bottles, so obtrusive earlier in her predicament, now proved elusive. At last. Here was one. Two more, as if attracted by the capture of their friend, rolled bumping against her legs. She gathered them up and prepared for action. How fortunate, they had screw stop-pers. She poured all three down the pipe that stuck through the floor. Apparently wanting to join the game, a cardboard box nudged her. She pushed it away. Oh—one moment. Wasn't there . . . Yes, packets of detergent poking from that box. Would they help? She pulled one out and started to tear the top. How . . . curious. She'd never known . . . such tough cardboard. There. That should do. Fumbling a little, she tipped the contents down the pipe. Satisfied that she had done all she could, she pushed the rubber cap back into place, hoping to lessen the stench that was making her head reel. At least, she reflected, with all this shaking, it should foam up nicely down there. The van rattled on its way. No good . . . it hadn't worked. Dizzying clouds, held at bay by action, began to engulf her mind. The van gave a polite hiccough. Could that be . . . ? No, they were still moving. Two more hiccoughs. Miss Seeton tried to take an interest. A series of hiccoughs. Very tiring, thought Miss Seeton dreamily—and could prove dangerous if prolonged. People had died of hic-coughs. Silence descended as the engine cut out and they coasted, swaying, to a stop.

"In trouble, mate?"

A ginger mop withdrew from under the bonnet, leaving its useless scrutiny and ineffectual fiddling. "Dunno. Guess it's sump'n in the pump. Plenty of gas but not getting through." He eyed the burly driver of a light-blue van which had drawn up just beyond him. "Guess you needn't worry none. Soon have it right."

"Not that way you won't. Here, give us that spanner." Faint tapping sounded from the back. "What you carting, mate, livestock?"

"No, dad. Just bits 'n' pieces and one old hen t'deliver."

The burly man undid the nut to the petrol feed. "Now we'll soon see." They did. Out spumed a froth of blue bubbles. "What you runnin' on, mate, soapsuds?" He threw back his head and roared with laughter.

"Help!" sounded faintly from within the van. His laugh cut off. He turned. A click. He swung back only half prepared for the attack. The knife ripped into his left arm instead of his stomach. His boot came up; contacted. His assailant screeched; bent double. The man's right fist came down and it was over. Catching hold of a foot he dragged the unconscious boy to his own van, reached in, took twine, bound the body, and threw it to one side. He strode to the back of the other car, twisted the bar handle and flung open the doors. He gaped.

"Strewth, miss. Take it easy." He held out his hand.

Head swimming and gulping fresh air, Miss Seeton pulled herself forward and managed to alight. She stood on precarious feet to thank her rescuer, but her knees buckled and she knelt before her salvation.

"So sorry," she murmured vaguely. "The fumes, you know. So strong."

He lifted her up and held her. "Easy now, miss. Feel swymy enough I doubt, cooped up in there."

She gasped. "Your arm. You're hurt."

He glanced down. Blood was dripping from his hand and seeping through his coat sleeve. "It's nothing, miss. Just a jab from your chauffeur there."

"You mean he actually attacked you? He must be out of his mind. I'm most dreadfully sorry. And grateful, too. I don't know how to thank you. I don't know what I should have done. What happened? Did he run away?"

"Not to say run, he's back there sleeping it off. I tied him up neat enough so he'll not come to no harm."

Miss Seeton was recovering. "Take that coat off," she ordered, "and let me see your arm at once."

The wound upon examination proved less serious than she had feared. She made a pad with a clean handkerchief from her pocket and bound it tightly with a moderately clean one from his. The burly man watched her with interest.

"I've got it. You're the lady in the papers, aren't you, miss? The one they call 'the Battling Brolly.' There was a picture of you. What you been up to this time? Chasing our ginger friend?" With quickening interest: "Is he the one that did that girl in London?"

"No, no, he's not. There's no connection—at least I don't think so." She looked doubtful. "I can only imagine it's a silly —well—joke, I suppose. Somebody tried to steal some eggs the other night. I woke up and managed to stop him. And either it was he, it was too dark for me to be sure, or it's one of his friends trying to get back at me."

The burly man looked doubtful. "If you say so, miss. What do we do now? We can't leave young Ginger lying about. Can't leave the van neither. I'll allow there's not much traffic this way. But it's narrow enough for passing. We'd best sling him in the back. I'll give you a tow."

"Tow?" She was disturbed. "Oh, I don't think I could. I've never driven a car."

"And you won't be driving this one neither. Nor no one else. Don't know what he filled her up with but it's coming out blue bubbles."

"I poured something down a pipe where the petrol seemed to be, hoping that might stop it. It was the only thing I could think of to do," she explained.

"It did that sure enough." He peered into the back, saw the bottles and let out a whoop of laughter. "Our Ginger stoned by Stone Ginger. That's rich enough, that is." Chuckling and delighted with his wit, he went to his own van, backed it up and returned with a length of rope. He began to tie the two vehicles together.

Miss Seeton joined him. Looking down at the trussed body, "Is he all right?" she asked tentatively.

"Right enough, miss. Should be waking up soon, or thereabouts. I doubt he'll have a stiff neck and a sore—well, he won't walk none too easy for a day or two. Do him good."

She picked up the knife. "What about this? We oughtn't to leave it here, do you think?"

"You're right, better give it me." Miss Seeton wiped off the blood as best she could on the grass and handed it over. "I'll turn it in to the police along with him."

"The police?" she exclaimed. "Oh, must we? No, no, of course you're right," she agreed, seeing his expression, "I do realize that. To attack you with a knife—quite unforgivable. It was just . . . I hadn't thought. So stupid of me. But the police—and then the newspapers. They're sure to think—to imagine . . . Oh dear, how very tiresome!"

The burly man stood up with a satisfied grunt. "There we are, miss, that should hold. Now we'll just get rid of Carrot-top here." He scooped up the body which was beginning to stir. "Starting to take an interest in things, is he? Well, it's time enough he was out of the way. I doubt he'll have a few things to say when he comes round which saving your presence wouldn't be fitting." He tossed the body into the back of its own van, closed the doors, and turned the handle to lock them. "Come on, miss, in you get."

Miss Seeton viewed the prospect with alarm. Nervousness made her voluble. "Of course, I do see that you're right, about not leaving his van here, I mean, on such a narrow road, particularly with him inside it, I mean, if there was an accident, he might be hurt and do you feel up to driving with your bad arm?"

"It's right enough, miss. Can feel it but it'll do."

"I can't think it wise for me to try and steer, you see, I don't know how."

"Nothing to it, miss. Come along, I'll show you." Miss Seeton got in and sat upright, apprehensive. He placed her hands on the steering wheel. "Now, remember, right hand down you go right. Left hand down you go left." She followed his instructions. "That's it, miss, but don't grip so tight. Take it easy. And this," he put her foot on a pedal, "is the brake. Keep your foot on it but not hard and press it when you want to slow. Aim to keep the rope tight between us. Only push the pedal right down if you want to stop. But don't do it sudden or you may snap the tow. Don't worry. I'll be keeping an eye on you in the mirror. And we'll take it slow and easy. Straight along here," he pointed ahead, "joins the Brettenden Road. We turn left there. Then it's dead straight except for the bends." He closed her door, grinned at her, gave her a thumbs-up and jumped into his own van. Gently, hesitatingly, they began to fluctuate down the road.

Why couldn't witnesses use their eyes? despaired Delphick. Two women, from cottages opposite, who had seen a van in the lane by Miss Seeton's side door had described the driver as tall, short, fair, red-haired, young, and couldn't-say-I'm-sure. And another woman, shopping in the street, remembered a strange van passing at approximately the right time driven by a "dreadful-looking man with a white face and gleaming eyes." The best description of the van was that it was low; dark, brown or black. The only certainty was that the man had headed north from Plummergen. It was such long odds, he thought, as the sergeant put the car into gear for their fifth sedate patrol of the Brettenden Road. These endless side roads. Nothing more they could have done. Road blocks to all main roads. All available motorcycle patrols out. He envied young Colveden rushing round scouring the countryside in that M.G. He almost envied Sir George lumbering about in a vast utility that looked like a trippers' coach. They'd get this man in time of course—bound to. But that wouldn't be in time . . . and catching him later, what proof would they have? Unless by a lucky fluke there were some clues left in the van. And that would prove too late to be lucky for her.

They pulled off the road at the double bend on the rise just above the spot where Nigel had ditched the car from the Singing Swan and looked down over the marsh. In the distance two vans, one hard on the wheels of the other, crawled from a side road and turned left toward Brettenden.

They alerted. The rear van was low. And dark. From here it could be either gray or brown. Delphick switched to transmission.

"Car 403. Car 403. Position: mile north of Plummergen, proceeding Brettenden. Two vans half mile ahead, approx., turned from side road, proceeding Brettenden. Slow pace, leading van large, color light blue. Rear van low, color dark gray or brown." Bob got under way again as Delphick's voice quickened. "Rear van driving dangerously. All over the road, pulling out to pass on bend. Swinging back . . . Trying again." His voice. "Car coming toward them—they'll crash. No . . . they're swinging back. Still trying . . . fighting to pass. Dangerous driving—could be quarry. Am giving chase. Over."

He looked at her. He turned his back on Bob's beaming face as the sergeant settled into the driving seat of the converted van to take over the tow. He looked at her. All his distressed concern of the past hour—all that worry—and there she'd been, skittering round the countryside, getting herself into danger, getting herself out of it, breaking all the laws of probability, blowing bubbles down the petrol tank, roping her man and bringing him in—and all she could say was, "How very fortunate, superintendent. I was so hoping we'd meet." So hoping . . . So help him. Delphick held the passenger door of the police car open. He looked at the battered hat, the disheveled little figure, mastering in his relief a strong desire to put her over his knee and smack her.

Nine

During the week that followed Miss Seeton's abduction adventure, Superintendent Delphick and Sergeant Ranger remained in Plummergen.

The actual grind of collecting information, much of it useless and the remainder to be sifted and collated in the hope that it might one day be of value in the building of a case, was a slow, laborious process unimagined by the majority of the press and public, alike impatient for finality.

On Mrs. Venning, the information so far gathered seemed innocuous except for one significant gap. She had been married at twenty-three to a rising executive in an engineering firm. The young couple, comfortably off and with an assured future, had lived a social life to the limit of their income, so that when the husband was killed in a motor accident he left his widow and two-year-old daughter with an expensive flat and no visible means of support. In neither case were the parents wealthy and, so far as could be checked, no financial help had been given to his widow. After a suitable interval Mrs. Venning had resumed her social life, dressed well and had engaged her old nurse, a Mrs. Fratters, to help look after the child and run the flat. Sonia Venning had paid her bills, had not been in debt, but her means of support for the next three years remained a mystery. Then she had set down in book form the stories she used to invent as bedtime entertainment for her little girl. A publisher had been interested and the book had proved a success. After the publication of her second book she had sold the lease of her flat and moved to Plummergen. From then on all was plain sailing. Highly strung, gay and gregarious, she was conspicuous in all local affairs until about a year ago when she stopped all her social activities and became in effect a recluse. Her books continued to appear at regular intervals but that was all now that was known of her. Her abrupt and mysterious retirement from the life of the community had provoked, still evoked, much speculation. The police too speculated. It could be no more than the evident trouble with her daughter, but it was tempting to take the two unaccountable chapters in her life and deliberate possible cause and effect. There appeared to have been no man other than her husband; although it would have been an obvious and easy solution to account for her solvency in the early days of her widowhood, no trace of such a man could be found. Again a love affair would have been a simple answer to her recent seclusion but in all the talk about her there was no hint of this and it was difficult to believe that the village gossips would not have seized upon the idea had there been any grounds. Indeed, with impulsive generosity, they would have provided her with not one man but a score.

In the case of Trefold Morton research was hampered by the need for delicacy. As a solicitor he could, and no doubt would, make things awkward if he got wind of their investigation. There was nothing against him. The police had no excuse for curiosity. Report made him more prominent than popular or, as one fellow councilor put in the course of conversation, "A gas bag with influence." There was nothing tangible, but the superintendent decided that there was a "feeling." Mr. Trefold Morton felt wrong. He was obviously well-to-do. It could be, though at this stage there could be no means of proving it, that he was better-to-do than might have been expected. The only facts which emerged and which Delphick filed as of possible interest were that in four cases clients whose affairs were completely in their solicitor's hands had come to unfortunate ends: or, more accurately, in three cases; in the fourth, though the present was unfortunate, the end was still to come.

A Mrs. Cummingdale, an elderly widow presumed to be rich, had died in a fire, supposedly caused by smoking in bed. Her nephew from Scotland had been loud in his surprise when she cut up for a little over six hundred pounds. The superintendent learned from people living around that she had been behaving oddly for some time before she died.

Ernest Foremason, a bachelor in his fifties, had driven his car into a wall: the wall survived. The police opinion was "Drunk in charge." Mr. Foremason had died intestate and having no relations his estate of a few hundred pounds and a mortgage on his house had gone to the Crown. Mr. Foremason, too, had been thought to be wealthy.

A Miss Worlingham, a maiden lady of sixty-three, had committed suicide. She had left a will written in her own handwriting on the morning of the day that she had died, witnessed by the milk roundsman and her daily help. The document was valueless however as her personalty failed to cover her debts. This caused no surprise, though she had been thought to be moneyed, since during the last years of her life her behavior had been noted as strange.

Miss Hant, another maiden of uncertain years, was in a private nursing home being treated for drug addiction and was regarded as incurable. No one visited her there except her solicitor. So far as was known she was without relatives or friends. She appeared to have had money though it was now rumored that Mr. Trefold Morton was helping with her expenses out of kindness.

Odd behavior, drunken behavior, strange behavior, and Miss Hant's behavior with her craving for heroin could not be counted as normal. All lonely people without close kin to question the aftermath of their death. All presumed to be rich yet all shown in the event to be poor. All except Miss Hant, and even there the hint of poverty was in the offing. Coincidences worth bearing in mind? The superintendent thought so, but, on the other hand, how many solicitors could not show a like percentage of unfortunate clients in the course of thirty years' practice? There was no way that he could see for the police to carry the inquiries further. It would be useless to interview Miss Hant in the nursing home for, although rational enough at times, according to her doctor, like all drug addicts she would give no helpful information to the police and he would have succeeded in advising Mr. Trefold Morton of his interest. It would be a pity to make no effort to see her while she was still alive, her doctor did not give her a long expectation, for once she was dead there would be nothing the police could do without more to go on than they had. In fact, as the superintendent admitted, they had nothing. The germ of an idea to achieve this object had occurred to him but he was still unsure whether to put the idea before his superiors or to risk acting on his own initiative.

From the viewpoint of the police, the investigation into Miss Seeton's abduction, which with the facts undisputed and the culprit in jail should have been simple, was proving to be the most difficult. They had so far failed to obtain further information of any kind and the case was verging on the ridiculous. The preliminary inquiry before the magistrate on the morning following the arrest had alerted the newspapers and reporters had flocked to the district. Birds of press had hovered round the chief actors in the drama, pecking at stories before settling in rows with a flutter of notebooks on the press benches in the magistrate's court at Ashford four days later.

The case was a blessing. Apart from cheesecake, it had all the ingredients to please a newsman: a colorful heroine, a gallant rescuer who had been wounded in the fray, and a mysterious villain.

The case was a curse. Apart from cheesecake, it had every ingredient to displease a policeman: a colorful heroine, a gallant rescuer who had beaten the police to it by a car's length, and a mysterious villain. This last was the greatest snag. Miss Seeton and her burly friend had handed over their prisoner to the law neatly tied, but unlabeled. The label was still missing. The prisoner refused to speak—at all. His fingerprints were not on file, which suggested the amateur. He had nothing on him which gave a clue to his identity, which argued the professional. The van he had used, an old Buick car converted and with the back of the body too large for the chassis, turned out to have been stolen overnight in Brettenden, the owner remaining unaware of the theft until it was returned to him. Attempts to establish the prisoner's identity by publishing his photograph produced the usual spate of replies, all useless. Identification parades were held for members of the Singing Swan, for Nigel Colveden, and for Angela Venning. The seven suspect members of the club and Angela were overloudly positive that they had never set eyes on him. This evidence, though it might convince the police to the contrary, with the overloudness muffled by defense counsel, would have the opposite effect on the court. Of other members of the club who had been present on the night of the hen house raid, one was certain and two were fairly sure that the prisoner had been one of a group at a corner table. Two more were definite that he had not been present. The evidence canceled out. Nigel thought that he was one of the two strangers who'd been in the car park but the light had not been good and he could not decide without hearing the voice. Evidence mute and inconclusive.

The police considered asking for more time but came to the conclusion that if the prisoner succeeded in maintaining his silence, the longer the case was delayed the more farcical it was likely to become. In any event, the gravity of the charges, abduction and unlawful wounding, presupposed that the case would be sent to the Assizes at Maidstone and this would automatically gain them time before the trial proper.

The youth had been granted legal aid and his counsel, not averse to publicity, entered the fray with enthusiasm. Having first pleaded that there was no case to answer since his client was more the victim than the aggressor, thenceforward, unhampered by any instructions from his client, he was free to let an unfettered imagination roam and it became clear at the Ashford court what line the defense would take. The police had kept the prisoner under observation in hospital and the doctor's written report was that he could find nothing physical or organic amiss nor any overt signs of mental instability. His verbal report was more lucid: "He's boxing clever!" A doctor called by the defense agreed with the physical and organic soundness but theorized that it was impossible to stipulate what effects shock and bound incarceration in the back of a moving vehicle might have on a highly strung mind; it could well lead to temporary amnesia and loss of speech. The prosecution doctor, recalled, had to concede the point but said he could see no ground for the supposition of a highly strung mind. The defense doctor, recalled, contended that the grounds for such a supposition were the evident results. Thus the medical evidence ended in a draw with a replay booked for the Maidstone Assizes.

On the question of abduction the defense seized upon Miss Seeton's assumption of "a prank in revenge for the egg stealing" to minimize the charge and with regard to the unlawful wounding the burly van driver played into their hands by saying that "young Ginger acted like a nut case." This last was a gift: not only to the defense; the Plummergen contingent who had hired the school bus for the day responded with delight, sniggers, and audible remarks, to the embarrassment of Miss Nuttel and Mrs. Blaine until silence was called for and order restored; the reporters, too, were made happy, the anonymous prisoner had a title at last. From then on it became known in all newspapers except the *Times* as "The Ginger Nut Case." The *Times* correctly followed the court which, after much searching for precedent and having tried *Regina* v. *Person Unknown,* deemed to have a certain frivolity, and *Regina* v. *Anon* which had an unfortunate ambiguity, settled with a sad lack of imagination for *Regina* v. *X.*

The way things were going, Superintendent Delphick reflected, this wretched little hoodlum was likely to be let loose on probation as a first offender with the sympathy of the court for his sufferings. The van driver would be fortunate if he was not charged with assault and Miss Seeton could count herself lucky if she escaped with a fine for wantonly immobilizing the defendant's vehicle.

The one subject on which the police made no inquiry produced information unasked: the subject of Miss Seeton herself. The advice came in the form of four reports—one from the police at Windsor, three from the Hampstead division—and was forwarded from New Scotland Yard to the superintendent as "Information of possible interest."

From Windsor. Re Miss Seeton, Emily D.

Subject recognized by P. C. Bock from photograph in press as woman attending race meeting here two years ago. Outsider won third race after favorite shied at umbrella blown inside out near rails in high wind. Subject collected winnings on race from bookmaker. Strong feeling roused in spectators. Known members of race course gang noted following subject and P. C. Bock suggested subject well-advised to leave meeting. Subject willing. For safety, P. C. Bock escorted subject from course.

From Hampstead. Re Miss Seeton, Emily D.

Four years ago subject chief witness in murder case. F. Swannel, artist, killed model known as Lyla by running down with car. Motive blackmail. First thought to be hit-and-run but subject witnessed killing and took number of car. Car traced to Swannel, who confessed. Never satisfactorily established how subject read car license number at distance. Subject stated, quote, I saw practically nothing at the time. I was too far away, unquote. Owing to confession of Swannel point was not pressed.

Re Miss Seeton, Emily D.

Newspaper photograph of subject recognized by P. C. Turner as woman who caused queues last year at fortuneteller's booth during August Bank Holiday Fair on the Heath. Gypsy Flora, owner of booth, left subject in charge during tea break. On owner's return queues necessitating police action had formed outside booth. Subject appeared to be telling fortunes without license. G. Flora lodged complaint.

Later retracted on seeing financial result of business. No action taken.

Re Miss Seeton, Emily D.

Subject observed five years ago by Traffic Controls, Chelsea, Westminster, Mayfair, St. Marylebone, Hampstead, travelling by taxi in company with skeleton uncovered and not under sufficient control. Caused traffic confusion en route and traffic block and crowds to gather in Hemel Road outside school where subject employed. Prosecution for obstruction considered but not proceeded with owing to difficulty of assessing legal definition of proper control in case of skeleton and hilarity of charge.

Sergeant Ranger frowned over the reports for some time. At last he remarked: "It seems like a sort of disease with her, sir, getting into messes." He relapsed into thought; perhaps dreaming of a cure, weighing a bottle of medicine against inoculation.

The superintendent found the reports illuminating. If the police had notes on four outlandish situations in which she had found herself, how many must there be unnoted over the years? It followed that Miss Seeton was likely to have become inured to the unusual by repetition and had leaned to accept it as part of the everyday pattern of life. It would explain why she could not, or would not, connect one happening with another, treating each on its merits as it occurred. The abduction was linked to the hen house raid, on that they were agreed; in fact it had been her own reaction, as otherwise the abduction made no sense; but that these events necessarily sprang from the Covent Garden murder she was not prepared to admit; she gave lip service to the possibility but there it ended. When Delphick had argued with her and pointed out the improbability of coincidence, she had retorted, 'But, my dear superintendent, if there were no such thing as coincidence, there would be no such word."

He was aided, too, by a meeting with the headmistress of the school where Miss Seeton was employed. Mrs. Benn had read the newspapers, broken her holiday in Cornwall, and arrived in Plummergen to see if her colleague needed assistance. Delphick was beginning to feel that anyone less in need of assistance than Miss Seeton and less willing to entertain it when offered would be hard to find.

As a schoolmistress, Mrs. Benn was something of an anomaly: as a person, contradictory. She was plain but attractive. Her short square build demanded heavy tweeds, shirt and tie; it received pastel suits and frilled blouses. She wore a monocle, and the fact that many considered this to be an affectation did not disturb her; she preferred that people should imagine that she was affected rather than that they should know that she was nearly blind in one eye.

The meeting got off to a bad start. Delphick was conscious that he was not in order in discussing the case with an outsider and, though seeking information, was prepared to give none. Mrs. Benn, equally anxious for information, was unwilling to discuss a colleague. It was not until the superintendent appealed to her for help and suggested that they should both put what cards they could on the table without actual indiscretion that Mrs. Benn gave in and agreed to play, both reserving the right to trump or withhold cards as they saw fit.

"I really do need," he explained, "to know a little more about Miss Seeton. I don't wish to ask her as I'm certain it would cause her acute embarrassment, but I think you'll admit that collected information on her which has come to hand gives a very curious impression to the uninitiated." As a first card down, he showed her the reports in confidence.

The headmistress was intrigued. "I'd no idea the police kept files on inoffensive people. Are we all docketed?" Delphick smiled without answering. "Well, well. Now let's see. Windsor. I knew she'd been to a race meeting. It was in connection with some lectures she gave on Motion in Art—but nothing of the circumstances more. Witness to a murder? That's complete news to me. Wait. I seem to remember her asking for a day off because she'd been a witness of some accident. How like her not to explain. Afraid we'd have worried, I suppose. Hampstead Heath. Fortunetelling—no, I've never heard of that. SOB, of course, I do know about."

"Sob?"

"Seeton's Old Bones. The children christened it and that bedeviled skeleton has been known as SOB ever since."

Delphick grinned. "I must admit even I was shaken. The other three I could take at a pinch, but to go for a ride with an uncovered skeleton—that did seem extreme and, in fact, illegal."

"It was partly my fault. Seeton asked if we could have a skeleton for anatomy drawing and I agreed if we could get one cheap. She advertised and some artist in Chelsea had an articulate plastic affair which was very reasonable if we could arrange cartage. Cartage and delivery would have been expensive, so Seeton went down to fetch it herself and brought it back by taxi. I did ask the police what they would have considered the correct traveling attire for a skeleton but they weren't very helpful. Anyway, SOB now has his own private winding sheet, so that's all right."

Delphick chuckled. "Mrs. Benn . . ." He hesitated, then plunged. "My object in showing you these reports is to lay the ground for asking your advice—unofficially and off the record."

She regarded him quizzically. "In connection with Seeton?"

"Yes. There is a side angle—or perhaps I should say a side issue—which may have nothing to do with the case, but which I can't afford to ignore. Sorry I can't be more explicit. Briefly, there is an elderly woman in a small nursing home just outside Plummergen. She's a heroin addict, incurable and according to the doctor hasn't long to give. I can't interview her myself. In the first place, it would be useless; in the second, it might get back to a third party who is concerned with her, which is what I want to avoid. Incidentally . . ." He stopped.

Mrs. Benn waited. Then: "Incidentally?"

Delphick roused himself. "I'm sorry. I was going to say there is an indirect connection between Miss Seeton and this third party."

"And it suddenly dawned on you that the connection might be more direct than you'd supposed."

"And more urgent. In short, I want Miss Seeton to go and see this Miss Hant in the nursing home."

"Seeton to interview a dying drug addict. Don't be ridiculous. How could she? And whatever for?"

He found it difficult to put into words. "It's . . . it's nothing more than a feeling I've got that she might come up with something. It was a drawing of hers that put us on to this angle in the first place."

"Drawing of Seeton's?" The superintendent told her of Miss Seeton's three sketches, giving no name except Lebel's. Mrs. Benn was fascinated. "Well, well. I thought I knew Seeton, but this is a side of her I'd never have imagined. Curious. Simplicity of mind allied to a satirical hand. No, that's wrong. There must be satire in the subconscious—but buried fairly deeply I should say. Intriguing."

"The point is," the superintendent pressed, "do you think it would unduly distress Miss Seeton to make this visit to the nursing home? That is if she'd agree to do it. I wouldn't want to upset her."

"I don't think anything distresses or upsets Seeton except bad manners. But I can't see what you hope to gain."

"A pointer. That's all I'm looking for. If anything is said, or even if she only gets an impression that points in the right direction, then I'll feel justified in digging a little deeper into the gentleman's affairs and take the risk of his finding out. Frankly, if my suspicions have a foundation, this inquiry could prove of vital importance to Miss Seeton herself. Miss Hant is one of four cases, all connected with the same gentleman, that I'm not happy about. And if I'm right, I think Miss Seeton has been scheduled as a fifth."

"Then my advice is ask her. If she agrees, go ahead."

Ten

If the police were hampered by rules of evidence and hedged about by unprovable facts, the villagers were not. Plummergen seethed. Unbridled imaginations were ridden bareback in any and every direction. Trade was brisk. Plummergen shopped in Brettenden as usual and spread the tidings; but, which was not so unusual, the whole district, including Brettenden, came to shop in Plummergen as the fountainhead of news, and unlooked-for visits were paid to the villagers by distant acquaintances, become overnight dear friends.

Among the stories that were rife was one that Mrs. Blaine and Miss Nuttel had evolved in retaliation for the sniggers in court over the "Ginger Nut," an engaging theory to account for the silence of "that poor boy." It was too likely—well, really, what other explanation could there be?—that That Woman "had given him a shot of some drug that had paralyzed his vocal cords." It was not made clear why Miss Seeton should have wished to silence him, but a nod and a beck—a wink would have been vulgar—conveyed all that was necessary.

The gentlemen of the press were thick upon the ground and there was always the chance if you came up with some particularly outrageous tidbit that you might get your picture in a paper.

"I don't like it, you know. I find it very worrying." Miss Treeves accepted a cup of morning coffee and took a biscuit. Last night at the W.I. Committee Meeting she had spoken her mind. Backed by Lady Colveden, she had called for solidarity: the village must stick together and put a stop to all these disgraceful rumors and gossip that were going around. They must, she had insisted, not only not repeat such tales themselves, but they must be very firm indeed with those who did. And everybody must be particularly careful what they said to any newspaper reporters. And as for stirring up trouble by inventing spiteful lies—and she had looked straight at Miss Nuttle as she had said it—that was downright wicked. Her present call was an example of this solidarity. It was a pity, as it turned out, that Miss Seeton was not in, but the example was still there. And this pleasant, sensible friend who was staying here was in some ways easier to talk to. "Arthur—that's my brother," she continued, "is worried too. As vicar he feels his responsibilities. It's helped in the garden, of course, as whenever he gets in a real tiz, as he is at the moment, he finds such relief in gardening. There's practically not a weed in the place. But I do feel sorry for him because I know that underneath it all he's very upset. You see, it's his village and he feels—well, as I said, responsible And when people behave badly and things get out of hand, he considers it his duty to do something. And I must say I think he's right to feel like that. Don't you?"

"Yes," said Mrs. Benn.

"How nice of you to understand. Though I fear your first view of Plummergen must have given you a dreadful impression. It's such a quiet little place as a rule. Though just now with all that's going on and all the talk, I feel you must be shocked and find it very strange."

"No, not in the least strange," said Mrs. Benn, with a mental picture of the teachers' common room at the school; though she was bound to admit that the police and the press were extra—they didn't as a rule have those.

"And, then, the police and the press," sighed Miss Treeves in unconscious echo, "poor Miss Seeton, I do feel sorry for her, she must be plagued by them. I can't think how she manages."

"Quite well. The few reporters that have caught up with her, she dealt with very simply. She agreed with, sympathized with, and then contradicted everything they said. I think they now write their interviews without reference to her. As she doesn't read them it doesn't matter."

"No, I won't have anything, thank you. I only just dropped in as I was passing to see if she was all right. How nice the room looks." Lady Colveden studied it. "And yet it's the same. What's she done? Oh, I see. She's taken down all those rather dreadful pictures and put up others. A great improvement. You know, I rather like that one—I can almost feel the wind." She moved to examine a large framed watercolor over the mantelpiece. The dark outline of a branch in the right foreground, a few scattered leaves still clinging, heightened the effect of distance to the gray sky where lighter and darker tones became massed and rolling clouds. Between, a sweep of moorland with heather bent before the wind. "Funny, it seems familiar. But then I suppose it would. After all, all moors look alike, don't they, like the Chinese?"

"Yes," said Mrs. Benn.

Lady Colveden peered for a signature. "E.D.S. No—never heard of him. But I still like it." She turned back with a smile. "You know I'm so relieved you're staying here. It worried me her being alone with all that's happening. I wanted her to remain with us, but she wouldn't. Of course I do understand the difference—being in your own home. And naturally we hope nothing more will happen—well, there's not much more that could, is there?—but if it does, it makes such a difference if it happens to two instead of one, doesn't it? That's why having a friend to stay just at the moment is ideal."

"We work at the same school."

"At the same . . . do you?" A trace of wistfulness. "It must be wonderful to have brains. Funny." Lady Colveden gave it thought. "You know I can't imagine Miss Seeton teaching. Wouldn't it be chaos?"

"She's a very good teacher. I don't suppose we get a lot of embryo Michelangelos, but what Seeton can do—and does— is to teach people to use their eyes and to understand something of what they see."

"But don't the children rag her?"

The monocle flashed. "Rag her? Certainly not." Mrs. Benn smiled wryly at the thought. Children knew when they were outmatched. Any rumpus the little horrors could dream up would look insignificant quite beside the confusion Seeton could produce naturally with a single good intention.

There was a cry of "Mother."

"I'm in here, darling," called Lady Colveden. She introduced Nigel to Mrs. Benn as he came in. "Miss Seeton's out at the moment."

"I know," he replied, "I think she's equipped with radar. This is the second time she's got out from under when the village was coming calling. She's at Knight's nursing home."

"At Dr. Knight's?"—surprise; "Is she?"—reflection; then she nodded. "Very wise. After all she's been through so should I be. Very comfortable and such good food."

"I don't think she's stopping there, mother. She wasn't carrying a toothbrush or anything, I just saw her going in as I drove past. And talking of driving past, you know the Rev. Arthur's becoming a public menace. He was striding headlong down the Street, so I stopped the car for safety, but he walked slap into it, leaned over the bonnet, and said, 'My boy, you're on the right side.' I wasn't, you know, I was on my left—he was on the right. 'Your mother's at Miss Seeton's and that's right, too, quite right.' I think he's working up into what Sister Molly calls 'a regular tiz.' So I thought if you were here you might like a lift home." He grinned cheerfully. "Poor Mrs. Benn, are you having to cope with the solidarity?" She looked a question. "Didn't mother explain? Our vicar's sister blew a blast on the trumpet last night at the W.I. and the walls of the Nut House are cracked if not fallen. She called for solidarity and a stop to scandal. That's why mother's here—she's being solid."

"Nonsense, nothing of the kind. I was just . . . actually, I was having a very interesting conversation with Mrs. Benn till you burst in."

"It's as well I did. The March of the Solids is practically upon us. There's Mrs. Jally, Mrs. Spice, and Miss Wicks at different points on the Street, but all with the same look of determination and all headed this way, at a guess."

"Miss Wicks?" ejaculated his mother. "Oh, help!" She put out her hand. "My dear Mrs. Benn, it's been so nice meeting you, but I must fly. No, not Miss Wicks. She's a nice woman and I do try, I really do try not to, but I can't help it, she makes me do it, too. Come along to us after it's over." She fled.

"Do what?" asked Mrs. Benn.

"It's the teeth," Nigel explained. "You'll see. When Miss Seeton gets back, come along for a drink and or lunch to recuperate. Good luck." He followed his mother.

Mrs. Benn was beginning to sympathize with Lady Colveden. It was indeed difficult not to "do it, too." Miss Wicks leaned forward and gave earnest point to every sentence. Afflicted with buck teeth, her speech had a sibilance: she resembled a squirrel and sounded like an ill-tempered swan. The effect was hypnotic. Mrs. Benn could feel her own upper lip curling, retreating; her own front teeth were lengthening by the second. It needed great self-control.

"So sorry Miss Seeton should be absent," hissed Miss Wicks. "Please be sure to say that I stopped by. I do so sympathize. This shocking business must be such a strain mustn't it?"

"Yesss," sibilated Mrs. Benn.

"Now, I mustn't stop as I'm certain you've things to see to

so I'll slip away. But please be sure to give Miss Seeton my message."

"I will indeed," said Mrs. Benn, determined that no betraying "s" should trip her. "Very kind of you to call. I know my friend will apprec- . . . be grateful."

"Of course I'll tell her, Mrs. Jally. How very kind of you."

"Very kind of you, Mrs. Spice."

"Very kind."

"Kind."

Well, well. If this was the response to the mere W.I.'s trumpet, let the Last Trump sound.

Miss Seeton appeared abstracted and restless on her return. Mrs. Benn thought it better not to mention the offer of drinks and or lunch, observed the fretful hands with interest and kept silent. Presently, deciding she would have a short rest before their meal, Miss Seeton went to her room. Mrs. Benn glanced up from her book and smiled.

Later, lunch prepared, she grew thoughtful. Was Seeton asleep? Had the visit to that nursing home upset her, after all? She'd better check. She stole upstairs and tapped softly at Miss Seeton's door. No answer. Asleep then? Carefully she lifted the latch and looked in. Miss Seeton, in a woolen cardigan and bloomers, her legs crossed and folded, her eyes shut, was sitting on the floor, holding her breath, and murmuring with deep concentration:

"Two, three, four, five, six . . ."

Mrs. Benn closed the door, crept downstairs, and returned to the sitting room. Well, well. Yoga yet. So this was why Seeton seemed spryer than recently. And she'd been imagining it to be the result of the country air. So this was why she could toss off being thrown in the back of vans with no ill-effects. Well, well.

After lunch Miss Seeton sat at her desk and sketched, while Mrs. Benn took her book into the garden. The superintendent arrived alone, sergeantless. Exercising tact, Mrs. Benn remained where she was.

The desk flap was closed when Miss Seeton showed Delphick into the sitting room. They sat down and the superintendent studied her.

"No luck?" he asked at last.

"I'm afraid not, superintendent. I did what you asked me to do. I went and saw that poor Miss Hant. Naturally I know it's all very tragic and one should feel sorry for persons like that and, of course, I do, in a way, but there are so many people in trouble through no fault of their own and I know it's very unfeeling of me, but I do find it difficult to sympathize completely with someone who's gone out of their way to bring trouble upon themselves. I did as you suggested and tried to show an interest and asked what had made her start on drugs in the first place, but her replies were very rambling and frankly I doubt if they were strictly true."

"I doubt it, too. Drug addicts and alcoholics have this in common: the truth is not in them."

"I felt that she resented my intrusion and I must say I really couldn't blame her. So I fear, after all, I wasn't of any assistance to you."

"No?" an eyebrow quirked. "It was your impression of Miss Hant rather than her version of herself that I was interested in."

"My impression?" Miss Seeton looked bewildered. "But I don't think I—well, I don't think I have one."

Delphick smiled. "Not even a sketch?" He looked from her to the desk; the flap was not quite shut and pieces of paper were protruding.

She followed his gaze. "That—oh, but that's quite different. I mean it has nothing to do with Miss Hant. At least not directly."

" 'By indirections find directions out.' It's starting to rain." Mrs. Benn put her book on a table and glanced back through the French windows. "Only a shower, I think, but not even for the sake of tact will I sit and soak. You'll have to build a summerhouse or something, Seeton, for guests to retire to when you're in conference. Sorry to butt in, superintendent, but the only outbuilding is occupied by hens and I refuse to perch with them."

Delphick laughed. "You're not butting in. We're out of luck, I'm afraid. As you know, I'd hoped Miss Seeton's visit to the nursing home might spark off something—that her inner eye might light on some point and might even produce another drawing that would in its turn shed some light on my problem. But I gather not. The visit was a failure and had no effect."

"No effect!" exclaimed Mrs. Benn. "It may have been a

failure but it certainly had an effect. Seeton came home all broody, retired upstairs to commune with herself before lunch, pecked at her food, and has been doodling away at her desk ever since." She turned to her friend: "For heaven's sake, show the poor man whatever it is you've been up to and put him out of his misery. If it doesn't help, that's that. At least it'll stop him feeling frustrated."

"I must admit," agreed Delphick, "that the mere fact that it's something that you felt so soon after seeing Miss Hant is enough to make it interesting."

Miss Seeton yielded. "But of course you can look if you really want to. I was trying to explain to the superintendent when you came in, it has nothing to do with Miss Hant. It's—it's rather unkind, in fact, and perhaps—well, a trifle vulgar."

Mrs. Benn's monocle gleamed, the other eye twinkled. "Then that settles it. If you've gone in for indecent drawing, it's time I knew about it. In any case, we're all more or less grown up here so we should be able to stand it." She opened the desk, sorted the papers, and picked out a drawing. "Wow!" said Mrs. Benn. On the paper capered an obese and elderly gentleman with a European face, clad only in his dark skin, a grass skirt, and a gloating expression. In his left hand he brandished a native spear; in his right hand he clutched aloft four shrunken heads—or was it five? Four had features roughly penciled in; the fifth was blank like an egg. "Well, well. When you take agin somebody you certainly don't pull your punches, do you? You know, I think you should do a series of portraits of the staff at school. I could pin them on the board. It should have a most salutary effect. Admittedly I doubt if any of them would ever speak to either of us again." For a moment she considered this idyllic state, then dismissed it as impractical. She handed the sketch to Delphick. "Tell me," she continued, "who is our grass-kilted friend doing the Headland fling?"

"It's my solicitor, I'm afraid," Miss Seeton admitted. "Or rather, to be accurate, of course originally he was Cousin Flora's."

Mrs. Benn let out a joyous laugh. "Then it's simple. Change your solicitor, my dear Seeton. Try one who wears clothes."

Miss Seeton was embarrassed. "I—I hadn't meant anyone to see it. And I'd no reason to . . . After all, Mr. Trefold Morton's been most kind and considerate. Of course he does boom rather."

Mrs. Benn watched the detective's face with interest as he

studied the drawing. "I gather it has some particular meaning for you, superintendent?"

He gave her a crooked smile. "To expand your very apt quotation when you came in, Mrs. Benn: 'And thus do we of wisdom . . .'" he bowed to Miss Seeton, "'with assays of bias . . . By indirections find directions out . . . You have me? You have me not?' In short it's the pointer I needed." He turned to Miss Seeton. "Was it seeing Miss Hant that put Mr. Trefold Morton into your head?"

"Oh, no," explained Miss Seeton, "he was going into the nursing home as I was coming out. I met him in the hall."

"Damn," said Delphick.

. . . "It's just been unfortunate in both cases. Very unfortunate. With—er, I can't remember his name. I don't think Noyes ever told me his name—but the tall boy shooting himself in the foot. And now Ginger getting himself arrested. But he won't speak, I promise you. Not a word." . . . "But that's the point. That's just the point. They did their best. The best they could. But they're not professionals at this sort of thing. Not professionals at all. Can't you send someone down?" . . . "But it's urgent. The woman must have been following me about. Getting in front of me even. This morning I went to see Miss Hant, she was there. At the nursing home. Just leaving. She'd been to see Miss Hant herself. Now what reason could she have for doing that? What possible reason? Dr. Knight had some trumped-up story that he thought it'd be a good idea for Miss Hant to have outside visitors. I don't believe a word of it. Not a word. That woman put him up to it. Or else the police must be behind the whole thing. Maybe she's working for them. Employed by them." . . . "But I gave this wretched Seeton woman some pills." . . . "Because she complained of a headache." . . . "No, I don't know whether she took any. I don't know what she's done with them. But if the police got hold of them—" . . . "Well, it wasn't my fault. It seemed a good idea—at the time. I thought if she took any it might make Ginger's task a little easier. A little easier altogether." . . . "She gets everywhere, I tell you. Everywhere. She even went and called on Mrs. Venning." . . . "I've no idea. No idea at all. But she walked straight into three of the boys. One of them was taking the car out for a spree, in spite of what Noyes had said. The other two had quite rightly stopped him. Quite rightly." . . . "The tall one? Yes, he was. But she didn't recognize him, thank heavens. Didn't notice

him at all. The woman's a danger. A public danger." . . .
"Can't you arrange something from London? Send someone
down who understands this sort of thing? Who's used to it?"
. . . "If you insist. But I'm not happy about it. Not a bit
happy." . . . "Very well, then. I'll wait here for a call."

Mr. Trefold Morton dropped the receiver, pushed the telephone away, and sank back in his chair. He took a crisp,
clean handkerchief and mopped his face. He stuffed the handkerchief back into his breast pocket where it hung, a limp
symbol of its owner, crumpled, soiled, and wet.

* INTERIM *

. . . "Your so-called position in a picayune community is of
no interest to me, except in so far as it can be used to advantage. You will be involved to the extent I decide and take
what risk I choose." . . . "You will drop this woman at the
crossroads on Plummergen Common tonight and leave her to
walk home. The ensuing accident will not be your concern;
except that you will be well-advised to arrange proof of your
presence elsewhere." . . . "Then as her solicitor you can remember some urgent paper to be signed, tell your hosts that
business prevents you from dining but that you will join them
for coffee, and you can give the woman a lift as far as the
Common on your way." . . . "Making it sound realistic is
your business. Has that fool of a boy's foot recovered? Can
he walk and drive?" . . . "Good. Tell Noyes to have the boy
pick up the Venning girl in her car and wait the further side
of the crossroads. He'd better give her a heavy shot to keep
her quiet. As soon as you pass them after dropping the
woman, he will start the car, run the woman down on the
Common, and make sure she's dead. He will then run the car
into a tree, finish off the Venning girl, and arrange the body
near the car as if she'd been thrown out on impact. The
whole affair will be an unfortunate accident caused by an irresponsible girl." . . . "The mother will keep quiet for her
own sake. She'll have no reason to suspect the girl wasn't
alone." . . . "I know Noyes found the girl useful as a trollop
to amuse the boys, but it was a mistake ever to get her
hooked. She's becoming too wild, too noticeable. It's time she
went." . . . "All right, if his foot won't let him run that far,
tell Noyes to have one of the others wait with a car farther
down the road. They can pick him up and he'll be back at the
Barn before the accident's discovered." . . . "Good. I'm glad

to hear it. And would it be asking too much for you all, this time, to carry out instructions; to do exactly as you're told, without letting yourselves be hypnotized by this woman, shooting yourselves, or getting yourselves arrested?"

The telephone receiver was slammed down.

Eleven

"It is very good of you to have taken such a forbearing attitude at my having interrupted your evening in this manner. Very good of you. It was remiss of me to have overlooked the need for your signature on that particular document. Most remiss. A little holdup of that kind, as you doubtless know, could delay the whole of probate. Or, maybe, you yourself are but a probationer in these matters." Miss Seeton winced in anticipation of the inevitable laugh. It came, but the boom was a little hollow. "However," Mr. Trefold Morton continued, "all's well that ends . . ." he faltered, recovered, "that is to say, that we should now catch the first post in the morning. Now you're sure—quite sure—that you don't mind walking home from the crossroads, if I drop you off there?"

"Not at all," murmured Miss Seeton.

"It is unfortunate that the friends with whom I should have been dining and whom I shall now have to join for coffee should live in exactly the opposite direction. Most unfortunate. But naturally I will take you right to your door if you insist. Naturally. However late it makes me. Or, if absolutely necessary, I could telephone my friends and say that I won't be able to get there."

"Please," protested Miss Seeton, "I wouldn't hear of it. You say it's no distance to walk—less than a mile. And, in any case, I have a torch with me. It's very kind of you to have brought me so far."

"The least I could do. The very least. Besides, by using this route to the village, as far as this is on my way. It's only here that our paths diverge."

He slowed as he approached the Plummergen-Ashford Road, pulled in to the side and stopped the car. Miss Seeton got out. Mr. Trefold Morton called through the window:

"Now, you know your direction? This part is called Plummergen Common. You turn to the right and the road leads straight down into the village. And you're sure you'll be all right? Quite sure? Because, if so, I'll be on my way. I feel dreadful—leaving you here like this. Quite dreadful. But needs must when the—er . . . Yes, indeed. Needs must."

Without giving her time to reply, the car jolted forward, clashed into second gear, turned left, and sped down the road.

How that man talked. Really, she was positively tired from listening to him. Of course it was very thoughtful of him to have sent a car to fetch her to Brettenden. But, to be honest, had she realized, when he offered to give her a lift back, that he meant to drop her off here she would have asked the driver to wait and take her home. Oh! Miss Seeton jumped as a noise like a shot sounded from a nearby field. Bird scarers? When it was dark? Ah, yes, she remembered now. Stan had said something about farmers using them at night to frighten rabbits and things. Surely it would have saved time if Mr. Trefold Morton had brought the papers for her to sign over to Plummergen in the first place and then gone on to his friends from there? However, she hadn't liked to suggest it on the telephone, when he'd told her that a car would be calling for her and was already on its way. No doubt it was just habit to attend to all business matters in his office. But he'd literally never stopped talking from the moment she'd arrived there. It was ridiculous, of course, but one might almost have said that he was nervous. Surely he couldn't have supposed that she might view a call to his office after hours in the light of an assignation. Miss Seeton smiled at the thought, took her torch from her handbag and switched it on.

Now, did one walk on the right side of the road or on the left? Cars drove on their—left, didn't they? And pedestrians? There was some rule about it. Either you did the same as cars —or exactly the opposite. Going down into a tube station there was a notice telling you to keep to the . . . She tried to visualize such a notice. Ah, yes. KEEP TO THE RIGHT. So probably the same applied. She shone her torch across the road. Well, that settled it. A hedge and a ditch on that side. One might easily miss one's footing and stumble into the ditch if a car came by. So awkward when there were no pavements— no, footpaths, she believed, was the correct term in the country. Whereas over here it was comparatively flat. Of course. This would be the Common.

The headlights of a car flared up suddenly some way in front of her. Miss Seeton stepped well off the road and turned aside to keep the dazzle from her eyes.

How effective. A lake. No—probably not big enough for

that. But a very large pond. She would wait by this tree till
the car had passed. Curious the falsifying effect of artificial
light. The leaves of the trees and shrubs overhanging the
water, even the branches, looked as though they were cut out
of cardboard. Yet, even as she watched, the light changed,
the third dimension was added, forms grew solid. Miss Seeton
glanced behind her. A car coming from the opposite direction. Distances were extraordinarily deceptive at night. The
first car appeared no nearer. Seemed not to have moved. Perhaps a couple . . . No, because then, surely, they would have
driven off the road. And then, again, they wouldn't have their
lights on. The lights of the second car were brilliant now.
Brilliant? They were coming straight toward her. Oh dear, oh
dear, there'd be an accident. What was the driver thinking of?

She waved her umbrella to attract attention, then turned to
run. Blinded, she bumped into the tree, knocking her hat off,
staggered round the trunk, and blundered forward. There was
a splintering crash as the car hit the tree against which she'd
been standing.

There. She knew it.

Horrified, she turned to go to their assistance, trod on nothing, lost her balance and fell backward with a splash.

Twelve

The village grapevine in action: Something observed here; something overheard there; a meeting or two, a few discussions, some telephone calls—and the picture was coming into focus.

Miss Treeves had observed Miss Seeton's departure. Going out to supper when she had a friend staying with her? That was unusual. And why hire a car from Pratt's in Brettenden instead of using Crabbe's from the village? She discussed this with Martha Bloomer when they met in the church to top up the water in the flower vases for the night and replace any dead blooms.

Doris, the waitress at the George and Dragon, had overheard the conference at table when Mrs. Benn had hurried into the dining room as the superintendent and his sergeant were finishing their dinner. Doris had discussed with the barmaid the facts: Mrs. Benn was in a state; Miss Seeton's lawyer had sent a car for her after hours about some paper or other to be signed; she should have been back; she wasn't; the police were ringing up all over the shop and that the young one, the big one, was bringing the car round.

The barmaid passed the facts on to Stan Bloomer as he was finishing his evening pint. Stan told Martha on his return home and Martha went straight over to Miss Seeton's cottage.

Seeing the light on when she got back, Mrs. Benn felt a wave of relief only to find that it was Martha having a Grand Slam in the kitchen. Between them they had a fairly clear outline of events and Mrs. Benn rang the Colvedens on the unlikely chance that Miss Seeton might have called there on her way back.

Lady Colveden, a late starter through not living on the Street itself, soon caught up with, then passed her competitors by the adroit use of her title and her telephone. She rang old Mr. Pratt's private number, learned that Mr. Trefold Morton had hired him, and it was he himself who had fetched Miss Seeton and taken her to the solicitor's office where he had been told not to wait as Mr. Trefold Morton would give her a

123

lift home. Undeterred by the fact that Mr. Trefold Morton's housekeeper said that he was dining out and she didn't know where, Lady Colveden demanded a list of possible names and addresses. She struck lucky at her third attempt, insisted on speaking to the solicitor himself and, when informed that he had dropped Miss Seeton off at Plummergen Common, leaving her to walk home, commented on his behavior in terms that would have raised blisters on the hide of a rhinoceros.

Sir George was out at a meeting. Nigel, once he had grasped the purport of his mother's telephone progression, jumped up and headed for the door. Lady Colveden called after him:

"If you take the M.G. without me, I'll . . . I'll . . ."

Threats failing her, she had to depend on tone of voice and expression. A short call to Mrs. Benn to bring her up to date, she downed receiver, snatched coat and head scarf from the hall, and ran out to join her son.

Mrs. Benn relayed the latest information to the police so that as the Colvedens swept round into the Street, Delphick and Bob Ranger were already pulling away from the George and Dragon opposite. The two cars stormed off, Nigel fractionally in the lead.

Mrs. Benn, too troubled to consider food, repaired to the kitchen where Martha was in full spate. She was put to work shelling and slicing hard-boiled eggs, chopping onions for a veal and ham pie made with some pork that Martha had found in the fridge—"You can't expect veal, not with the prices osculating as they do"—and some bacon. She found the noise, the activity, and Martha's determined optimism comforting.

Finally Martha crashed the oven door upon their joint enterprise. "There! Twenty minutes for the pastry, cover it and we're done in a couple of hours. She can have it hot tonight or cold tomorrow. All depending. No need to get yourself into a fret and a fritter, I've told you she'll be back right as rain, you'll see. Won't she?" demanded Martha and burst into tears.

Arms flailing, groping hands clutched, held. Miss Seeton struggled to gain a foothold—found one—and discovered that by clinging on above and by standing on tiptoe below she could keep her chin above water.

Entirely her own fault. So very careless—not to look where

she was going. Of course she had been dazzled by the lights, but she should have remembered how near she was to the pond's edge. So very fortunate, too, to find something to . . . She looked up. Her immediate surroundings were silhouetted against the light which shone across the water in front of her. Why—it was her own umbrella, hooked on a branch above her, that she was grasping. Some of the younger mistresses might laugh at her for carrying an umbrella in all weathers, but you never really knew. And, after all, it was practical. Now—could she, by pulling on it, get herself out? She must try to see if she could help whoever had been in that car— they might be injured, perhaps badly hurt. She heard the sound of movement and peered through the twigs and leaves. Yes. There was the car; one side crumpled against the trees, the remaining headlight still on. The car door opened and a figure got out. A young man. Well, probably. The young dressed so alike these days; very sensible but a little muddling sometimes. Miss Seeton opened her mouth to call. The figure limped forward into the light, examining the ground ahead. Dark hair; tall.

It couldn't be—it—it was. One of those boys in Mrs. Venning's lane. From the Barn. And his foot—the hen house. Miss Seeton realized she was very cold. The water of course. She shut her mouth.

The youth returned to the car, leaned in, then backed out, dragging another figure. A girl. He hefted the body, swung it above his head and . . . Oh, no, he couldn't—no, please—he mustn't—oh, no, how truly shocking—

. . . smashed the head against the door jamb.

A frantic effort to get out. To stop him. Her feet slipped, her hand slipped; she slipped under water.

"Glp!" screamed Miss Seeton.

He stumbled to the bank and threw the body down so that it lay on the brink with the head under water. He moved forward. Looked about, around, down. A report cracked as another cartridge from the bird scarer exploded. He sprang round, crouched, pistol in hand. Lights in the distance approaching. He straightened, hesitated, made for the road. The car which Miss Seeton had first seen stationary was approaching slowly, the passenger door open. He reached it. Jumped in. The door slammed. The car accelerated.

"It's no good, Mr. Colveden. Apart from the head injury, the neck's broken. She was dead before she hit the water."

Reluctantly Nigel laid the body of Angela Venning back on the grass and stood up. "We'll know more when we get the doctor's report," Delphick went on, "and when we can examine the ground by daylight. But it looks as if she lost control, tried to jump out, crashed the tree before she could make it and hit her head on the door as she was thrown out. If you'll stay here, sergeant, till the ambulance arrives, I'd better get back on the road and try to find Miss Seeton."

"Would you take my son with you, superintendent? I'll . . ." Lady Colveden took a deep breath. "I feel that I should go and break the news to Mrs. Venning."

"Would you? I should be grateful, it would be kinder, I think. We'd better get on then, Mr. Colveden. Other mobile units should be along soon but we can't afford to waste time." Delphick returned to his car. As a sleepwalker, Nigel followed him.

Lady Colveden turned for a last look at the girl's body, at the wrecked car. Looked again. Ran forward and knelt.

"Sergeant." Her voice was sharp.

Bob Ranger joined her. His torch shone on the remains of Miss Seeton's hat crushed under a front wheel. Without a word, he started circling, like an enormous hound casting for a scent. His second cast brought him to the bank.

"Hold the torch."

Lady Colveden hurried to him, took the torch, held it steady. There, from a branch above the water, as it were an arrow to mark the spot, hung an umbrella. The sergeant stripped to his undershorts, stepped to the edge. The torch beam wobbled. In his clothes he was big. Out of them he looked like a colossus. If he jumped there'd be a tidal wave. And he might land on—crush . . . Lady Colveden relaxed as Bob Ranger lowered himself gently into the water. The torch aimed down, probing. The sergeant, chest-deep, then deeper, knelt and vanished underwater, to reappear a moment later holding a sodden bundle. He put the bundle over one shoulder and clambered out.

Tragedy imminent; the night cut by a swatch of light. Danger imminent; the night a festering shadow. A primeval monster rises dripping from the swamp, his capture in his arms. A horror film in action. It was too much. Lady Colveden fought to repress incipient hysteria.

The sergeant loosened the clothes, laid the little figure face downward on the grass in the light of the remaining headlamp, knelt astride it and turned the head. He placed his hands low down on the back and began to exert pressure. After a moment or two, Miss Seeton yielded a quantity of pond.

Lady Colveden, reaching precariously, retrieved the umbrella, collected the sergeant's clothes, took them over to her M.G. and put them in the boot. She reversed the car and left it, engine running, facing toward Plummergen.

After this moment of normal activity, the improbable reality of the scene struck her the more. One body lay half-shadowed, the other full-lit and crouched over it the bared body of a man. Emotion outrunning her capacity, Lady Colveden bit back a giggle of fright. The Monster snarls over his prey.

The sergeant thought that he detected the first faint signs of breathing. He continued the rhythmic pressure until he was certain, then turned Miss Seeton over and began to pat her face.

Some . . . where. Somehow. Some thing. Must tell . . . Important. Hen house . . . limp. The Barn. One of them from the . . . Bob Ranger bent low to catch the murmur. "Ba-a-a," bleated Miss Seeton.

He began to pat her face again. Wearily her eyes flickered open to strain through shifting mist: focused. Black against the light, a naked man squatted over her, one hand upraised to strike; descending.

Oh, no. No, please. Miss Seeton fainted.

Grateful for practical action which helped to dispel the nightmare quality of events that was threatening to overwhelm her, Lady Colveden fetched a rug from the car and as the sergeant wrapped Miss Seeton's unconscious form:

"Dr. Knight's. That's the quickest," she told him. "We turn right before the village and it's almost opposite the lane to the Vennings'. I'll drop you there and then go on to the Meadows to tell them of the accident."

As they were starting, the ambulance arrived. She stopped. The sergeant left a message for Delphick, gave brief instructions to the men to await the superintendent's return and they were off.

Drawing up outside what had once been the old Cottage Hospital, Sergeant Ranger got out, rang the bell, went in, still carrying Miss Seeton, and the door of the little nursing home swung to behind him.

Lady Colveden's M.G. pulled away and took the turning opposite, to the Meadows. She drove slowly down the lane, dreading the coming interview. It proved to be worse than she had feared. Sonia Venning flatly refused to believe her; refused to discuss Angela; refused to go upstairs and check that the girl was, as she maintained, in her room, and stated that the car was in the garage which was locked, producing the key to the padlock from her bag as proof. Helpless in the face of this rejection, Lady Colveden began to feel desperate. Mrs. Venning turned abusive, shouting that the village, the police, that everybody was against them, persecuting them. That Angela had been a little thoughtless and wild, but that she was completely able to deal with her. And had. Disturbed by the noise, Mrs. Fratters came from the kitchen to see what was the matter. Lady Colveden appealed to her.

Mrs. Fratters beamed. "Miss Angie? Oh, no, m'lady. She's upstairs in her bed, she's not been well these last few days, you see. She had her supper in bed, I took it up to her myself."

But the police would come, questioning. And find them unprepared. Lady Colveden struggled to free them, to free herself, from this fantasy, this engulfing miasma of disbelief.

"She's not in bed. She's dead, I tell you, dead. Oh, God, how can I make you understand? She's dead. She's by the pond on the Common, lying there, dead. Her car hit a tree. She nearly killed Miss Seeton. She's . . ." Catching the note of hysteria in her voice, she set her teeth hard on her lower lip.

Mrs. Fratters had left the room. The two women remained frozen. A sobbing wail and the housekeeper was back.

"It's true, ma'am. She's gone. The window's open. And there's a ladder. She's gone. Oh, ma'am, m'lady, what are we to do?"

"Liar!" shrieked Mrs. Venning. "You're all lying." She swung round, plunged blindly out.

Lady Colveden grabbed the telephone and dialed. "Dr. Knight? Meg Colveden, at Mrs. Venning's. Can you come over at once? She needs help."

Sonia Venning stood in the doorway, wild-eyed, in her hand a padlock, hasp and staple, splinters of wood still clinging to it. "You were lying. An accident, you said. What accident put a ladder to her window?" Her voice rose. "What accident did this?" She shook the padlock. "Angela never forced that, she hasn't the strength. Who did it? Who phoned her? Answer me. Who telephoned this evening? Who was with her?"

"Why, nobody," stammered Lady Colveden. But something glimmered in her mind: "She—she was alone."

"She wasn't," snarled the other. "The Seeton woman was there. You said so. Who else? Go on, tell me, who else? Who did it?"

"There was nobody." Again the glimmer. Yet surely, there must . . .

"There was. There was." The voice cracked higher. "There must have been. You killed her. And you call it an 'accident.' "

Dr. Knight hurried into the room. One glance and he forced the distraught mother to a chair, stood across it, caught her arm, and imprisoned it against his side.

"She drugged by accident," the frantic voice babbled on, "that accident was mine, my fault, the fault was mine. She died by accident. Whose accident was that? Not mine. Oh, God, not mine."

"In my bag, on top, the hypodermic in a tin box, cotton swabs, and the bottle of spirit next to it, quickly, please." The doctor's calm voice was a moment of sanity. Lady Colveden fumbled, found them, held them ready. The doctor peeled back the sleeve, swabbed, filled the cylinder, inserted the needle, and pushed the plunger home.

"Tell me," the voice was screaming, "tell me, go on, tell me, murderer, whose accident was that?" The raving faded to a mutter and stopped.

Except for Mrs. Fratters' helpless sobbing, silence stole across the room.

A nursing home? There must be some mistake. Bob gaped at the rather plain little girl in pigtails who had paused halfway down the staircase to stare back at him in a moment of equal bewilderment. She pulled her dressing gown tighter— not such a little girl as he'd supposed.

Not another accident? What a day. Well, at least they weren't dripping blood all over the place—like that poor wretched plowman this morning who'd cut half his finger off —Good Lord, it looked as if he'd got that Miss Seeton who'd called on the Hant female. Not dead. Or he wouldn't have brought her here. And if there was no blood, they were certainly dripping. She ran back up the stairs, calling over her shoulder:

"Up here. First door on the right."

His clothes and Miss Seeton's umbrella under one arm,

Miss Seeton herself cradled in the other, Bob went up after her. Entering the first door on his right he found that an electric fire had been switched on, the bars beginning to redden, and a large bath towel laid in front of it. The plain girl with the pigtails was taking a nightdress and some small towels from a chest of drawers. On a table by the bed glowed the orange light of an adjustable electric top blanket. Bob dropped his clothes and the umbrella near the door and laid Miss Seeton on the carpet beside the towel. Working together with the silent efficiency of a practiced team, they stripped her, dried her and slipped her into the nightdress.

In the doorway Dr. Knight stood watching them. "I would of course be the last to interfere if this is a purely private affair. However, should you need the services of a doctor at any time, don't hesitate to call on me."

The plain girl looked up with a smile. "Ah, there you are, dad. Good. I was just coming for you as soon as we'd got her into bed. I think she's all right. The breathing's not bad and the pulse is quite strong, though a little fast."

"Right, Anne. I'll have a look at her. To save time, you might fetch my bag. Anything I want will be there. I'm sure that your probationer is quite strong enough, from the looks of him, to put the lady to bed on his own. I'll be here to keep an eye on the proprieties and to see that he knows which end the head goes and technical points of that kind."

Bob picked Miss Seeton up and laid her on the bed as Anne went out and the doctor leaned forward, pulled back an eyelid to examine the pupil, then felt the pulse. Anne came back with his bag. He took his stethoscope, listened to Miss Seeton's chest, then straightened.

"Shall we turn her for you, dad?"

"No-o. I don't think that's necessary. At a guess, I should say immersion followed by shock." He took a hypodermic syringe from a box in his bag while Anne produced cotton wool and a bottle of spirit from a drawer in the bedside table and swabbed Miss Seeton's upper arm. "A sedative," the doctor went on as he injected, "that's the best thing. She'll sleep right through and that, with warmth, should take care of the shock. As to the immersion, I doubt there'll be any complications, but at her age you can never be sure. We shall know tomorrow. Since it's that Miss Seeton that everybody's so interested in, I think, Anne, you should ring the George and Dragon and tell that superintendent fellow that we've got his lady friend here. You had better, perhaps, mention that it would appear that she had been bathing, unseasonably and unsuitably clad. And that he can see her tomorrow morning, but not before."

"Right, dad." Anne crossed to a corner cupboard, collected a kidney-shaped white enamel bowl, took a hypodermic from it, dropped the used one in its place, clipped the fresh one into her father's case and slipped it into his bag. Carrying the bowl, she turned to the door as the telephone rang.

"Blast!" said Dr. Knight.

"Shall I take it, dad?"

"No, my dear. I'd better go and learn the worst. It's bound to be somebody giving birth to a clowder of kittens. It always is. And they always do—after hours. And the later the bigger the litter," he called back as he sped down the stairs.

Anne became conscious of Bob staring at her and embarrassment made her brisk. "I was on the point of having a bath when you arrived. You'd better take it over, it'll only need some more hot water. If you'd like to bring your clothes, I'll show you where the bathroom is." She picked up Miss Seeton's sodden garments, balancing the enamel bowl on top.

It dawned on Bob, in horrid revelation, that he was not dressed—not dressed at all—for a social occasion. As his face flamed and he bent to retrieve his clothes, he had a moment's fleeting thankfulness that he didn't wear those rather tight triangular briefs that were so fashionable. At least his own loose undershorts were decent. He glanced down. But not, he realized, when wet. His color mounting to a rich shade of petunia, he dropped his clothes, grabbed the towel from the floor, and pulled it round his waist. He hung Miss Seeton's umbrella on the door and recovered his clothes. Anne watched him with an expression of grave interest, but Bob caught the glint of laughter in her eyes.

"Of course," she remarked, "I don't know if you can talk. But so long as you can understand . . ." Bob sweated and cleared his throat, preparing to apologize—to explain—to say . . . what on earth could he say? "Don't try," Anne reassured him kindly. "There's no need to speak. It's just nice to know that you probably could. If you wanted to. Come along."

She closed the door behind them and set off down the passage, Bob following: a leviathan in tow to a tiny tug.

With Bob settled in the bathroom, she disposed of Miss Seeton's clothes and the basin, then repaired to her bedroom where she rang the George and Dragon, left a message, sat down at her dressing table and looked at her reflection.

Damn. Damn. Damn.

And again, damn.

Her face was hopeless, of course, but her hair was pretty and her figure good. It would be just her luck, concluded Anne as she studied her reflection with distaste, that the former should be screwed up in pigtails for a bath, while the latter was hidden under pajamas and a serviceable but shapeless dressing gown. She pulled the offending ribbons out of her hair, brushed it, dressed quickly, choosing something red that clung, then ran downstairs.

A drink. And a snack. Perhaps coffee? He must have something after plunging about in the canal, or the pond, or wherever—or he'd catch a cold. Her mother had gone with friends to the cinema in Brettenden and wouldn't be back yet, so she was free to forage. She noted her father's message on the telephone pad by the hall extension "Gone Vennings," wondered briefly what was up, dismissed it, and continued on her way to the kitchen. Once there, she paused. What would a snack be for someone of that size? A whole ham, a loaf of bread, and suet pudding to follow? She began to put things on the cart. Slices of ham, mustard, pickles, bread, butter, cheese, and a jam tart. That should do. She pushed the cart into the sitting room, plugged in the percolator, put out the drinks and, hearing Bob on the stairs, went into the hall. The front door opened and her father came in followed by the superintendent.

Just her luck.

Thirteen

Many of the villagers had a busy and satisfying evening. Facts were plentiful, fancies abounded, and rumors flew.

Miss Seeton was missing, gone off in a car—fact. The sound of shots had been heard—fact. Nigel Colveden, with his mother, had raced down the Street, hotly pursued by the police—fact. The Vennings' car was smashed against a tree by the pond on the Common—fact. An ambulance had driven away from the scene of the crash—fact. Lady Colveden had driven in the opposite direction accompanied by a man without a stitch—fact. Nigel Colveden was in a police car with the superintendent from London—fact. Two police cars were drawn up by the pond and the officers refused to allow anybody near—fact.

Nigel Colveden was under arrest—not exactly a fact, but what other explanation could there be? Angela Venning was drunk and had driven off the road with several of her friends from the club; they were all in the ambulance—well, if not a fact, it was only too likely, wasn't it? There were things by the pond too horrible to be seen—must be a fact, surely. There'd been a gun battle on the Common—an audible fact. Miss Seeton had fled—evidently a fact. Lady Colveden was old enough to know better—an undisputed fact.

Miss Seeton had fled; possibly to London; probably abroad. Miss Seeton had caused the accident, attacked Angela Venning and her friends and, always ready with that revolver of hers, had shot three and wounded one; the bodies had been taken away in the ambulance. The bodies were laid out in a row by the edge of the pond and guarded by police; the ambulance had rushed a wounded man to the Ashford Hospital for a blood transfusion. There had been a moonlight bathing party which the police had raided; Lady Colveden had got away with Nigel, but without his clothes. Lady Colveden had absconded with one of the men. Angela Venning and one, two, three of her friends had been drowned and taken away by ambulance. Angela Venning had crashed her car trying to escape and she and two, three, four of her friends had been

133

rushed to the Ashford Hospital, by ambulance, in a critical condition. Miss Seeton had made a getaway driving the ambulance. Miss Seeton had been found drugged in the pond and had been taken away by ambulance. Miss Seeton was still in the pond, refusing to come out and the police were on the bank trying to persuade her. Nigel Colveden had been arrested: for fighting Miss Seeton; for fighting Angela and her friends; for fighting the police; for indecent exposure.

It was deplorable. It was tragic. It was shocking.

Admittedly all these allegations were but kite-flying. However, they were worth the enjoyment spent on them, since there was the knowledge, born of experience, that with a little tailoring here and a touch of embroidery there a fair proportion of them would be deemed to have achieved factual status by the morning.

Most of the police had a busy, if not wholly satisfying, night. Delphick blamed himself. He should have cottoned on to the fake accident. He should not have allowed the body to be moved, nor let people trample the ground, until the police surgeon and the murder squad had arrived. He should have found Miss Seeton earlier. He should have been able with luck to get a statement from her.

"She said nothing, Bob? Nothing at all?"

"No, sir. Not really. I think she was trying to say something. But she only made a sort of noise. It sounded like— well, a bit like a sheep, sir. Then her eyes opened and she suddenly looked scared silly and passed out cold."

He should not have allowed the killer time to get clear before a call could be put out. He should have broken the news to Mrs. Venning himself. He should not have allowed Dr. Knight to put the only two possible witnesses incommunicado until morning. Above all, he should have managed somehow to have been in three places at once.

"Stop beefing, Oracle, about all the might-have-beens and the never-looked-like-its. Start counting your blessings for a change." Chief Detective Inspector Brinton of the Ashford Criminal Investigation Department picked up a small pile of papers and began to deal them face upward onto his desk, as if preparing for a game of solitaire. "Now, the Venning girl first." He took the top of three overlapping sheets. "A preliminary canter from our medic. 'Time of death . . .' Well, we know that near enough. 'Cause of death. Fracture of left temporal area and a fracture-dislocation of the left cervical vertebrae . . .'—all that the Latin for she died of a hole in the head or a broken neck—or both. 'There are also signs of contusions around both ankles . . .'—chummy probably gripped her by 'em. 'Marks on both thighs give a strong suggestion of the use of a hypodermic needle: may well have been a drug addict . . .'—all this, of course, is subject to the usual ifs and buts and why can't we wait for a proper post-mortem—except that he'd call it autopsy because it's more difficult to pronounce—when he'll tell all." The chief inspector considered the next paper. "Ah, yes, our Scientific Branch. Clever lot. Write Greek. 'Latents on steering wheel and door —'What's the poor twit think he's talking about? If it's latent it's damn well invisible. He probably thinks latent is the Chinese for fingerprints. I'm all for science, but save me the jargon. I'd be in favor of a computer if I wasn't afraid it'd give me the answers in Arabic. What it boils down to is: the girl's dabs on the car, padlock, and garage door are mostly overlaid by smudges—so chummy wore gloves and was probably driving." He pushed the paper aside and looked at the next. "Ah, yes. The car. Nothing wrong with it. No brake failure or what-have-you. No skid marks on road. So it was deliberately driven off the road and into the tree. But not very hard. Just enough to mess up the front a bit. Chummy wanted it to look like an accident, but was careful not to hurt himself. Oh, land yes—a woman's hat, crushed under the near front wheel."

Sergeant Ranger sat up. "That was Miss Seeton's."

"Was it? Didn't you say, Oracle, that she was fit to be tied because they mucked up her titfer when they bagged her in the sack?"

Delphick grinned. "Yes. I think it was what annoyed her most."

"On recent form she'd do better with a crash helmet." He glanced at the next set of papers. "Trefold Morton. Looks like you've hooked a tidy fish there. We picked him up for you at his friend's house and bunged him over to Brettenden to cool off. The inspector wanted to bring him here, but I said no, I thought he'd do better in his home town. Very impressed the inspector was and said, 'Ah, yes. Bringing psychological pressure to bear,' which is French for using your nut."

"How's he coming along, Chris?" asked Delphick.

"Morton? Oh, quite nicely, I think. Very blustery to start with, but the wind's dying down a bit now." He pushed the top paper to one side. "I had a chat with Brettenden on the phone half an hour ago and they think he's beginning to come apart at the seams. Anyway they'll sit with him and hold his hand till you want him. By which time he should be ready to sob it all out on your shoulder. Particularly if you find anything in his office or in his house." Brinton scanned the next note. "That's all laid on. I rang Sir George Colveden. He'll have the search warrants ready and you can pick them up on your way back. He sounded delighted. At a meeting and missed all the fun earlier on, I gather."

"Yes," agreed Delphick, "but luckily he was back by the time I took young Colveden home. I felt sorry for that boy. He's a trier. Your first corpse is no fun; especially when you're young and it was someone you knew. I made him drive me. Not strictly according to regulations perhaps, but it helped to keep his mind on the road, instead of other things. His father should be able to sort him out. They're a close family."

"One more thing about Morton." The chief inspector prodded another piece of paper. "Remember, Oracle, you rang me from the Yard about the Singing Swan?"

"I did. On a tip-off from Miss Seeton."

"It would be. That woman gets her umbrella into everything. Well, I told you that we'd raided once or twice, but were pretty sure that they caught the whisper. We've found where the leak was. Or rather it's up and found us. When Morton was taken into the station at Brettenden, one of the local flatfeet said, well, good gracious, him. If it weren't Councilor Trefold Morton—him that was always on about what a disgrace the Singing Swan was. It came out that every time we were going to raid, this idiot in uniform proudly told Morton, to show how on the ball we were and because he didn't like criticism of the force. Well, he's now learning all about criticism of the force at first hand." Brinton leaned back in his chair with a sigh. "Well, that's the lot, I think. I suppose you two want to get weaving if you're ever to get to bed tonight, though I wouldn't give much for your chances. By the way, sergeant," he eyed Bob severely, "what's this note from the ambulance men, that you were gamboling about Plummergen Common in female company and driving round the countryside all starkers?"

Bob's face flamed. "I was all wet, sir," he explained.

"I see." The chief inspector nodded. "Well, I won't argue with you, you should know and they say self-knowledge is the first step to wisdom."

"Lay off him, Chris," laughed Delphick. "If it hadn't been

for Bob and his skin-diving act, we should have lost Miss Seeton."

"Quite. Well, I haven't met the lady myself, but before she came we just had nice quiet larcenies, dopings, muggings, and the like. But since her arrival it's been shootings, abductions, and now murders—the lot. I suppose you wouldn't like to take her back to London with you and give us all a rest?"

"I believe she's considering settling down in Plummergen, Chris," Delphick told him cheerfully.

"She is, is she? Well, at the rate she's going we'd do better to call in the army and settle for martial law. Break Morton down if you can, Oracle. At the moment he's only assisting us. But if we're to hold him we'll have to work out what charges. I'll stay put till you're through with him. Even if it means dossing down here for the night."

Delphick and Bob Ranger picked up Mr. Trefold Morton's keys at the police station in Brettenden on their way to his house where they rang several times, knocked, and were on the point of letting themselves in with a key when the door was opened for them by an elderly woman in dressing gown and slippers, with a shawl round her shoulders. She had a broad face which should have been jovial, had it not been for the tiny, pursed mouth, and she stood, blinking nervously at them, barring their entrance. The superintendent explained that they were police officers and apologized for the lateness of the call. She stepped back and, as soon as they were in the hall, shut the front door, then pointed to an oak bench against the wall. Delphick produced one of the search warrants, but she shook her head, pointed once more toward the bench and moved to the stairs. Nonplused for a moment, Delphick went after her holding out the warrant. She waved it aside, drew herself up and, the little mouth pinched even tighter, jabbed her forefinger twice toward the bench with an air of command.

The sergeant was surprised to see the Oracle suddenly smile and bow.

"Very well, madam. We will wait. But we should be grateful if you'd be as quick as possible."

She gave him a brief, final nod and scuttled up the stairs.

Bob followed his superior as Delphick moved to the bench and sat down.

"What's up, sir? I don't think she's all there."

"Your powers of observation do you credit. She's not.

However, I think she's repairing the omissions. We'll hope it doesn't take too long."

"But hadn't we better make a start, sir? It's getting a bit late."

"True. But I think it might save time in the long run to have a guided tour. Also there's no point in upsetting the old lady more than we need. Remember that, whatever we may think of this wretched solicitor, she probably thinks the sun, the moon, and several stars shine out of him. Again, if we're lucky enough to find anything here, a witness who's prejudiced in his favor is to our advantage."

"Good evening, gentlemen."

Bob turned and his jaw dropped. Down the stairs sailed the same dressing gown, the same shawl, the same slippers, but a woman transformed. Spectacles, with a heavy black frame, made her eyes appear large, shining, and genial. The firm, wide mouth, stretched in a welcoming smile, seemed to Bob's awestruck gaze to be crammed with glistening white teeth. The whole face glittered with glass and plastic.

"I'm the housekeeper," she went on. "Can I help you? I'm so sorry to have kept you, I'm sure. The bell woke me and thinking it was him and having forgotten his key I came down quick as I could and went and quite forgot my glasses. And it wasn't a mite of good you going on about what you wanted until I'd fetched them because what you can't see you can't take in if you know what I mean. Now, what's he gone and done? There was a Lady Colveden or some such name rang up earlier wanting to know where he was but as I told her I couldn't tell her not knowing. But she wouldn't take no and asked who he might be dining with so I gave her a list of possibles. But he did take his car that I do know. Has he had an accident?"

Delphick was fazed by this spate of verbiage after her determined silence at their first encounter.

"No," he assured her, "nothing like that."

"Not? But you said you were police." She beamed upon them inquiringly. "What's he been up to? Got himself into trouble?"

The superintendent chose his words with care. "There are certain matters that need an explanation. At the moment Mr. Trefold Morton is helping us with our inquiries. Have you been with him long?"

"Well, 'long' depends how you look at it, doesn't it? Now it would be—let me see . . ." the housekeeper considered, "yes, it would be a matter of twelve years come Christmas."

"And yet the possibility of trouble doesn't seem to surprise you?"

"Not to say surprise no. Too smooth by half I've always thought him."

"Have you had any trouble with him yourself?"

"Not to say trouble bar a couple of run-ins first off when I came. He said the food was too expensive and I ought to be able to manage with cheaper. I told him. You can't make an omelet without breaking eggs I told him and if you want to eat the shells, sir, you're welcome if that's what you want and I'll have the eggs but lower myself I won't. He never said no more. You have to be firm or people take advantage. And then there was the wages. He wanted to keep back part of my wages and put it into something for me. I told him straight. You put my wages into my hand I told him and any further putting that needs doing I'll do myself. Too smooth by half I thought that."

The sergeant had moved unobtrusively behind the housekeeper, his notebook in his hand, and Delphick decided to glean what he could while she was in the mood for reminiscence.

"Tell me," he asked, "have you noticed anything strange? Any odd goings-on?"

The housekeeper bristled. "Certainly not. Nothing of the kind. Goings-on and I'd not have stopped. Nasty he may be and not to be expected different it being his nature poor man but respectable I'm bound to give him."

Delphick pacified her. "No, that wasn't what I meant. I was thinking more of any unusual type of visitor. Or anything unusual, in fact, that you remember."

The housekeeper moved to a chair and sat down. "Well, there's one man. He comes here quite a bit, you might say he was unusual, anyway his clothes are and his hair's done in a sort of bob with a fringe. I've seen him about the town and somebody did tell me his name but it's gone, they said he runs a club or some such out Les Marys way."

"And you say he comes here quite a bit?"

"Well, you could say quite a bit—about once a week regular. Mostly latish, I've only let him in a few times myself, but sometimes when I've heard the door go late I've looked out the window and seen him leaving."

"Any others?" Delphick queried casually.

"Not to say unusual, no." She pondered a moment, then

laughed. "Of course, there was the young gentleman from Scotland, but that was years back."

The superintendent's face took on a look of sympathetic interest. "Yes?"

"Well, he called, and I asked him to wait, but when I went in and gave his name, he said to say he wasn't at home, so I went back and said he wasn't in, which wasn't true of course but I couldn't say different having been told, and the young man wasn't half wild, said he'd come all the way from Scotland to bury his auntie and where was the money? I told him I couldn't say I'm sure and he stamped off saying he'd have the law on him. That made me laugh, I mean how can you have the law on a lawyer, doesn't make sense."

Delphick gave another gentle prompt. "Anyone else?"

"Else? Well, let's see now—there was that Miss . . . no, her name's gone, though it was all in the papers after, she came twice. The first time he saw her and they didn't half have a row, I could hear them in the kitchen, she was shouting and screaming and she was crying when she left and he said I wasn't to let her in again if she came. But she did come, oh, a long time after, must have been above a year, it was in the morning and I said she ought to try his office but she said she'd been there and they'd said he wasn't in. She seemed in such a state I felt sorry for her, poor thing, and took her into my own room and gave her a cup of tea. She kept saying the bank must have made a mistake and she couldn't be poor, she shouldn't be poor, and did I think she was poor and things like that. Well, I told her I really couldn't say, not knowing. And she said look what things had brought her to—well, she did look bad and that's a fact. And she said if she wasn't poor, she kept harping on that, well, anyhow if she wasn't, she'd fooled him she said and he'd find out soon enough because she'd made a new will only that morning with the milkman. Well, that didn't make sense because milkmen don't make wills anyone knows that. Then she said never trust a solicitor, so I told her I wouldn't and was there anything I could do and she said no, there was nothing anybody could do now. And off she went. I felt quite upset. Then I read in the papers next morning how she'd gone and jumped off a roof that very afternoon after leaving here. It gave me quite a turn. I knew at the time that tea wasn't doing her any good."

"And?" Delphick still spoke quietly, afraid to break the flow.

"And?" repeated the housekeeper. "Now, let's see. The

only other one I can think of is a Miss Hant. Yes, now I come to think of it she wasn't so long ago, a matter of months. She turned up all wild-eyed and starey like that other Miss . . . funny how that name's gone and it's on the tip of my tongue too if only I could put my hand on it." She frowned.

"Miss Worlingham?" murmured Delphick.

"There, of course, Worlingham, I knew I knew if if only I could call it to mind. Well, as I was saying, this Miss Hant came of an afternoon, I didn't take to that one, when she must have known he wouldn't be here and was very surprised he was out or said she was but I didn't believe her, she was sly that one. She said he'd promised her some pills, well, he's not a doctor I told her, but she got a bottle out of her bag and said would I pop up to his bathroom cupboard and see if there was one like it there and get it for her."

Delphick seemed almost asleep. "What kind of bottle?"

The housekeeper smiled and nodded. "Well, now it's funny you should mention that. It was sort of different in a way. It started off more like a tube for tablets and then right at the bottom it opened out like a bottle. I gave her the rightabout quick, the idea that I'd go handing out his things to people at the door without directions, whatever next, and anyway there was no bottle like that in his cupboard as I should know having dusted. And he wasn't half wild when I told him, he said the woman was mad and ought to have a certificate. I hardly liked to look at the papers the next few days in case she'd done herself too, but I've heard since that she's in hospital so she'll all right, I think the National Health's wonderful, don't you?"

Delphick rose hastily. "Now perhaps, if it's not keeping you up too late, you could just show us round. Have you any idea where Mr. Trefold Morton is most likely to keep any private papers?"

"Papers?" The housekeeper deliberated. "No, I couldn't say, I'm sure, excepting for his office. Of course there's that safe he's got hidden behind some books in his study, you might try there, I suppose." She crossed the hall and opened a door. The detectives followed her. One wall of the study had been shelved making a floor to ceiling bookcase. They exchanged glances. The conducted tour was paying off. The housekeeper took a few volumes from one of the middle shelves, disclosing a small wall safe. "There. I came on it when I had the books out for dusting but I never let on I knew not being my business, but seeing you're police with a warrant and his keys I suppose it's all right."

More than all right, Delphick reflected; blind luck. It could have taken them hours of searching, certainly more time than they had that night, to find the safe. He was intrigued, too, by the housekeeper's relation to Mr. Trefold Morton and the fact that she would not—probably, though unconsciously, could not—bring herself to mention his name, always referring to her employer as him or he. In view of such dislike it was curious that she should have stayed with him so long. He caught himself wondering what Miss Seeton would have made of the housekeeper in one of her portraits. He selected a key from the owner's ring, opened the safe and removed the contents: a few old jewel cases; and papers. He put the cases back, handed half the papers to Bob and began to riffle through the remainder.

Entries in a small black notebook caught his attention and he put the rest to one side. The entries were under four main headings; each heading being the shortened, underlined version of a name. Under these headings followed lists of figures and dates, the earliest dating back some fifteen years, with occasional initials. The names Delphick could guess. C'dale would be Mrs. Cummingdale; the young gentleman from Scotland's auntie. F'son, Mr. Foremason, who had died in a car crash. While W'ham must be Miss Worlingham. And H't could only stand for Miss Hant. A right-hand column in each entry was given over to addition and under the total was drawn a heavy black line. Delphick was struck by notes in red under the black lines: 25%, then a figure and, after subtraction, a final total. Who, he speculated, had been milking Mr. Trefold Morton for 25 percent? Miss Hant's entry was unfinished, the addition incomplete, the black line as yet undrawn. The entries were too cryptic to be resolved without a key, but his own suspicions allied to the housekeeper's revelations to the transfer of bonds, stock and share certificates, and the like, but advice from the various banks on their late clients' original holdings should soon decipher the whole. He shut the book.

"Anything in your lot, sergeant?"

"I was wondering about these, sir." Bob offered a packet of papers held by an elastic band.

"What are they?"

"There's no name or anything, sir, just figures. But they're dated for each week and they look like a list of outgoings and incomings. I got the idea, from what this lady told us," he smiled at the housekeeper, "that they might be a weekly state-ment of accounts from that club the Singing Swan."

Delphick took the papers, glanced at them, then, with the notebook, put them into his pocket. He opened the smaller of the packets: a cardboard box holding a number of two-inch-square transparent envelopes with a small quantity of powder in each. The superintendent split one of the envelopes, wetted his finger, tasted it. He laid it aside and turned to the other package: a sealed container. The sergeant watched, intrigued, as Delphick broke the seal, but knew better than to ask ques-tions. As Delphick again tasted, Bob looked round the room. On the writing desk was a roll of Sellotape in a plastic tear-off. He fetched it. Delphick nodded thanks, resealed both pack-ages and pocketed them. He returned the rest to the safe, locked it and replaced the books on the shelf. He addressed the housekeeper.

"Thank you for your patience. We shan't want anything else tonight. I'll arrange for a full search in the morning. I'm only sorry that we had to get you out of bed."

She smiled. "Oh, that's all right, it makes a change." She closed the study door. "Will he be coming back tonight?"

"No," said Delphick. "Not tonight."

Her smile broadened. "Well, it just goes to show doesn't it, I told you he was smooth."

Delphick's curiosity got the better of him. "Frankly, I'm surprised you've stayed with him so long."

"Well, it suited if you know what I mean," she explained. "He knows his place and I know mine and we don't interfere with each other above half. It's not as if he were married or had a family with everybody wanting things different."

"And yet I gather that you've never really liked him?"

"Not to say like no," she admitted amiably. "I can't abide him, never could take to him not from the first. When some-body's too smooth like he is then somebody else is going to get the rough of it I always say."

Which was as good a sum-up as any of Mr. Trefold Mor-ton and his activities, decided Delphick, as he and the ser-geant returned to their car.

At the solicitor's office in the High Street they found nothing of immediate interest except for a small, unlabeled bottle of pills in a medicine cupboard on the wall of a wash-room adjacent to Mr. Trefold Morton's sanctum. It was a replica of the bottle that the housekeeper had described. Held in the hand it resembled a phial, but in fact the base widened out like a miniature decanter.

"Makes it easier to stand up, I suppose," commented Bob.

"That, yes," agreed Delphick. "But more important, I should say; without being particularly noticeable, it's sufficiently different not to be mistaken for anything else."

"What was in those packages, sir?"

"On that, Bob, I can give you no authoritative statement. It's not my field. But, off the record and subject to findings from the lab boys, I should say that the envelopes contained heroin ready for distribution and that the other is raw opium. Which means, if it isn't concealed somewhere in his house—unlikely, I imagine, since his housekeeper would have been sure to have come across it in her dusting—that there is a processing factory somewhere near, in the running of which our Mr. Morton must be deeply concerned."

The clock at Brettenden Police Station showed one minute to two when the superintendent and the sergeant arrived. They went straight to the office where Mr. Trefold Morton was being detained and took over the interview from the two weary officers who had run out of questions, out of ideas, and had but one thought between them, sleep. Without speaking, Delphick sat down at the desk and began to read through the notes left ready for him, ignoring the solicitor's protest.

Listening, Bob decided that there was little of literary merit in Mr. Trefold Morton's repetitious phrases and contented himself with entering in his notebook: "T.M. snorting and blowing like a grampus." It took Delphick less than seven minutes from the time of their entry to cut through the skin and reduce the whole to blubber. The superintendent had used one of those minutes before he pushed the papers to one side, stared at the solicitor, then introduced himself and the sergeant by name and rank.

Mr. Trefold Morton jumped to his feet, taking his stand on Outrage. It was an outrage, he insisted, an outrage, he repeated, in fact he repeated it several times, that he should have been kept there so long simply because he had given Miss Seeton a lift in his car. If anything had happened to her after he had dropped her—he knew nothing, of course; he had been told nothing; merely questioned like a common malefactor—but if anything had, it had nothing to do with him.

Nothing at all. Nor, he ended triumphantly, if unwisely, could it be proved.

Delphick cut the ground from under him by agreeing that, on the evidence that they had so far, he was, as yet, merely an important witness in a case of murder and attempted murder. The solicitor's eyes bulged. The question of complicity would be gone into—and gone into very thoroughly—at a later stage. And that, if that had been the only reason for his detention, it would indeed have been an outrage.

"I understand," he continued, "that the manager of the Singing Swan was a regular visitor at your house and I should like an explanation of—these." He slapped down on the desk the packet of papers from the safe that Bob had given him.

Mr. Trefold Morton goggled for a moment, sat down again, then admitted to having financed the club. He denied having any say in, or knowledge of, the way the club was run. He insisted that it had been a speculative investment undertaken from altruistic motives; that he had no thought of profit, merely a laudable desire to provide the youth of Brettenden with a social club that would keep them out of mischief. If his generosity had been abused in any way he, himself, could hardly be blamed.

Delphick made no comment on this, but keeping his eyes on the solicitor, said:

"I should also like a full explanation of the entries in this." He withdrew the black notebook from his pocket and held it in his hand.

Mr. Trefold Morton gazed at it, hypnotized. Delphick laid it down. "And—of these." He placed the two packages on the desk beside the notebook.

Of their own volition Mr. Trefold Morton's hands made a small wringing movement. Seeing that he had broken, that he had, finally, come apart at the seams, Delphick cautioned him and picked up the telephone.

"Get me Chief Inspector Brinton at Ashford, please. . . ." "Chris?" . . . "The holding charge will be embezzlement and breach of trust." . . . "There'll be further charges, I imagine. But that's not my pigeon. It'll be up to Narcotics. I've a couple of expensive birthday presents for them here that should interest them and keep them busy." . . . "Right." . . . "And to you." . . . "Good night."

Fourteen

"Nasty piece of work, wasn't he, sir?" observed Bob as he and his superior set out for Plummergen the next morning.

"Yes," agreed Delphick, "I'm bound to admit that I find myself in entire sympathy with his housekeeper; I never could take to him, not from the first. How she stuck him for nearly twelve years . . ."

They had stuck him until after three o'clock that morning, when Mr. Trefold Morton had been removed to a cell for what was left of the night.

Faced with the proof of his frauds, on that particular subject the solicitor had whined quite freely, the recurring theme of his chant being sorrow for himself. His attitude was that, except in the case of the nephew from Scotland of whose existence he had been unaware, none of the clients concerned had either near relatives or friends to inherit. In consequence the properties would have gone to charities or to the Crown and he felt, he felt strongly, that considering his position he had as much right, indeed more right, to the money than they. That he had beggared his clients whilst they were still alive, he admitted to be true, but what else, he asked tearfully, could he have done? If he had waited until their deaths, it would have been too late to take action.

When Delphick, restraining anger, pointed out that certainly in the case of Miss Worlingham and probably in that of Mr. Foremason, he had not only robbed people who had trusted him but had also been directly responsible for their deaths, Mr. Trefold Morton shrugged. If people were too stupid or too indifferent to look after their own affairs, to look after themselves, what else could they expect?

On the question of drugs, they could wring no admission from him. He denied ever having seen the curious-shaped bottle before, declaring that if it had been found at his office premises, it had either been planted, or else that it must belong to one of his staff and Delphick was in no position to press that particular issue further until an analysis had been

146

made of the contents. The story of Miss Hant and her bottle
Mr. Trefold Morton dismissed as the ravings of an unbal-
anced mind. He insisted that the pills that he had given to
Miss Seeton out of kindness, purely out of kindness, were
some proprietary brand of headache cure whose name he had
forgotten and, as Mrs. Venning had destroyed the bottle in
question, and Miss Seeton was not there to testify, there the
matter had to be left.

Asked about the contents of the two packets, he set his
mouth, stared at the floor, and refused to speak; began in fact
to show a certain kinship with the Ginger Nut. He was obviously terrified; too frightened to risk a word. It was to be
hoped that Narcotics would be able to glean some intelligence
from him at a later date, but again Delphick was unable to
pursue the matter until an analysis of the contents of the
packages should confirm or disprove his guess.

When Mr. Trefold Morton had been taken away, the duty
sergeant had produced tea and camp beds. Superintendent
Delphick had settled to sleep in reasonable comfort, while
Sergeant Ranger for whom the camp bed was far too short,
had settled in unreasonable discomfort on the floor.

Bob slowed the car. "Do you mind if we stop here for a
moment, sir? There's something I want to get."

"Go ahead."

Delphick watched Bob enter a florist's shop, then relaxed in
his seat to plan his next moves. As usual, Miss Seeton's latest
assailant had disappeared into thin air. There must be good
organization behind them. Still that was only to be expected.
Drugs meant big money. Big money meant big resources.
Were these repeated attacks upon her in the nature of a personal vendetta by Lebel, either acting on his own behalf or
through friends? Or were they on orders from above? It was
a profitless speculation, Delphick decided. Whatever the reason, someone seemed determined to continue having a go,
which was what chiefly concerned the police. It would have
been pleasant to have nailed Trefold Morton for his part in
last night's attempt, but it didn't look as if there was going to
be a chance of proving it. Thank the Lord that, owing to the
solicitor's confession over the embezzlement, he himself
hadn't been needed at the magistrate's court this morning.
Chris Brinton had arranged for someone else to present the
police case and to ask for remand without bail, with the possibility of further charges. He'd passed all his gen on to Narcot-

ics and they could take it from there. It might be worth their while to have a go at Miss Hant. There was the chance that Trefold Morton had been slipping her doses of the hard stuff when he visited her in the nursing home. If so, she might blow the gaff on him when her supplies were cut off. He must have a word with Dr. Knight. In the meanwhile the solicitor should cop a good stretch for embezzlement. So that was one unpleasing specimen knocked out of the ring, who would never in any real sense get off the floor again. Dealing with drug traffickers was like dealing with an ants' nest. You trod on a few unimportant workers, but you never seemed to get to the heart of the nest. To the inner ring of workers. Let alone the queen. Or was it a king? Anyway, the leader. Boiling water was good for ants. He watched himself striding down the labyrinthine corridors of an ants' nest, with a kettle in his hands, demanding "Take me to your Leader." The kettle tipped, spilling boiling oil. Now, that was an idea. If he could use . . . boiling oil . . . that should prove . . . it should definitely prove . . . something.

He jerked awake as Bob returned carrying an enormous sheaf of flowers and the largest box of chocolates that Delphick had ever seen. Bob laid his purchases on the back seat, got in and started the car.

"I thought as we were calling at the nursing home, sir—well, I thought . . ."

"And a very nice thought, too, Bob. Provided she's there."

Bob was confident. "Oh, she will be, sir."

Delphick was less confident. "I wish I could feel as sure. She's got amazing powers of recuperation. After a good night's sleep, she's just as likely to be skittering round the countryside with her umbrella, stirring up mayhem in all directions. Speaking for myself, for a nice twelve-hour kip, I wouldn't need to be given an injection—just the chance."

At the nursing home, Bob got out and collected his offerings from the back of the car. Delphick remained in his seat.

"I'll stay put, Bob, till you've checked whether Miss Seeton is really here."

"Right, sir."

Bob pushed past the swing doors and looked round the empty hall. Anne Knight, in nurse's uniform, came quickly through a door on his right.

"I saw your car from the window. I'm afraid you're too late. Miss Seeton's gone. She didn't seem any the worse for last night, and as soon as she'd had her breakfast she said she really couldn't laze about in bed any longer. And off she went." Bob gazed at her dumbly and Anne realized what he was carrying. She smiled. He looked so like a lovesick suitor. What a shame Miss Seeton hadn't been there to receive him. "Oh, what a charming thought. How sweet of you. I know she'll love them. If you take them along to her cottage, I think you'll find her there."

Bob advanced upon her, his face crimsoning, and thrust his purchases into her arms.

"For you," he said. He turned and walked out.

Mrs. Knight, coming downstairs, found her daughter sitting on the bottom step, clutching what appeared to be half the garden wrapped in paper and a small crate of chocolates.

"Darling. Have you got an admirer?"

Anne raised a tear-stained, smiling face. "Have I, mummy? I'm not sure. He's only spoken two words since I met him."

"What were they?"

" 'For you!' "

"Then you have," decided her mother. "But I shouldn't cry about it. It's good for the flowers, but ruination to chocolates. Come along."

She helped her daughter cart the booty into the sitting room.

"Miss Seeton's left, sir. They say she's gone home."

"Oh." Delphick refrained from comment on Bob's flushed face and wooden expression, forbore to glance toward the back seat, even managed not to smile. "I see. Then we'd better get along there. Carry on, Sergeant."

"A fight to the death. Both took up their swords.

"Wham. Bang. Bang. Whang. Wham. Scrrounch.

" 'Stop. Stop,' cried Jack the Rabbit.

" 'Why?' asked Wally Weasel.

" 'Because I've broken my sword,' said Jack.

" 'That makes mine longer,' said Wally. 'I shall win. Remember it's a fight to the death.'

" 'Of course it is,' said Jack. 'But look, my sword's got long jagged splinters. I might hurt you.'

" 'Oh!' said Wally.

" 'We shall have to call it off,' said Jack.

" 'Yes, I see that,' said Wally.

"Jack held out his paw. So did Wally.

"Little Lucy sat on the umpire's knoll and smiled.

"Arm in arm the two enemies walked into the rising sun.

" 'I do wish people would look where they're going,' said the sun."

THE END

She pulled the sheets out of the typewriter, picked up two more and began to insert the carbon. Her mouth twisted. She wouldn't need a carbon of this. At least they wouldn't be able to say she'd failed them. In that respect, anyway, her conscience would be clear. They'd paid her an advance and the book was finished. The story was finished. She put a single sheet of paper into the typewriter, rolled it to the middle and typed:

THE HUTCH THAT JACK BUILT

She sensed a movement, looked up and saw Miss Seeton standing in the doorway. They stared at each other for a long moment. Then:

"If you'll wait one minute while I finish this." She turned back to the typewriter and completed the title page:

by Sonia Venning

She laid the page on top of the completed manuscript, slid the whole into a large stamped envelope addressed to her publishers, and stuck down the flap. Mrs. Venning pushed her chair back, rose, and went to the fireplace. She held cold hands to the blaze, but felt no warmth. Without turning her head, she spoke:

"Will you sit down?"

Miss Seeton hesitated, then moved into the room. "I know you won't wish to see me. But I had to come."

"Of course."

Miss Seeton sat on the edge of a chair, her bag and her umbrella in her lap. "I did knock. But there seemed to be no one about. And then I heard the typewriter, so I came through the kitchen and knocked again."

Mrs. Venning's gaze was still on the burning logs. "I'm sorry. I didn't hear you. Mrs. Fratters isn't here. I wanted—I thought it better for her to be out of the house for a day or two. She's staying at her sister's."

Miss Seeton leaned forward. "I didn't mean to interrupt you."

"It doesn't matter."

Miss Seeton tried again. "I know it doesn't help to say I'm sorry. But I am. Most dreadfully, dreadfully sorry."

"That doesn't matter either." Still contemplating the fire, Mrs. Venning straightened and leaned against the beam across the inglenook. "In any case I see no reason why you should be sorry. Quite the reverse. Mrs. Fratters heard the whole story last night from Lady Colveden and the police and told me." Her mouth hardened. "I understand that my daughter and some friend of hers tried to run you down in a car. He then killed my daughter and you were lucky to escape with your life."

"Oh, no. No," breathed Miss Seeton. "It's wicked, wicked. How can they—dare they say such things? I was so afraid it would all get twisted. That was why I felt I had to come. I know it can't help you now—but it might later. Your daughter knew nothing of what was happening. She didn't suffer." Miss Seeton made a helpless gesture. Then went on: "I feel I should have been able to help. To do something. But when he ran the car into the tree, I slipped and fell into the water. And then it was all so quick. I saw him drag your daughter from the car. But she was quite limp. She couldn't have known. And then he—" she caught her breath and closed her eyes tightly; forced herself to go on—"he killed her. But, believe me, she couldn't have felt—anything. I think I tried to scream. But I don't remember any more." She frowned, uncertain: "Except . . ."

"Except?"

Miss Seeton made an effort to remember. "Except that he —the boy, I mean—looked like . . . Of course, I can't be sure, but he was tall. And he did seem lame. Which might have been the hens. It was only a glimpse. And the time before, in the lane, I didn't really notice. But it did look like one of your tenants."

"My tenants?" echoed Mrs. Venning. She turned away; moved to stare out the window.

"From the Barn," clarified Miss Seeton.

"My tenants?" A harsh laugh. "My tenants," she repeated.

The silence that followed was so long that Miss Seeton decided that Mrs. Venning had forgotten her presence. Quite understandable. And very natural, too, that she should wish to be alone. Indeed, she herself would never have dreamed of intruding, only it did seem so important Mrs. Venning should know the truth. Should know that that poor girl hadn't

suffered. And had been in no way to blame. It might eventually, if only a little, ease the pain of remembering. She
didn't, of course, want to appear rude, but perhaps if she
could just slide out of her chair and steal quietly away. Yes.
That would be best. She was beginning to ease herself forward when the other spoke. Miss Seeton gave a guilty start
and sat back.

"Tenants." Mrs. Venning's tone was reflective. "So
inevitably it was my fault. Nobody to blame but myself. My
fault—all mine."

"Yours?" Miss Seeton was startled. "But . . ."

"Mine," the detached voice affirmed. "Do you know who
my tenants were?"

"Well—no, not exactly. Some sort of holiday club, I
gather. Nigel—that is, Mr. Colveden . . ."

"He knows nothing," Mrs. Venning remained dispassionate,
"neither do you. My tenants were converters and distributors
of drugs. They destroyed my daughter's morals, her health,
and her life. They've destroyed me. Those were my tenants."

"But surely . . ." This was dreadful. Quite dreadful. Miss
Seeton felt lost. Poor Mrs. Venning couldn't know what she
was saying. And to sound so—so remote. Almost uninter-
ested. Somehow that made it worse. It couldn't be true. At
least not in the way . . . Mrs. Venning shouldn't be allowed
to go on thinking . . . It was, well, morbid. Because, in any
case, one would have known. She tried again. "But surely—I
mean references, your agent."

Sonia Venning returned to the fire, picked up the poker;
forgot to use it. She smiled distantly. "No references. No
agent. Just a trick. A trick played on fear. I was afraid, always afraid of poverty. Years ago when my husband died, I
was afraid then. I became a pusher."

"A—?" Miss Seeton looked helpless. "I'm sorry. I don't
understand."

"No? And yet when you first came here I thought you were
another. Or spying. Either for them or the police."

"I . . . I . . ." Miss Seeton boggled.

"Have you ever been to an all-night chemist in London late
at night?"

Miss Seeton stared. Poor Mrs. Venning. The strain, of
course. "Chemist? Only once, I think. A friend had scalded
her hand. We were having a pot of tea. Ointment," she explained. "I had to wait, I remember. There was rather a
queue."

"A queue? And it didn't occur to you to wonder what the queue was for?"

"Why, no. I—I supposed people had run out of things."

"They had. Supplies. And it wouldn't have occurred to you to wonder what started many of them in the first place? Me. And people like me." Miss Seeton caught her breath. "You must have read about it often in the newspapers; even with the young these days. The usual progression; soft drugs to hard. That's how it's done. Get someone used to a stimulant. Step it up a little until they're dependent on it. Then progress to a mild form of opium or cocaine. On to morphine. Finally heroin. All in the name of progress." She stopped for a moment. "Progress," she repeated thoughtfully. "Whether it's children egging each other on for kicks or adults doing it for gain. They choose people with social contacts and position to maintain, but in need of money. It was easy enough. Be a little gayer than usual at a party and if anybody asked you how you managed it: 'But, *dahling*,'" viciously she parodied the social manner of previous years, "'haven't you heard? These new pills, too *terribly* divine and happy-making. I'll let you have a bottle.' If anyone had a headache or was out of sorts: 'But, *dahling*, so sad-making and unnecessary. You *must* try these new pills. Too *madly* herbal and harmless, I believe. But quite *too* miraculous. I'll give you some.' And you were well paid. Oh, I don't mean that everyone who took the damned things went on to drugs. Quite a small percentage, I imagine. Most of them probably threw the bottles away. But the social amateur is paid for trying, not succeeding. You only had to give the names and addresses of people who were likely to be worth a follow-up by the professionals. With drugs, profits on one success offset a lot of failures."

Miss Seeton shifted uncomfortably in her chair. Really, this was a quite appalling story. And so private. One felt very sorry for poor Mrs. Venning. And, obviously, she believed that her daughter's death was in the nature of a retribution. Well, to be fair, Miss Seeton admitted, she herself thought not in the least understanding, had sensed something of the kind. Should one say that one was quite sure that Mrs. Venning was in no way to blame—to blame, that is, for her daughter's death? But then, again, it was all so long ago. Surely it would be better not to dwell on it and, Miss Seeton repressed a sigh, most certainly not to speak of it. What could one say? And how could one tactfully, and without appearing unfeeling, suggest that one must be going?

Miss Seeton, having thought herself to a standstill, lost her chance as Mrs. Venning put down the poker and continued:

"A trick. Played on fear. You don't know what fear is, do you?"

"I?" Miss Seeton blinked.

For the first time Sonia Venning turned and spoke directly to her visitor. "You go into battle without thinking. I think. And don't go. When I started putting the stories I'd invented for Angela as a baby in book form I was lucky. They were successful. And finally I felt safe enough to cut all connection with my former life and move down here. It worked and we were happy. Would still be happy, but for fear. Fear of what would happen if I were ill. Or my imagination withered and I couldn't write."

Really. Mrs. Venning did jump about so. And what odd ideas people had. After all, one knew one's own faults. That one was, perhaps, too timid. And worried too much. But, as for fighting . . . Well, really. Of course writing—even children's stories—must be very difficult, one saw that, but, even so: "Couldn't you have found something else?" asked Miss Seeton.

"It found me. One of the local council came to see me with a proposition that I should convert the old barn at the end of the field. He would advance the money against a mortgage on this house and would guarantee to find me a tenant. It meant an assured income: security. I agreed. It was let to this man Noyes. I didn't care particularly for the look of him, or his boys' holiday club. But as I rarely saw them and the rent was high, I'd no cause for complaint. With Angela growing up and spending time over at the Barn, I liked it even less. About a year ago I gave Noyes notice. He laughed at me and referred me to my friend on the council. The drug business, like all big concerns, keeps files and personnel records. They'd chosen this place deliberately and were running a factory at Meadows' Barn; processing—they call it converting—raw opium into morphine, into heroin. Like all big concerns they also have branches. My friend on the council was what I suppose you could call an area manager for Kent. If I opened my mouth, they would provide the authorities with proof of my past association with drugs, foreclose on the mortgage, and produce faked proof that I was behind the racket at the Barn. And that I was using Angela as a pusher to get youngsters started on drugs at that club, the Singing Swan. I was too frightened to fight it. I tried to control Angela and keep her away from them; to give myself time; hoping to work out what to do; hoping for courage; living on false hope with fear. Failing in everything." Her voice trailed off; her gaze back on the fire.

Miss Seeton didn't know what to say. Poor woman. It was quite dreadfully sad. And one felt so useless—it couldn't be good for her to keep staring at the fire like that, so bad for the eyes—but of course it must be stopped. And stopped at once. Mrs. Venning must see that. This business at the Barn.

"Forgive me," she asked, "do the police know about these people in the Barn?"

Mrs. Venning stirred; looked up. "I should have told them last night, but the doctor gave me an injection that knocked me out. First thing this morning I got rid of Mrs. Fratters and went over to face them; to bring in the police. They'd gone. I don't know what your quarrel with them has been . . ."

"Mine?" interjected Miss Seeton.

"But you put one of them, a red-headed boy, in prison. Noyes and the other three must have got out last night when they realized they'd failed to kill you—knowing you must have seen the killer and would be a witness."

"But I simply don't understand," protested Miss Seeton. "I didn't know them. Didn't even know about them." But behind her protest there was an uncomfortable feeling. Witness to a killing? Both the protest and the situation held a familiar ring. "But what about this gentleman from the council?" she suggested. "Couldn't the police . . . ?"

"Trefold Morton?" Sonia Venning sounded tired. "There's nothing they could prove against him."

Miss Seeton gasped. "Mr. Trefold Morton? But he's my solicitor. It was he who gave me that sort of phial thing with the headache tablets that you—"

"The fool. So I suppose that's how you got involved with them. I suggest you leave your solicitor and go to the police."

"Oh, but the police know," Miss Seeton assured her earnestly. "I told them. Oh, not that they were drugs, of course," she added hastily, "because, naturally, I didn't know. And then I—" remembering how Mrs. Venning had slapped it from her hand, "I didn't actually have the phial with me any more. You're quite sure that they were? Drugs, I mean?"

"Quite sure. That bottle—phial, whatever you like to call it —was designed to be unremarkable, but unmistakable."

"Well, of course," Miss Seeton acknowledged, "I'm bound

to say that I don't really like him. I find him rather tiresome. But that a solicitor should . . . someone in a position of trust . . . Drugs . . . Somehow I find that quite shocking." Quite shocked, Miss Seeton stood up.

Mrs. Venning rose. "Well, now that you do know, tell the police. Tell them everything I've told you. It will probably save trouble." She held out her hand. "Good-by. And thank you. You've been kind. I apologize for having used you as a confessional."

Miss Seeton took the outstretched hand. "There's nothing I can do?" she asked tentatively. "Nothing I can get? No shopping?"

"No. Nothing, thank you. Wait—yes." She went to the desk and picked up the manuscript for her publishers. "There's this." She handed the envelope to Miss Seeton. "If you're going through the village, perhaps you'd be kind enough to take this to the post office. It will probably—save delay."

"With pleasure. But please don't come out. I can find my own way." At the door Miss Seeton stopped, worried. "You're sure you'll be all right?"

"Quite sure," replied Mrs. Venning. "I've done with fear. I've nothing to be afraid of any more."

People's lives, reflected Miss Seeton. So terribly involved. And so sad. Of course most people would consider her own life humdrum and dull. But at least it wasn't complicated, she decided with satisfaction. Though, whatever Mrs. Venning might say, she did not feel that she could tell the police that dreadful story about her past. After all, what good could it do now? It was all over. And surely that poor woman had been punished enough. The less one discussed, or interfered in, other people's affairs the better. The Barn, of course, was a different matter. Mr. Trefold Morton . . . well—that was rather difficult. After all, there was nothing completely definite. Only her own prejudice. And now something that she'd been told. And one did so dislike gossip. But perhaps if she dropped a hint to the superintendent that she'd been told —without mentioning names, of course . . . Didn't the French have a word for it? Ah, yes. An on-dit . . . that he wasn't very reliable. The superintendent already seemed interested in Mr. Trefold Morton, so he would probably find out everything. Mr. Trefold Morton and the drug traffic disposed of, Miss Seeton entered the post office.

Miss Nuttel and Mrs. Blaine, who were on the point of

leaving the same establishment, stopped, smiled, bowed and said "Good morning."

How tiresome. One could not, of course, make a scene in public. One would have to smile and bow in return. Or, at least, nod. Miss Seeton looked straight through the two women, then deliberately turned her back. Oh dear. Now she'd been rude. But, thinking of Mrs. Venning and what those two dreadful women had said, she really could not bring herself to . . . oh dear. She crossed to that nice Mr. Stillman and handed him the envelope. As he took it from her to weigh it and check the postage, Miss Seeton found herself loath to relinquish it.

"There's something wrong," she murmured.

"No, nothing wrong," Mr. Stillman assured her cheerfully, "in fact, it's overstamped." Miss Seeton gazed at him, unseeing, shook her head, then hurried from the shop. Poor old thing, thought Mr. Stillman, all these goings-on had been too much for her. From what he'd heard, she'd have been better off to stay at Dr. Knight's for a bit.

On the Street Miss Seeton found herself at a loss. This was ridiculous. She'd go straight home. She turned and walked rapidly in the opposite direction.

"My dear Miss Seeton." Both her hands were caught and held. "How fortunate. I've just been to Dr. Knight's to see you and they told me you'd left already. Remarkable. The human frame is wonderfully elastic. But is it wise? I'm sure my sister would say the same. Rest, the great restorer. And while there I called at the Meadows. I've seldom met Mrs. Venning—not one of my congregation I fear—but, more important, one of my people. A tragic loss. Nothing I could say, but I felt bound to say it. I'm shocked to find that she's away. The house is locked. She won't have heard. What a homecoming. Perhaps my sister will know her address. Poor, silly child. Youth is so reckless. To go bathing late at night. If only I had been there. But I didn't hear until this morning. And then you. To plunge to her rescue as you did, they tell me—a simple act of heroism. An example to us all," declared the Rev. Arthur Treeves. He descended from the heights to shake his head and look severe. "If only some that I could name would follow your example. Other stories are going about. I am disturbed. Perversions of the truth. Malicious lies." Emotion colored his face and deepened his voice. "Ill-natured gossip is a wickedness that spreads like poison gas. I will not have it. I shall put my foot down and stamp upon it. I shall speak my mind."

Miss Seeton stared blindly at the vicar. Of all the sincere and well-intentioned bumble but one word had penetrated. She pulled her hands away.

"Gas," said Miss Seeton.

She moved quickly round him. She began to run.

Fifteen

Miss Seeton was not at her cottage. Representatives from the newspapers were. News of the previous night's events was spreading and the newshawks, who had withdrawn to hover with watchful eyes, were once more swooping to the attack. Mrs. Benn had kept them out of the cottage itself, but she was powerless to prevent them from flocking round the gate, pecking about the front garden, and making occasional forays into the main garden at the back. The Battling Brolly was headlines again and it was understandable that editors and reporters alike should wish for some story, preferably based on fact, to follow in smaller print under the main heading. Such accounts as they had gleaned around the village were too libelous to print and too diverse to be anything but patently inaccurate. One piece of good fortune, shared equally between Miss Seeton and Dr. Knight's nursing home, was that news of her visitation there had not been disclosed.

Superintendent Delphick and Sergeant Ranger's arrival at Sweetbriars was greeted with enthusiasm, but their disappearance into the cottage without comment or statement was not so popular.

Mrs. Benn had no idea where Miss Seeton could be. She was expecting her back for lunch. But meanwhile she might have gone shopping. Or she might conceivably, seeing the crowd around her cottage, have taken refuge elsewhere.

The superintendent was in a quandary. It was essential that Mr. Benning should be interviewed as well, but he came to the conclusion that Miss Seeton's whereabouts must take precedence. A few discreet telephone calls having produced no results, Delphick and Bob decided that their only course was to seek information in the village.

At the post office Mr. Stillman proved helpful. Yes, Miss Seeton had been in. She'd come in with something to post. Actually, he thought she was doing an errand for Mrs. Venning as the envelope was addressed to her publishers. Mrs. Venning's publishers, of course. And he knew the name because Mrs. Venning always posted her things here and the envelope was overstamped, as Mrs. Venning often did. Well, now that they came to ask him, Miss Seeton had seemed a bit vague. And was in a bit of a hurry when she left.

The vicar, who happened to be in the shop with his sister, added his quota. Yes, he had met dear Miss Seeton upon the Street; had stopped to have a word—to congratulate her, he could do no less, upon her heroism of last night. Remarkable at her age. And such a tragedy, too. And then, with Mrs. Venning not at home, that made it worse. It was to be hoped that she could be reached in time. But he would put a stop to it. Too much had happened, and a great deal too much had been said. It was his bounden duty . . . No, Miss Seeton had said nothing of her intentions. She had seemed—well, preoccupied.

"But what did she do?" demanded Delphick.

"Do?" answered the vicar. He was at a loss. "She didn't do anything. She—just ran."

Miss Treeves was exasperated. "Oh, Arthur, do pull yourself together. Where did she run?"

"Why, home, I suppose," her brother told her. "Really remarkable. Most ladies, after a certain age, trot. But she was running. Running like a girl. Really remarkable."

Delphick restrained himself and spoke as to a child. "You saw Miss Seeton run home?"

"Well, no. Not exactly home," admitted the vicar. "She was going in the other direction." Inspiration came to him. "She was going back to Dr. Knight's, I expect."

"And she didn't speak to you?" asked Delphick.

"No," replied the Rev. Arthur.

"Nonsense," cried Miss Treeves. "Do try to think, Arthur. She must have said something."

Her brother became fussed. "Now don't muddle me, Molly. I don't need to think. I'm perfectly clear about it. I tell you she didn't say anything. At least only one word. And, quite obviously, she was thinking of something else."

"What?" pressed Miss Treeves.

"What?" echoed Bob.

"What word?" urged Delphick.

"Gas," said the vicar.

Outside the post office Delphick and Bob instinctively looked for their car before remembering that on this occasion they were on foot. They began to run.

Miss Treeves, the vicar, Miss Wicks, Mr. Stillman, and the rest of the customers surged onto the Street to join the crowd of villagers and reporters, grouped outside the shop. All watched the fleeing figures of the two detectives. They started to follow. They began to run.

Bob, with more length to his leg, more breath, and less years to his credit than Delphick, won the race. The side door, next to the big wooden gates in the boundary wall of the Meadows, was open. Bob pounded through it, down the path by the garage, rounded the hedge, skidded to a crunching halt by the back door and looked down: broken glass, a broken umbrella, and two heads with pink faces lying in the open doorway. He drew a deep breath, choked on the reeking gas fumes, then dragged the two bodies onto the path as Delphick panted into view.

"Leave—you, sir—hospital—quickest," gasped Bob.

Delphick, no breath to waste on words, nodded and, holding his handkerchief to his face, plunged into the kitchen.

Having left his blown superior to throw open all the ground-floor windows and to pass on the news by telephone to Ashford, Bob's re-emergence from the lane, on his way to the nursing home, with Miss Seeton draped over one shoulder and Mrs. Venning slung over the other, was greeted with cheers by the villagers, shouts of approval from the pressmen, and flashes of light from the photographers.

Dr. Knight, appearing from his surgery at the back of the hall, took one look and sniffed.

"Gas?"

"Yes, sir."

"How long?"

"I don't know, sir."

The doctor stood back from the surgery door. "In here. One on the table. One on the couch. Anne," he called up the stairs, "ask your mother to come down and help me—urgent. Oxygen. Your probationer's back again—overdressed this time, wearing a couple of women as a stole. Prepare two beds, please."

There was nothing to do but wait.

Delphick waited at the Meadows. He had rung his chief at the Yard to bring him up to date and to prepare him for the sensation that the newspapers were certain to make of the morning's sequel to the events of the previous night. They had agreed, in view of the wild rumors circulating locally, that as soon as he could get a statement from Miss Seeton, Delphick would be well advised in his turn to give a reasonably full and factual statement to the press. He had paid a brief visit to the nursing home to confirm that the two witnesses whom he was anxious to question were once again asleep; although on this occasion he could hardly hold the doctor to blame. Dr. Knight had spared a moment to tell him that Miss Seeton was a "cert and shouldn't be too long now," adding with enthusiasm that she had already vomited twice, which appeared to please him. Mrs. Venning, the doctor diagnosed as "only a might." Provided that she did not relapse, provided that pneumonia did not supervene, and provided a host of other technicalities that Delphick failed to understand, "she might make it. No reaction so far; no retching; not even a contraction." The doctor had shaken his head in disapproval. "They'd have to see."

Delphick had retreated, baffled, to the sitting room to collect Bob for a search of the Meadows, but Anne Knight's entrance had changed his mind. She had come in to explain that one of the staff was with Miss Seeton, that her mother and father were busy with Mrs. Venning and, as there was nothing she could usefully do at the moment, her mother had sent her down to entertain the detectives. Could she get them coffee or anything? Delphick had picked up his cue. Where Mrs. Knight led, he could surely follow.

"Not for me, thanks. I was just going. No, not you, sergeant," as Bob moved, "you'd better stay here till Miss Seeton recovers. And let me know as soon as she can talk. I shall be over the way at Mrs. Venning's. I hold you responsible for her. She's not to get loose again till I've seen her. There's no knowing what she might get up to. She's not to go out. If necessary, arrest her, take her umbrella away, anything you like, but keep her here until I arrive."

"Oh, sir, I nearly forgot." Bob reached into his raincoat pocket and withdrew Miss Seeton's umbrella. It was broken. He placed the remains gently on the arm of the sofa, where it lay bedraggled, like a bird with a broken wing. "It was lying near her," Bob went on, "so I stuffed it into my pocket. It—well, it didn't seem right somehow to leave it behind."

The two detectives regarded it in silence. Watching their respectful attitudes, their somber faces, Anne had the impression that they were mourning the death of an old friend.

Delphick sighed. "I'm sorry about that." He picked up the relic. "I'll ask Miss Seeton, of course, but I doubt she'll want it back. And, if not, I think I should like to keep it as a memento." He moved to the door. "By the way, sergeant, you might ring Mrs. Benn for me and explain that Miss Seeton is back here and why. Otherwise she'll be worrying." Delphick took his leave.

Outside, P. C. Potter had rounded up the local inhabitants, herded them back into the village, and sent them about their normal pursuits. Delphick got rid of the reporters by promising to give a press conference, at the George and Dragon, as soon as he was free. Potter, who had stationed himself at the nursing home gates in order to prevent any further attempt at unlawful assembly, turned to the superintendent with eagerness.

"Anything further you'd be wanting me to do, sir?"

Delphick gazed at him absently for a moment, then: "Why, yes, constable. If it won't interfere with your other duties, I should be glad if you could help me search the Meadows."

"Yes, sir. Certainly. A pleasure, sir."

"See if we can find any trace of a connection between the girl and Lebel or between her and Trefold Morton. Any trace of drugs. Anything at all. We shan't, of course, but we have to look. Even if we can only trace the whereabouts of that woman—what's her name?—who looks after Mrs. Venning, it would be something." Delphick began to walk down the lane.

P. C. Potter, personal assistant, in person, to a superintendent from Scotland Yard, paced beside him. "Mrs. Fratters, you mean, sir. I'm afraid she's gone off, sir."

Into Delphick's mind, which had wandered ahead of him, intruded a picture of Mrs. Fratters suddenly, inexplicably, having started to decay. He pulled himself together. This lack of sleep was beginning to tell. "Gone off? Where?"

"To her sister's, so she said, sir, when I saw her this morning getting on the Ashford bus. And none too happy about it, too, sir, as I understood it, sir. Not wanting to go. But said that Mrs. Venning had said that she wanted to be alone for a day or two. I suppose you can understand it, sir."

"Yes," agreed Delphick, "I suppose I can."

Bob, waiting at the nursing home as instructed, put down the telephone and returned to the sitting room.

"I got on to Mrs. Benn all right," he told Anne. "She was a bit shocked and wanted to come here, but I said I thought better not. She said she'd have something ready for whenever Miss Seeton could get back. And it wouldn't matter about the time as there was a cold veal and ham pie." He sounded wistful. "Poor Miss Seeton. I don't suppose she'll be feeling much like food."

Anne handed him a plate of cakes and poured the coffee that she had prepared while he was telephoning. She laughed. "Don't be too sure. I don't think anything Miss Seeton did would surprise me. Remember she's been taking a lot of exercise. And lost her breakfast into the bargain. She ought to have been feeling pretty sorry for herself this morning, but she wasn't. Dad says he's never seen anybody like her for her age. He says she's tough as a boot and can't think how she does it. What exactly did she do, by the way?"

Bob looked puzzled. "Well, we don't really know. She was talking to the vicar and apparently she suddenly said the word 'Gas' and ran off like a scalded cat. But we don't know how she knew." He sat down on the sofa beside Anne and started to eat a cake. "The kitchen window at the Meadows was smashed. That must have been how she broke her umbrella. And then she must have climbed in—or rather dived in; it's only a tiny window—over the kitchen sink, switched off the oven, unlocked the door and dragged Mrs. Venning out. They were both lying in a heap in the doorway when I got there. The place reeked."

"So you just picked them up and brought them to us."

"Well, yes," acknowledged Bob. "We hadn't got the car, you see. I did think of ringing for an ambulance, but it would have wasted time. It seemed quicker really to cart them over and dump them here."

Anne smiled at him. "Which probably saved Mrs. Venning's life."

Bob brooded. "She won't thank me for that."

"Not now, maybe," she conceded. "But if she does win through, she may later. I think if people are meant to die they do and if they're meant to be saved they are and that's all about it."

Bob gazed at her, lost in admiration for this simple, splendid philosophy; this simply splendid girl. Anne grew embarrassed under his steady regard.

"Oh," she said, "how awful. I haven't even thanked you for the flowers and chocolates."

It was Bob's turn for embarrassment. He looked out the window, eyed the blaze of color in the beds around the lawn dismally and apologized. "I see now. Stupid of me, I didn't think. Coals to Newcastle."

"Rubbish," she replied. "I've always thought that Newcastle's probably very grateful for the coal. Think of the work it must save them." She eyed the blaze of color in the vases around the room happily, picked up the box of chocolates and offered: "Have some. They're very good."

Bob put down the empty cake plate, took a chocolate, bit into a caramel, and was rendered speechless.

Anne gurgled. "I thought you were bringing them for Miss Seeton. You know, I like her. She's a funny little thing and I hardly know her at all, but I like her a lot. I think she's a pet, don't you?"

"M'm'm!" said Bob, fighting to free his teeth.

"Some of them are awful. Take old Miss Hant. For all of me, anyone can take her; she's a horror."

"Doesn't make any difference," mumbled Bob.

"Believe me, it does," she contradicted him, "if you have to cope with them. Miss Hant's been creating half the morning."

Bob, having won his fight, swallowed quickly and burst into speech; it came out louder than he had intended. "It doesn't make any difference!" he shouted. He blushed, turned down the volume, and continued, "I mean it doesn't make any difference as to how you feel about them. Not always, I mean. I mean you can suddenly see someone and know exactly how you feel about them. Know that's it, I mean. Know that you always will feel like that about them, I mean." He reviewed his exposition and wondered if he had made his meaning clear. The call of duty echoed in his thoughts and he came down to earth. "What was that about Miss Hant?" he asked. "What's wrong with her?"

Anne was disappointed. Bother Miss Hant. Just when the conversation had been going so well. "There's nothing wrong with her—at least nothing more than usual. Apparently she was expecting a visit from her solicitor this morning and was upset because he hasn't been yet."

"And he won't," said Bob.

"Oh, I expect he will," she replied. "As I told her, he's probably busy. He might look in this afternoon, or else tomorrow morning."

"No, he won't," said Bob, "he's in quod."

Anne gasped. "In prison? Mr. Trefold Morton? But he can't be. He's a solicitor."

"That's why." And Bob proceeded to give her a résumé of his and the Oracle's late-night final.

Anne was shocked. Impulsively, she put her hand on his arm. "I think it's wicked. You can hardly have had any sleep at all. You must feel awful."

Bob placed his hand over hers. "I feel fine."

"And to think of bringing me flowers and chocolates when you must have been so tired."

"That was easy," Bob told her. "I was thinking of you all the time."

"But . . ."

He leaned closer. "You know—you must know—how I feel about you."

Anne tried to draw her hand away. She failed. "No, I . . . Yes, I . . . But you can't. Oh, you don't understand," she cried in desperation. "Look at me—I'm plain."

He looked; past the trim figure, the neat uniform, to let his eyes linger on her face. "Yes," he agreed.

She turned her head away. "Well—there you are."

Bob addressed the back of her head. "I love you," he said.

Dr. Knight opened the door. He stopped. "I imagine it's compulsive," he observed.

Still holding Anne, Bob leaped to his feet, realized, then hurriedly lowered her to the floor.

The doctor watched them with interest. "Yes, obviously compulsive," he decided. "As you know, Anne, I would be the last to interfere, but I feel it only right that you should be apprised of the facts and be warned."

Anne grinned at him. "What's compulsive, dad?"

Her father looked severe. "This habit he's got. Picking up women, carrying them about, and then putting them down somewhere else. Once could be an impulse. Two—especially two at a time—must be viewed with grave concern. But three —that's compulsion. To the best of my knowledge, it's a conpletely new symptom and I doubt there's a cure. I'm only speaking for your own good," he told her. "You will have to give due consideration to the fact that, whatever you may be doing at any particular time, you may be suddenly grabbed off your feet and put down somewhere else in a completely different position. That is . . . h'rm." Realizing that his flight of fancy had taken him further into the stratosphere than he had intended, the doctor cleared his throat, abandoned the flight, and bailed out. He brightened and turned to Bob. "On the other hand, young man, if any time you need a job, let me know. Should we ever be slack, we could always drum up trade by sending you out as a retriever."

Bob stood, huge and hugely embarrassed. His mouth opened in preparation for speech; to explain; to apologize. Inspiration failed him and his mouth closed.

"In view of your very natural anxiety," continued the doctor with glinting enjoyment, "and to forestall those eager questions which I feel sure a natural diffidence, rather than a lapse of memory, is restraining you from asking, I had better give you the latest news of your patients." Bob started: Mrs. Venning, Miss Seeton—he'd forgotten them. "Which was the reason for my interrupting your—um—discussion with my daughter. Mrs. Venning may do, I think; though I suspect a slight heart condition there. No question of an interview, I'm afraid. Even with complete quiet, it'll be touch and go for the next day or two. Miss Seeton, on the other hand, is as bobbish as can be. Extraordinary resilience. Wish I knew her secret. She must be made of India rubber. You can talk to her any time you like. She wanted to go home, but I've forbidden it. She ought to need rest, even if she doesn't, so I've ordered her to stay in bed."

Behind him, Miss Seeton gave a polite cough. Dr. Knight spun around, blocking the doorway. "Get back to bed, woman, I told you to stay there."

Miss Seeton smiled at him and held out her hand. "Yes, I know, doctor, a most kind suggestion, but I'm quite all right now and I wouldn't dream of troubling you further. The nurse tells me that Mrs. Venning is a little better. Such a relief. So thank you again," she withdrew her hand. "I really do feel that I must go."

Sergeant Ranger felt fine. Miss Seeton's gratitude, in double measure, for her rescues had embarrassed him, but left a glow. The Oracle had been pleased to find, after they had driven her home, that Miss Seeton had actually been an eyewitness of last night's murder. What with that and acting like a rodent officer in clearing the Barn of rats overnight, you'd got to hand it to the old girl. When it came to action she was spot-on. Her evidence, too, would help in building the case against that solicitor chap. Also, since the old girl had somehow winkled the whole of Mrs. Venning's life history out of her, the Oracle wasn't feeling so frus- —cheesed off. Everything was working out, Bob felt. In fact, he felt fine.

Mrs. Benn had decided that, though late for lunch, and still a little early for tea, the troops needed sustenance. She had slipped over to the George and Dragon and returned with a couple of bottles of champagne. Miss Seeton had sipped half a glass and sneezed with enjoyment; one glass had satisfied Mrs. Benn; the superintendent had had two and the sergeant, under pressure from his superior, had drunk the rest. Martha's veal and ham pie had come into its own—and gone. Shortage of sleep, sufficient food, and a surfeit of champagne had induced in the sergeant a euphoria. He relaxed in his chair and thought mostly of Anne Knight.

Anne . . . Even a telephone call from the Narcotics Squad, who had traced their whereabouts from the George and Dragon, failed to disturb him. They'd picked up the equipment and some dope at Meadows' Barn, but still seemed peeved that the chums had scarpered. What did they expect the poor old thing to do? Hold 'em at umbrella's point till Narcotics were ready to pick 'em up? They wanted detailed descriptions. So what? They could have 'em. It was all down in his notebook—even if the last couple of pages looked a bit off. Anyway he knew the gist of it and could work it out. It would all work out. In the end. As for young César—or anyone else who wanted to have a go—he'd settle their hash. He could settle anything. Let 'em all come. He felt fine.

* INTERIM *

". . . and there will be no mistake this time. Those bungling yokels have allowed that confounded woman to jeopardize the whole southeast area: Morton and the red-haired boy in prison, the factory gone, and Noyes and the other three on the run; with a clear description out of that fool who shot himself among the chickens. While her fatalities total one handbag, two hats, and a ducking. It's time we had a professional on the job. I'm not risking setting things up down there again until she's out of the way." . . . "Because as a stranger in a small place like that you would have been picked up at once; especially with the police hovering round her like wasps round jam." . . . "It won't apply. They consider it's over. It'll be perfectly safe then. The fuzz, as you call them, will all be at Maidstone for the trial; so will she. And the whole village will be making a day's outing of it."

. . . "No, by motorcycle—less noticeable. You will be given a map of the district, the layout of the village, and a plan of her cottage. You will get in while the place is deserted and wait, either in the bedrooms above, or there is a large cupboard under the stairs. As soon as she returns and you're certain she's alone, finish the business at once and come back to London." . . . "It's unlikely there'll be any alarm. Nothing will be found till next morning." . . . "Right. Oh, and, César —for my personal satisfaction and, no doubt, yours—it would give me a small pleasure if, before you left, you broke her umbrella as well."

The telephone receiver was gently cradled.

Sixteen

It was over. Superintendent Delphick felt depressed as he and Sergeant Ranger journeyed back to London by train. The Assize had gone well enough. As for young X—or the Ginger Nut, as the papers called him—his dumbness had got him no place; detained during Her Majesty's pleasure, under medical supervision; so he'd be kept locked up until he spoke and if he spoke they'd lock him up for having spoken—which settled him. His defending counsel had been doing well and it had looked a bit tricky until Miss Seeton had started complaining about the damage to her hat—trust her to pull a rabbit out of it. From then on, once the laughter had died down and they'd restored order in court, there'd never been any doubt. The foreman of the jury could hardly wait for the end of the judge's summing up before bouncing to his feet to announce his popular, if unconventional: "There's no need for us to retire, Your Honor, if it's all the same to you. He's guilty of all you said and a sight more besides by our reckoning." Trefold Morton, too, had gone down for a nice stretch for embezzlement. And by the time the Narcotics boys had finished with him it'd be a long while before he'd see daylight again. Chris Brinton and the Ashford lot were a bit shaken up to find out how much had been going on in their manor. Chris seemed inclined to feel Miss Seeton was responsible for stirring it up and disturbing the peace. But after all, even if she did go beating the coverts with her umbrella and putting up villains on the wing in all directions, she could hardly be blamed for the birds being there in the first place. And if she flushed them out, it was up to the police to shoot them down. Which, give or take a few, they'd done. But, for himself, there was no blinking the fact that his assignment had been to watch over Miss Seeton and catch Lebel. And he hadn't. The only person who'd seemed to set eyes on César was Miss Seeton herself. As for the other types who'd been trying it on, she seemed fully capable of dealing with them in her own way—the police well to the rear. If there'd been another attempt on her this past week, when they were ready and set up for it . . .

170

But obviously they'd given her best and chucked it in. She shouldn't be safe enough now. And the local bobby'd keep his eyes open. With regard to César, he'd pop up somewhere else and they'd pick him up eventually. But meanwhile, for himself, he had to admit—he'd failed. Though they could chalk it up to their credit that if it hadn't been for Bob, Miss Seeton would have been drowned. But after all they weren't in business as lifesavers. No, scrap that—fundamentally, he supposed, that was what they were. Delphick grinned. He was going to frame that broken umbrella of hers and hang it on his office wall as a reminder not to get smug. With Lebel identified, it had seemed so easy. From the moment she had poked him in the ribs in Covent Garden and said "Naughty" or words to that effect, Miss Seeton had laid it on the line for them and they had followed along behind, mopping up this and that as they went, until he'd let himself be hypnotized into believing that she'd produce César and hand him over, neatly trussed and garnished, on a plate. Actually she had produced assorted villains and done most of the trussing herself. Funny, that trick of hers of being able to see into people's motives and backgrounds, without always fully realizing what it was she saw. Or rather drew. As for that Niobe sketch, with the girl lying in the water almost exactly as they'd eventually found the Venning girl—uncanny. They could do with her on the staff at the Yard. A good thing really Narcotics weren't going to try and press charges against Mrs. Venning. One way and another you could say she's paid her account. In any case, there was only Miss Seeton's report of a conversation; the Venning herself was too ill to make sense and at last they'd picked up a lot of dope and equipment, though they appeared to take the factory as a personal insult, maintaining that the conversion should have been done in two stages abroad. And for the amateur sales racket: there'd been an article in one of the Sunday rags recently, saying they ranged from diplomats to students and calling them the New Mercenaries. New? The pearl Cleopatra dropped into Anthony's wine probably contained a nicely calculated dose of poppy seed.

It was over. Somehow he'd known it would be from the moment Miss Seeton had broken her umbrella. Arm her with a brolly and all hell was let loose. But take it away and everything quieted down at once. Pity they hadn't picked up young César, but they'd picked up a couple of other chums and you couldn't do everything. César wouldn't be any use to his own bosses now that he was marked and Miss Seeton could finger him for the Covent Garden do, and if they thought there was any danger of his talking, they'd probably wipe him out themselves, which would save a lot of trouble all round. Anne Knight. It was a beautiful name. Anne . . . Anne Ranger. Somehow that went even better. It was more natural. He'd got leave this week end, she'd promised to come up, and they'd have dinner and do a show on Saturday, and on Sunday—he must think of something for Sunday—and . . . Bob gazed out the carriage window at his private view of a heart-moving future. It was only just beginning.

It was over evidently. She left the window and sat down as Crabbe's two buses drew up at the garage opposite and spilled out the returning villagers.

"They're back, Eric. Too stupid. I can't think what everybody wanted to go over to Maidstone to the trial for. As if it was a holiday excursion or something."

Miss Nuttel was subdued. "Went to the hearing at Ashford ourselves."

An echo of sniggers remembered. "Yes, and too unpleasant it was. After all, we only went because we thought we ought to support somebody who was living here and give them the benefit of the doubt. We should have known better. Anyway, this time there's no doubt at all. We've learned far more by staying here and only proved how too right we were all along."

Her friend demurred, worried. "Still think we ought to get on to the police, Bunny."

"Nonsense, Eric. They'd only believe her and she'd make fools of them as she always does. It's too obvious to me that she was in league with that young murderer from London and has been all the time and I've always said so. And this afternoon has proved it. Watching that young man creep into her house like that as soon as everything had quieted down and he thought the village was empty and no one would see. I'll bet he's hiding there waiting for her to come back. She hasn't had a chance before, with that friend of hers staying there and police all over the place. It's all too clear. As soon as she gets back—and trust her to have wangled a police car to take her and not use the bus like anybody else—she and that boy'll get together and there'll be trouble. You'll see."

Well, it was over and, really, it had not proved as bad as one might have feared. It had been unpleasant, of course, having to give evidence against that young man with the reddish hair, whose name nobody appeared to know and, indeed, his counsel had been almost rude, trying to make out that she and that nice lorry driver had been responsible for damaging his brain—the young man's brain, that was—by leaving him to roll about in the back of his van; but, after all, it hadn't been for very long and, as she had pointed out, she had been in the back of the van, rolling about, for much longer—and with a sack over her head—and it hadn't damaged her brain, only her hat. Actually the whole case was over much quicker than she had expected. The judge—such an understanding-looking man—had made it all so very clear. And then she had imagined that there would have to be a wait while the jury retired, but they hadn't. As the proceedings hadn't taken very long, perhaps they hadn't needed to. So extremely lucky, too, that she wasn't after all called as a witness in Mr. Trefold Morton's trial in the afternoon. Though, of course, it had meant waiting about in case. But, apparently, he had admitted to embezzling other people's money—really, quite shocking for a man in his position. In any event, she didn't see how she could have helped them over embezzlement, even if they had asked her because, quite frankly, it had never occurred to her that he did.

The police car drew up at the gate of Sweetbriars and Miss Seeton, thanking the driver who had jumped out to open the door for her, alighted. He smiled at her, saluted, got back into the car, and set off on his return journey to Ashford.

So thoughtful of them to have provided a car for her. Now she came to think of it, she had to admit that she did feel rather tired. Oh dear, should she have tipped the man? It was so difficult to know. He didn't look as if he'd expected it. But then, again, in the ordinary way, the less people looked as if they expected a tip the more they did in fact expect. No, of course, one never tipped police. It was called bribery. Though, from what she'd read, one did in certain countries abroad. And, of course, in America, where the system was probably quite different.

Miss Seeton stood for a moment in happiness looking at her cottage before walking up the short path to unlock her front door.

How nice to be home. And alone. Though, of course, it had

been very kind of Mrs. Benn to cut short her holiday and
come to stay as she had. And most helpful, too. But it had
been, in some ways, a relief when she had gone back to London to get the school ready for opening. It had been so pleasant, having the cottage to oneself these past few days. To
think that there were only two more days before she, herself,
had to go back to London for the beginning of the new term.
How the time had flown. What with one thing and another,
she never seemed to have had the chance to get down to
learning about gardening as she had meant to do. Though this
past week, after that dreadful affair by the pond, had been
quite peaceful. Poor Mrs. Venning. Such a relief that she had
recovered. And yet, Miss Seeton wondered, would it perhaps
have been better if she hadn't? Should one perhaps not have
interfered? The trouble was one acted on the spur of the moment without really thinking of the consequences. Dr. Knight
had told her that Mrs. Venning had now had a complete
breakdown and that they had flown her out to some sort of
nursing home in Switzerland, to get her away from all the
past unhappy associations. And, of course, the air there—so
very pure. Good gracious, what was that?

A long, flat parcel lay on the table in the passage. Miss Seeton picked it up.

Now, who could have . . . ? She didn't remember having
ordered anything. Beautifully wrapped. It must be from a
shop. And with that clever sticky tape to hold it down that
was so quick and easy to do and so quite—she wrestled with
it—impossible to undo.

Eventually there emerged from the torn brown paper a
narrow white cardboard box. Inside, wedged into place with
tissue paper, gleamed under its polythène sheath a slim black
silk umbrella with a card tied to its yellow handle.

Miss Seeton pulled the handle toward her in order to read
the card. From behind her there came a click.

What? She turned. Oh, yes, of course, she'd knocked the
cupboard door shut. How stupid. One forgot how narrow the
passage was. She looked at the umbrella's ferrule—no, she
hadn't damaged it. Martha had warned her to keep that door
bolted because the latch was inclined to slip and one could get
a nasty bang in the dark. But, surely—yes, surely—she had
bolted it. This morning before she left, after putting the vacuum away. Well, obviously she hadn't. Because Martha had
gone to Maidstone this afternoon and nobody else would have

been here. How very careless, she might easily have been hurt.

Miss Seeton shot the bolt. Prudently she moved into the sitting room to read the card. "Superintendent Alan Delphick, C.I.D., New Scotland Yard." Miss Seeton turned the card over; on the back there was a handwritten note.

"In reparation for your loss in the course of duty. A.D." She felt quite overwhelmed. Really, how very kind. And to realize that one preferred a crook handle, so much more practical, to a strap whose stitching was always giving way.

Miss Seeton noticed a mark on the handle; looked closer.

But, good gracious, it wasn't steel at all. It was gold.

Proudly, Miss Seeton placed her new umbrella in one of the clips on the passage wall above the drip tray.

It was a little late for tea now. And she was tired. No, she would go upstairs and do her exercises. It would be a pity to miss them as they did seem to be doing her a great deal of good. And then she would fetch her tray, take it up and treat herself to supper in bed.

The bell of the egg timer rang and Miss Seeton, in the corner of her bedroom, lowered her feet to the floor.

She was improving. She was coming down much more slowly now. Though her feet did seem to have landed with rather a thud. She remained huddled on the floor for a moment with her head down, taking deep, regular breaths. Surely . . . Perhaps it hadn't been her feet. Yes, surely someone was knocking downstairs. She caught up her dressing gown, hurried into the front bedroom and looked out the window. No—there was no one there. Either she must have been mistaken or it must have been at some other house.

Seven . . . eight . . . nine . . . She stopped counting her breaths in order to listen. There was quite definitely someone knocking. And it was here—she could feel the vibration. She straightened her legs, got up quickly, and staggered. Oh dear, of course one should take one's time—a little massage and then bend forward—before trying to walk. She put on her dressing gown again and went downstairs.

There was no one at the front door. She hesitated. Two more taps sounded, fainter than the previous ones. It was probably a branch against a window, decided Miss Seeton. She repaired to the kitchen.

She'd collect her supper tray and take it up now that she was down. After all, there was only one exercise that she hadn't completed, and really she didn't feel that she could start again.

At the foot of the stairs she heard a slithering sound and then a bump against the cupboard door. She stooped to lower the tray.

Oh dear. Probably the vacuum. She'd been in a hurry this morning and hadn't been sure at the time that she'd balanced it correctly on that box. She must have a proper clear-out of that cupboard and make more room. But—no. Not tonight. She was too tired. Miss Seeton straightened and began to mount the stairs. Martha and she could sort it out tomorrow. Whatever it was that had fallen down in there could be picked up in the morning.